Praise for P.D. Singer's work:

This story is extraordinary, with characters that are immensely complex and pacing that is so fast I felt as if I were riding a wave that kept on building. *The Rare Event* absolutely blew me away and changed my perception of the world of hedge funds.

Reviews by Jessewave, *The Rare Event*

It held me captivated from page one, often looking at the clock at work to see how much longer I had before I could get back home to Warren and Chad.

Bayou Book Junkie, *A New Man*

Overall, an excellent, well-crafted story that was a perfect blend of romance and cycling…a rare find!

Mrs. Condit and Friends, *Spokes*

The mountains, the town, and the people they meet are vividly drawn and very much a part of city-boy Jake's new experiences, and the firefighting that Kurt and Jake occasionally have to do leaps off the page.

Reading Reality, *Fire on the Mountain*

If you are looking for a book about two men who are perhaps both a bit naive and yet love each other very much; a book where the romance is balanced with exciting action sequences, with humourous situations and with tense and thrilling scenes; then this book is for you. Highly recommended with a grade of 'Excellent'.

Jenre's Well-Read, *Snow on the Mountain*

… I really enjoyed Blood on the Mountain. Read it for a cracking plot, and a wonderful couple that deserves their Happy Ever After.

Mrs. Condit and Friends, *Blood on the Mountain*

Also by P.D. Singer

Novels

Spokes
The Rare Event
A New Man
Fire on the Mountain
Snow on the Mountain
Fall Down the Mountain
Blood on the Mountain
Return to the Mountain

Novellas

Donal *agus* Jimmy
Prep Work

Shorts

Cross the Mountain
O'Carolan's Seduction
On Call: Afternoon
On Call: Dancing
On Call: Crossroads
Training Cats
On Call: The Collection
Set Up (in the Out in Colorado II anthology)

OTTER
Chaos
INCLUDES TAIL SLIDE

P.D. SINGER

ROCKY RIDGE BOOKS

Tail Slide © P.D. Singer 2015
Otter Chaos © P.D. Singer 2015
Cover art by Dar Albert of WickedSmartDesigns.com

Black is the Color of My True Love's Hair - traditional Appalachian tune

ISBN-13 978-1-62622-030-0

Published by:

Rocky Ridge Books
PO Box 6922
Broomfield, CO 80021
www.RockyRidgeBooks.com

Thanks to the wonderful folks who encouraged, cajoled, beta read, and otherwise assisted me in getting Lon and Corey's adventure out into the world. Eden Winters, Lynda Benn, Z. Allora, Angela Benedetti, Cari Z, you all rock.

Becky Condit, thank you for being the Ideal Reader who had to be pleased with this story. You kept me striving.

George Seaton and Jackie Morgan, many thanks for assistance with names, and JP Kenwood for clarification of geography. Kate Pavelle, you helped with koi more than you know.

Tail Slide

Pulling the car into the wide spot beside the narrow highway, Brian said, "Sure you aren't coming up to the ski area? They have lifts...." He trailed off suggestively.

"There's two feet of fresh snow out here in the back country," Lon told him, even if the country wasn't very 'back' when it butted up to a road. Access to the newly-fallen, unmarked powder snow didn't have to cost an arm and a leg and come with crowds. "You have fun cruising the groomers with the rest of the two-plankers." He swung out of the little Dodge and popped his board out of the roof rack. "Pick me up about five o'clock, okay?" Five was about half an hour from true dark. They'd both get plenty of runs in, but Lon was sure he'd have the better time.

"See you later!" Brian waited just long enough for Lon to click the rack shut before he rattled off toward Eldora.

Five or six cars could line up along this section of road, though none parked there now. That might change later, but at the moment Lon had a really decent snowboarding hill to himself. He stepped over the guardrail, into his bindings, and aimed down the untracked, unpacked snow. Who wanted to pay for groomed snow with all this champagne pow pow to schriff on for free?

Curving ever so gently, Lon bombed through the fresh powder. The chilly wind kissed his nose with the scents of pine, spruce, and with every curve, less highway and more deer. Trees loomed before him on more level ground—he threaded a path between them and ran out of steepness before he ran out of momentum. He sailed far into the stand of trees, close enough to hear but not see the stream that ran toward Boulder Creek. Stroking the green needles of a ponderosa pine, he considered trudging to the stream or heading back uphill.

Uphill won. He cut east toward the highway, and when he reached pavement, he stuck his thumb out. Some friendly driver, like this guy in the pickup truck, would give him a lift to the top. Lon threw his board in the back of the truck and climbed in after it. "Just to the parking area!" he told the driver, who grinned and said, "I know."

Bet he played ski lift all the time. Lon hopped out with thanks, feeling his beard crackle in the cold with the movement of his grin. Wind was changing, too. He ran a hand across his face, smoothing the crisp brown hairs that framed his mouth but didn't cover his cheeks. Felt good.

Still no others had come to his playground. Lon strapped on his board again to sail down the hill. Shifting weight to his heels, this time he carved a transverse path below the highway, first one way, and then with a sinuous turn of his hips, back the other way. Letting his arms carry his balance and his spine absorb the bumps, Lon slid downhill under the impossible blue of the Colorado sky, cutting toward the road again. One more run—he had plenty of time.

Another motorist collected him after ten minutes of holding out his thumb to the sparse traffic and dropped him at the top, leaving him to the solitude that might vanish with the next vehicle to round the bend. Taking the nearly straight path down, Lon let his speed wrap his senses, the wind slapping his jacket and pants against his body and taking cold nips around his sunglasses. He tasted the air and the emptiness—the deer had fled at his earlier foray into the trees.

2

Lon had enough momentum to pass his last stopping point, traveling into denser stands of growth where the snow lay in shallow drifts. He unbuckled his board and picked his way between the white hills, ducking below the branches and leaving as few footprints as he could. The creek babbled louder with each step, calling him more surely than the moon called the wolves.

Tucking his snowboard beneath a juniper, Lon threw some snow over the protruding edges lest its bright colors attract notice, though who would come so far on the flat? Time, oh, yes, it was time. He shrugged out of his clothing and bounded to the chuckling waters.

At 4:45, Lon poked his phone to silence and brightness. *Found SOME1 cuter thN u, hitch om.* Fucking Brian and his horndog ways! Lon definitely needed a more reliable set of friends. Stripping off his gloves to text back "U wont git it up, (_o_)," Lon contemplated his choices. Plenty of traffic headed from Eldora back to Boulder, all of it on the other side of the highway, and with no place to stop.

A rusty little sedan and a newish blue RAV4 had parked on this wide strip since Lon had made his last trek to the top, and the drivers, whoever they might be, were losing the light as surely as he was. Rather than risk getting squashed, he'd try the kindred souls who ought to be reappearing shortly.

"Whoa!" came from the other side of the guardrail—Lon was there in a flash to grab a flailing arm and pull its owner over the rail. The snowboard that had come uphill with the climber skittered down the slope without him.

"Damn. Only had that board a month." Lon's new companion peered down the hill. "Guess I better go fetch." Taller than Lon by about three inches and with a light stubble across his cheeks, he might have the skills to get down the hill without the snowboard, but better to keep him and those nice car keys in his pocket safe.

"I'll go down and get it, and you meet me at the second turn." Lon didn't laugh aloud at this built-in good will. "And if you're headed to Boulder, mind if I ride along?"

"I'd owe you more than a ride to town for that." His new companion grinned at him, locks of medium brown hair flipping around to lick the corner of his smile.

"We'll work it out on the way back." Lon stepped into his bindings for a last run that really would be more fun to take on his belly, but he had an audience. Probably wouldn't amount to more than a shared pizza, but the guy was attractive, in a late-twenties, happy-go-lucky way. Had to be secure in himself or he wouldn't have rainbow pompoms on the tassels of his Sherpa hat. Either that, or... Might be more in it than pizza after all. Lon shaved powder down to the lost board.

Ten minutes later, he sat in the warm cab of the RAV4 heading back to town with his new buddy, Corey, who looked even better with his hat and parka off. "Some great snow there, huh, Lon! Way better than up top with the gaffers."

"Super crunchy," Lon agreed, his lips curved with the memories. "Need to build a kicker next time it snows though." The only things he really missed about the ski area were the premade features and the half pipe. He'd stack snow for a jump if there was enough to make it worthwhile.

"I'm not much of an airdog," Corey admitted, guiding the little SUV through the river of headlights. "I like the speed and some nature."

That Lon could agree with. "The tricks are fun, but the quiet's better."

Corey nodded, making the ends of his hair dance. His hat had forced curls to form, inviting Lon's fingers to comb through them. "You'd never see an otter up at the terrain park."

Lon glanced sideways, all thoughts of running his fingers through Corey's curls gone. "You saw an otter?"

"Yeah, way cool little guy! Just slipping and sliding, having fun. He'd packed down a chute to slide into the creek, and just splashed in, *kerplop*, and got out to do it all over again. You know how they run with that bouncy gait? Maybe it's just how they get around but it screams, 'having a good time!' I watched him for a while until he disappeared downstream. Magic. That's why I come to the mountains." Corey slowed the truck—they were nearly back in town and there was a light up ahead.

"Me too." Lon relaxed against the headrest. Yeah, otters definitely had a good time.

So did men. Corey's home turned out to be a modest three-bedroom house on the south end of Boulder. "I'm between roommates right now," he explained, turning his key in the front door, and didn't have to mention that an associate professor in economics at the university would have trouble with property prices in Boulder.

Lon could sympathize. "I have three. It's always noisy." Not that he didn't contribute his share of the noise, but it made bringing someone home problematic, and it complicated other things.

Corey either went for simplicity or saw no reason to replace leftover grad-student furniture, but if the spindly lamp and the futon for a couch suggested leaner days, the big painting on the living room wall and the tribal rug over hardwood said he had good taste. Lon admired the green glass sculpture that kept hundreds of books company and wished it was on a much higher shelf.

An orange tabby cat ambled around the corner, only to hiss and flee. "I hate when that happens." Lon sighed. He liked cats.

"She's not very social," Corey apologized. "When she gets used to you, she'll be friendlier."

They played more 'getting to know you' games over the pizza: "*Where did you learn to board?*" "*What did you study?*" "*Did you do the Mall Crawl this year?*" Lon didn't ask if the futon

5

they sat on would flip into a bed, though he hoped they might try it. When the last round of pepperoni disappeared they arrived at the important question. Lon thought he could answer without Corey telling him. "Are you seeing anyone?"

With his face buried in Corey's neck, Lon inhaled deeply and trusted in Corey's "no". "Me either," Lon whispered, tickling soft skin with his whiskers.

"Good," Corey mumbled back. "Because I'd like to see more of you, starting with what's under this sweater."

Clothing flew to the floor and their hands heated trails across flesh. Pepperoni kisses gained momentum; Lon licked Corey's lips, finding his tongue and relishing the rasp of their whiskers, little skin kisses. Twisting and writhing together—Corey turned out long and lean under his baggy boarding pants—swept arms against backs, legs against legs, and cock against cock. Lon thrust upward against Corey's belly, content to be trapped beneath so much desire.

Corey rose up on his hands, looking at what he'd uncovered, and Lon wanted to squirm under that appreciative gaze. He was strong but he wasn't buff, not the way Corey was, with muscles standing in relief in his upper arms. Corey pushed against Lon's groin, his belly rippling with the thrust—Lon reached between them to grip both rampant cocks. Corey moaned, closing his eyes, letting Lon do what he would with his handful.

Good as Corey felt, he'd have to taste fine, with the tang of his day on the mountains and the glorious musk that was all man. Lon twisted from under, landing on his knees on the kilim rug that wouldn't be much padding but who cared, because Corey sat before him, his knees spread wide with welcome.

Lon took that welcome, parting his lips to brush over the straining head of Corey's cock, a crystal drop of fluid winking at the tip. No time for delicate teasing licks—a few swift swipes cleaned the droplet away before Lon plunged down over Corey's shaft, full and purplish, a glorious mouthful. Too much for a mouthful—Lon added a hand and set about bringing Corey to bliss. The tiny veins jumped under his fingertips like minnows darting. Corey stroked both hands through Lon's short, thick hair, following more than urging him on, because Lon needed no urging.

"You feel so good," Corey moaned, and Lon flicked his tongue against the tiny cord below the head of Corey's cock, because lifting away to say, "So do you" just wasn't happening. With one hand full of Corey's thigh and the other of cock, Lon dove again, down Corey's length, over and over, until a warning cry of "Gonna come!" brought him to the surface to watch jets of thick cream spurt across Corey's belly, catching in the crisp hairs.

Corey leaned back, sucking great gouts of air in through his mouth and letting them out through his nose, until he could curl forward to wrap his arms around Lon's shoulders and rub his cheek on top of Lon's head. "Wonderful," he breathed, and Lon pressed his face to Corey's chest in silent agreement. He eventually fished a blue T-shirt from the puddle of Corey's clothing to satisfy the silent demand of Corey's waving but too-short-to-reach arm. A quick swipe and they were standing long enough for a sweetly deep kiss that lasted until Corey pushed him down to the cushions.

"Now you." Corey breathed small gusts of warm air across the tingling head of Lon's cock and followed them with his lips.

Oh, yeah—Lon lolled back under Corey's wonderful attentions, the licks and swipes and warm pressure from his lips. Finally he could wind his fingers into Corey's curls, and flex his hips to drive more deeply into the heat Corey offered. Maybe not so much flexing— with one hand flat over the silky pelt covering Lon's groin, Corey firmly gripped the base of Lon's erection, holding him down against the futon.

All that sliding made Lon's balls draw up, but Corey chased them closer to Lon's body, his hand rolling the soft spheres under the skin. Lon wanted to say, "Too much!" but it wasn't, it was perfect, just too soon for a man who wanted this to last. Instead he moaned, the soft *hrrr* of each breath growing louder until the waves of pleasure coursing through him made him cry out. Corey held him through the pulsings, letting the hot strings of come splash against Lon's belly.

"Oh, that was good," Lon mumbled, letting one hand drop and the other massage the back of Corey's neck. The man gave seriously good head, and his hands felt so nice, stroking the last shivers away.

"Geez, this is soft." Corey bent to rub his face against Lon's thick, short, pubic hair. "Do you put conditioner down here or what?"

"Something like that." Lon squinched his eyes and hoped Corey wouldn't ask more questions. "I don't want to shave."

"If everybody's pubes felt this good, nobody would." Bestowing a quick kiss on Lon's softening shaft, Corey got another chin-swipe across Lon's groin. "It's nice. Feels like your hair."

"Yeah." Lon reached for the T-shirt and interrupted any more commentary with another kiss.

"Stay the night?" Corey offered.

"Wish I could, but I have to be to work at eight, and either I'm up at 5:30 for the bus or you're out of bed way too early with me." Professors, even the adjunct sort, got winter holidays, but not Lon. His desk at the bank didn't care if he found someone more enticing to spend a Monday morning with, Christmas break or not.

"Horrible." Corey climbed onto the futon to pull Lon into a hug. "I really want to know you better. Maybe dinner this week? And let's plan on going boarding on Saturday— there's snow forecast for late in the week."

"Sounds like fun." Lon snuggled closer to Corey and wished he didn't have to leave that night.

The sky gifted the land with close to a foot of fresh snow, champagne powder, crisp and dry. Lon and Corey'd finished their dinner date Friday evening with a snow fight in public and much warmer caresses in private. Lon woke in Corey's arms Saturday morning, and they almost hadn't gotten dressed to go boarding. Corey'd laughed when Lon pressed his nose against the window to admire the snow, and went to find his wool socks.

Little caps of snow balanced on the pine boughs at the bottom of a wide expanse of untracked white. "Ready to shred?" Lon lifted his face for a kiss—he felt entitled to a smooch now.

"You bet!" Corey obliged with a grin and a swipe of tongue. "No more 'til you get to the bottom!" He stepped into his bindings, flipped the latches, and put the first trails into the unmarked snow.

Lon swooped after him, his shout of joy ringing off the mountains, a plume of crystals rising up in his wake. Corey's private storm glittered against the cerulean sky, stinging Lon's cheeks as he passed through it, collecting a drift around his mouth. He swiped the flakes away from his beard—muzzle hair, Corey had called it the other night, tugging the coarse sprouts with his lips—and felt the pull of the snow. Other things called him from the base of the hill, where Corey waited with open arms, and that was the only pull Lon heeded. For now.

They hitched to the top rather than climbed, waiting longer for rides because there were two of them, but enjoying each other's company enough to stand in the cold with thumbs out. Lon kept one eye on the sun. It had swung to the other side of the sky while they'd enjoyed themselves.

"Think we'll see the otter this time?" Corey mused from the back of a pickup, his arm around Lon's shoulders.

"Might." Lon didn't want to make promises.

The hill was well and truly criss-crossed with tracks, theirs and others. Corey started down, cutting east toward the road. Lon let a clump of boarders get ahead of him, and sailed west, deep into the trees with desperate speed. He needed to evade everyone else on the hill. Losing the grade stopped him long enough to jerk his feet from the bindings, and he darted deeper into the woods, shedding clothes. The water called from just ahead; Lon ran to its cold embrace.

He'd stopped shivering by the time he'd climbed the hill—the exertion warmed him and he didn't have very long to wait for Corey, who tumbled out of the back of an SUV less than ten minutes later.

"Where'd you go, you muntjac?" Corey demanded. "One minute you're behind me, an hour later you're here."

Closer to an hour and a half. Lon had pushed steadily and knew exactly how long it took, and then he'd had to find his board and climb. "What does the bear do in the woods?" he teased.

"You could have said." Corey wrinkled his nose. "I thought you might have pulled a bono and were lying under a tree with a broken leg. Or neck."

"Sorry. The need came on fast." Damned fast. Lon had barely made it to the water.

"Too bad. I got a couple of runs in. Did you see the otter?" Corey brightened. "I watched him play in the creek."

"You did? Wow." Lon would have liked to watch Corey watch the otter; the man enjoyed everything he did. Lon would like to watch the otter too, but that just wasn't happening.

"Let's go that way. Maybe he's still there." Corey adjusted his hat over his ears. "You need to see him, he's really ace."

"I got some glimpses," Lon admitted. He'd go whichever direction made Corey happy, even if it meant climbing back to the top. Even though they wouldn't see the otter.

❧

Snowboarding with Corey was the high point of Lon's week, right up there with their evening spent at a movie, or walking the Pearl Street Mall looking at the fairy lights strung in the trees and listening to the street musicians who dared the cold. They'd eaten Thai food another night, spicy enough that Corey had welcomed the chilly slices of sashimi Lon requested from the sushi joint downstairs, and he'd been happy to accept the morsels of *hamachi* and *masu* from Lon's fingertips.

And now they were on their way to the mountain. Lon would need to slip away for an hour or so, but he'd tell Corey this time and not risk being followed or worried about. He was the more skilled boarder—he should be the one worrying about Corey's frangible skeleton.

Crap snow this time, damn it. Corey pulled a plax before they'd gotten halfway down, maybe catching his edge of his board on a death cookie hidden under the thin layer of new powder, and faceplanted hard after finding a rut. Lon dirfed it once for no reason other than ice. They thumbed their way to the top, discussing their prospects.

"Try once more, farther to the west?" Corey suggested.

One more wouldn't be enough. Lon didn't want to keep Corey waiting, but would he have a choice? They headed down the slope again, but in less than twenty yards, Corey bit snow hard. Head first, and his legs flipped into the air, curling his spine, maybe past the breaking point. The fun went *pfft* out of the day.

"Corey—what hurts? Does anything hurt?" If he couldn't feel anything—! Lon yanked one foot out of his bindings to kneel beside his fallen lover.

"That was fucking crashtastic," Corey grumbled, twitching and moving limbs when Lon begged for information. "Is there any point to staying out here? It's all choppy choppy, and I swear the next fall is gonna kill me."

11

"You want to go on up to the ski area?" Lon hoisted Corey to his feet.

"No, I want to go home while I still have a spine." Corey leaned against Lon, shaking slightly. "There'll be a lump on the back of my head from that scorpion." He wrapped both arms around Lon, who had nearly broken sympathetically when Corey had curled over far enough to conk himself with the edge of the snowboard. "Let's go back to my place. We'll pretend we had a good time up here, take a shower, go to bed, have a *really* good time, and skip any further near-death experiences. This slope is nothing but ice."

"We could penguin it." Lon's heart sank. Corey didn't want one more minute out here after that last fall, and who could blame him? But Lon needed some time.

"So I can find that chunk of ice with my face? No thanks." After one last squeeze, Corey knelt to unbuckle his bindings. With his snowboard under his arm, he started trudging up the hill, kicking hard into the snow but not finding much purchase, slipping back a step now and then.

The poor guy was miserable, and Lon was torn between Corey's needs and his own. He could yell, "Pick me up downhill in an hour!" but could he expect to get more than a polite "Bye" when Corey dumped him off at his own place and drove away? And without explaining, how could Lon hope for anything else? With a regretful look down the mountain to where the stream burbled its winter jokes, Lon knelt to release his bindings.

They drove back silently, Lon silently juggling time in his head with his hand on Corey's thigh, and Corey no doubt contemplating his mortality.

Getting back to the house perked Corey up a bit. "I'll throw a frittata in the oven, we'll have food in about an hour, and we can spend the day in bed." He pulled Lon over for a kiss. "Way better than killing ourselves on horrible snow."

If there weren't other considerations, Lon would have agreed wholeheartedly. He puckered under the kiss, his whiskers lifting forward, brushing Corey's cheek. They both shivered with the tickles. The marmalade kitty poked her head around the corner and disappeared before Corey could scoop her up. "Get used to him, Pumpkin."

"You want to take first shower, or do you want me to scrub your back?" Corey murmured.

Back-scrubbing, for sure, but Lon didn't dare ask for it. "Um, I might be a while."

"That 'sudden need' again?" Corey razzed him.

Absolutely, but it wasn't what he thought. Lon shrugged. "I'll yell when it's safe."

"Hokay…." Corey drawled, and headed to the kitchen.

Lon ran for the bathroom. He might have bought himself enough time; shedding clothing with every step, he prayed that the walls were thick enough that Corey wouldn't hear anything. This was bad—he tried never to be home at these times for good reason. With the bathroom door closed and locked, Lon turned the taps, jammed the plug into the drain, and let the water take him.

Hurrr, hurrr, warm. Lon almost never had warm water, but he didn't care, except for the novelty. His thick, oily fur kept the wet away from his skin except at his paws, nose and eyes. He paddled the few scant inches the tub let him move before flipping over, sloshing waves against the porcelain. He came back the other way, rising under the tap. Water bounced off his flat head and splattered into little drops around him. They didn't all stay in the tub, but they'd just make slippyslidey when he got out.

He sniffed the soap in the tray, wrinkling his nose and refusing to lick. It might taste better than it smelled. Nosing a bottle of shampoo until it fell into the water gave him something to bat around. The bottle bobbed under his splayed, webbed paws. Pushing it down to the bottom and then letting go made the bright plastic jump into the air—Lon dove at it like a trout. Trout would be good. Or char or kokanee. *Mmm.*

13

Darn. His stomach was growling. Nothing in this tiny room smelled good enough to bite into. He whuffled in the water, making the bubbles dance. Food would come along. Maybe. Other swims, he had to nose into the crevices between rocks for single bites of pinchies that didn't like to be eaten. They fought back with claws, pulling whiskers and nipping noses. Paws, too, if they were big and he was slow. They needed to be torn apart to get at the good stuff under the crackly anyway. He investigated the bottom of the tub. No rocks, no pinchies. He patted the drain, but it wasn't hiding any pinchies either.

The water was getting deeper, deep enough to do a flip turn tail over head. Fun! He did it again to be sure, this time under the waterfall. He had just enough room to spin a circle. Bunch of circles! Whee!

Hey! He could get up on the ledge, he could tiptoe around the water. And there was a slide! A little slide, but slidy. His claws chattered against the hard tub. *Hurr, hurr! Grab tight!* He launched down the slant of the tub, splashing into the water. Some of it jumped out of the tub, but the waterfall was bringing more. *Hurr, hurr! All good!*

Noises outside! Lon sat up, balancing on his tail, placing one webbed forepaw on the lip of the tub.

"Lon? Are you okay in there?"

He cocked his head at the sounds. Words, right, those were words. Lon knew words. Sometimes he knew a lot more words. He knew his name. He knew who made the words— Corey, yummy Corey that he nibbled but didn't bite, who petted him so wonderfully. When he couldn't swim. Corey didn't know how well he could swim. *Corey wasn't supposed to know Lon could swim!*

"Lon? I hear water, you can't still be on the pot. I'm coming in. I'm getting sore and I want to get into the shower."

Coming in—he understood that. He dove to the bottom of the tub, but he couldn't swim upstream and he couldn't swim downstream, and down wasn't very deep.

14

"Lon?" The door opened, and tall, yummy Corey stood in the opening.

Maybe Corey wouldn't be afraid. Lon stood up to his full height again, braced against his tail, his head about the height of Corey's belly. Resting both forepaws on the tub, he cocked his head, seeing Corey through the sprouts of whiskers around his nose. He blinked and lifted one paw.

"Lon? There's an otter in the bathroom." Corey peered around the door at the flushy noisy thing that Lon never played with. "Why is there an otter in the bathroom? Uh...." He dragged his eyes away to search the small room. "Lon? Where are you?" Corey turned back to lock eyes with him. "Lon?"

Corey recognized him! Even with his fur on! He slithered out of the tub, stopping on the soft not-grass on the floor. Drippy—he was drippy and shaking would make everything slippy. *Corey doesn't like slippy.* He bit the soft white thing hanging off the wall and yanked. It fell over him. Fun! He could play peekies! First to roll, rolling was good. More fun in mud, but he had no mud, just softalmostfuzzy. Twisting around in it made his fur puffier, and he could peek at Corey, who'd sat down on the flushy thing. Made a big thump. Corey didn't usually thump. He didn't like his thump earlier, he fell and made Lon leave the snow. The stream called but Lon couldn't answer, because Corey went thump.

"Uh...." This was a little thump, and then another little thump—Corey got up enough to reach over and make the waterfall stop. Darn! He liked the waterfall. Why was Corey moving so slow and careful? Did he think Lon would bite? Never!

Maybe Corey didn't like the waterfall. It made a rushy noise, like rapids that weren't fun to swim in, they had rocks and bashed. Corey had a bash, he probably didn't want another and the waterfall made him afraid. Okay. Ponds were fun too. In a minute. Right now he needed to sniff Corey, 'cause Corey didn't look so good. Maybe a little

15

wobbly, like he'd been through the rapids and bounced off a rock. Leaning elbows on knees like he might tumble. Wouldn't be a fun tumble.

"There's an otter in my bathroom and my boyfriend is nowhere to be seen," Corey mumbled.

That was silly, Lon was right here! He came to snuffle Corey's fingers, dangling at a good height for sniffing without standing. He whiskered Corey's hand, which smelled of yummy things, and felt Corey tense through his vibrissae. Could learn so much stuff with vibrissae! He whiskered again and pushed his head into Corey's palm. *Come on, Corey! Pet!*

"Therefore, my boyfriend is an otter." Corey finally stroked Lon's head. "Which is absurd. But here you are."

Well of course he was here! Lon petted himself against Corey's hand. Just 'cause he had his fur on! Course, Corey wasn't supposed to see him with his fur on when he'd know it was Lon, but Corey liked otters, and he liked Lon, so it should all be okay, shouldn't it? Lon dropped to the floor to roll on Corey's feet. Tummy up was irresistible!

Not irresistible enough—Corey hadn't reached down yet. Lon pushed all his whiskers forward in his best otter smile.

Corey finally reached down to stroke. "You're so soft." Lon wiggled under Corey's hand. "You're really an otter. Shifter. Otter shifter. Or were-otter. Or something."

Hmmph! Something! Show him otter! Lon twisted to his feet to jump back into the pond. What else would he be with his long body and strong tail? He was all wet again, but that was fine—he rolled to his back with his face out of water, his paws over his chest. A tiny swish with his tail made him bump his head on the slidy, so he floated. Of course he was an otter!

Except—Corey still looked tumbly. Cute wasn't doing it. He needed words. Lon *pushed*, but it wasn't time yet.

Okay, no words. Lon scrambled out of the tub. He was slick so he started to shake, one of those great-feeling "start at the front and get all the way to his tail" shakes, but Corey

16

looked scared. Of shaking? He didn't want to scare Corey. The soft thing would work, so Lon rolled on it again to get fluffy. Corey liked fluffy. Lon rubbed his belly on the soft thing. Get fluffy all over. Corey relaxed. He even smiled.

"Thanks for not soaking the bathroom the rest of the way." He ran a hand over the back of his head. "I conked myself and now my boyfriend's an otter. Some head injury." Corey stood up. "Are you hungry?"

Oh yeah! Hungry hungry! Lon bounced to the kitchen, reveling in the way his spine humped and stretched. He could run indoors, even if he couldn't swim more than a few inches. Something good for Lon! Corey followed—Lon made sure, circling around his feet.

Lon scraped at a cupboard door, making it swing out an inch and *thunk* back before he could get a claw into the gap. Corey opened it the rest of the way. "You want something in particular?"

Standing up again, Lon surveyed the shelves. A stack of flat cans! Lon knew what came from flat cans! He snagged the stack and pulled it forward. One fell, bouncing on the floor.

Corey shoved the stack back. "You want cat food?"

Ick! No catfood! Lon cuffed the can under the kitchen table.

"Nope, you don't want cat food." Corey bent to retrieve the can. "Bet you want tuna."

Yes, yes, fishie in a can! Weaving between Corey's ankles and *chirring* should convince him! Lon couldn't smell the difference before the seal was broken. One whiff of cat food would have sent him under the bed. Where the cat was probably hiding. Maybe she'd play with him when he wore his fur? *Hurr, no.* The last cat he tried to play with didn't care if he had his fur on or not, and swatted. He covered his nose with one paw.

"Yeah, it is pretty stinky, but Pumpkin likes it." Corey returned the cat food to the cupboard and found another can that looked the same to Lon. There was a way to tell the difference, but he couldn't remember it right now. But

17

Corey knew. He shook the tuna out into a bowl and squatted to set it down on the floor. "Dolphin-safe albacore. Good stuff, huh?"

Very good! Lon rubbed his chin on both of Corey's knees before diving in. Cooked, not his favorite, but still tasty. He bolted the flakes of fish and chased the scraps around the bowl with his slender pink tongue.

"More?" Corey asked, opening the cupboard again.

Maybe not fishie, but what else was there? Lon checked out the shelves, bumping a box which toppled. The contents rustled. And crackled when he pounced! What a great sound! He mashed the box with both forefeet, to Corey's yelp. Have to teach Corey how to play! Lon pounced again, skidding across the floor, trailing little round things that crunched when he stepped on them. He stepped on several—they went to sand under his pads. More? He gave the box a good shake. Lots of little rounds flew out like water splashes! *Hurr!* He shook again.

"Stop! Stop!" Corey yelled. He dove after the box.

Corey was playing, so why was he yelling? Lon backed under the table with his prize, but the box caught on the chair. Corey wrestled him for it. What a good game! More rounds flew out. Corey won the game! But he shut the box and put it back in the cupboard.

Spoilsport! All grumpy with his arms crossed like that. Tug-of-war was supposed to last longer, even if Corey was losing. Lon could still play with the rounds. He dashed out from beneath the table to skid through the drifts on the floor.

"You get to clean that up when you have hands again." That wasn't a playing voice.

Lon peered upward. *Lighten up, man!* He crunched a round and licked up a few more, showing how they stuck to his tongue. Didn't want to munch all the rounds, though.

"Don't try cute on me. It doesn't work." But Corey made his own *hrr.* "Come back to the bathroom. I still want that shower."

More waterfall! Lon scampered back to the fake pond and jumped in. Not much room to paddle, less with Corey standing in there with him, but Lon could play twisties around Corey's feet. Except the pond was escaping! Water gurgled after Corey took the plug away, but then he turned the waterfall back on, so everything would be okay. Lon didn't like the pond much once Corey soaped and shampooed, so he didn't mind that the water ran away. More fell on him, dribbling off Corey's elbows and dick. He tried to catch some drips, but they were soap-flavored. He went back to sliding, aiming between Corey's feet.

Did Corey still have soap on him? Lon checked.

"Agh!" Corey grabbed at his butt with both hands. "Don't do that!" He glared at Lon, who cocked his head. What was the problem?

"I've just been goosed by an otter." Corey took one hand away to rub his face. "Must have hit my head harder than I thought. When do you turn human again?"

Lon wrinkled his lip. *When did he?* He *pushed,* but he didn't change, even though his tail tingled. *Soon.* He tried rolling to his back and waving his forepaws.

"You're too cute. Just keep the teeth away from my junk." Corey cradled his groin with both hands.

Hmmph. If Corey still had soap on his butt, Lon didn't need to check any other parts. He ran a paw over his whiskers. Corey went back to rinsing his hair but didn't stop staring at Lon, his eyes slitted. *It was one little sniff, dude.* Lon flattened his head against the bottom of the pond and let the waterfall patter on his belly.

But Corey turned off the waterfall and stepped away to rub himself with a softalmostfuzzy. Lon's still lay on the floor, except it was a soggy now. Lon rolled on it anyway.

"You're trying." Corey knelt to stroke him. "But if we stay in here, there's less likelihood of you trashing the rest of the house before you change. Or are we stuck until the moon gets full?"

A beep sounded from beyond the door. "Wait here." Corey scooted through the door and shut it tight, so tight Lon couldn't open it even with his webbed front paws. Too slick. Stuck in here, 'til Corey came back. Not even clawing the rolly-come-apart stuff by the flushy thing made him feel better, although the shreds floated to the ground like aspen catkins in spring. He *whuffed* them across the floor. They wilted into the wet spots.

Corey slid back in. "The fritatta's—oh, Lon! Did you have to make such a mess?" He knelt again to scrape up the wet blobs. "Two weeks to the next full moon; I checked. I'm not going to have any house left." He flung the blobs into a round thing Lon hadn't sniffed yet and pulled him against a warm, solid leg. Lon flopped sideways and pressed the top of his head to Corey's skin. "What are we going to do with you?"

Lifting his chin for Corey's strong fingers to rub better, Lon considered. He needed some room. He liked Corey's scritches though. And once he put his fur away, Corey might never scritch again. Lon whuffled and sank flat to the not-grass.

"You're adorable, but...." Corey rested his hand on Lon's back.

But. Lon didn't want to put his fur away, but he needed his words to talk to Corey. He whuffled again, and huffed. Corey stroked to the base of Lon's tail and stopped touching.

Lon *pushed.* His legs grew, his arms extended, his fur went away, and Lon was left crouching on the bathroom floor on a sopping bath mat that he'd have to wring out as part of drying the room. Damn, but he hated wearing his fur indoors. He'd lift his head, stand up, and get started on the damage, except that would mean meeting Corey's eyes.

A warm hand landed on the back of Lon's neck, to massage gently rather than stroke. "Hey, Lon. You okay? Hungry again?"

20

Lon spoke to the floor. "You're taking this well." He didn't rise. Corey's hand remained on him, and Lon wanted to soak up the last caresses.

"Probably because I had an hour to get used to you being an otter and wanting the form that talks to come back." Covering more of Lon's skin with each stroke, Corey worked his way down Lon's back. "I can't believe I'm saying this, but the evidence is pretty persuasive." He reached the base of Lon's spine and stopped.

No, he didn't have a tail at the moment; he wouldn't have a tail again for days. Nothing there but Lon's rounded ass, with the crevasse Corey'd already explored pretty thoroughly. It was just a butt now, and Corey didn't have to treat it like something weird. Lon sat up, making Corey drop his hand.

"Yeah." Lon began to collect the rest of the shredded toilet paper. The remains of the roll hung in tatters. He threw a squashy handful into the trash and began to scrape up more. "Sorry about the mess. I'll clean it up and go."

"Don't." Corey reached out again, stroking Lon's shoulder.

"Have to. I wrecked the house." The fun was seldom worth the clean-up. The wreckage this time would be greater than any smashed cereal or clawed tissue.

"Clean up, yeah, but I meant 'Don't go'." He pulled Lon, and after a moment's resistance, Lon leaned into the embrace, his back warmed against the sparse pelt on Corey's chest. Corey added another arm to the hug. "Please don't go."

"This is my big chance to disappear and let you think you imagined it all in a concussion." But Lon covered Corey's hand with his own, weak now with fingers and an opposable thumb that let him open doors without help.

"But the frittata's ready, and then we were going to go to bed." Corey's lips against Lon's neck were awfully persuasive.

"And somewhere in there you're going to ask a million questions I don't want to answer. Better I just fade into the undergrowth." Lon pulled away. Wringing the soaked towel over the tub gave him something to hurt.

"I'm an economist, not a biologist. Yeah, I have a million questions, but it's not like I want to study you for a paper. But I'm used to observing and drawing conclusions, and being proven totally wrong by events. Not usually as spectacular as my boyfriend turning into an otter, but still wrong." Corey's voice dropped. "And I thought we were getting along pretty well these last few weeks."

Oh yeah, they'd been getting along beautifully, enough to lull Lon into risking a change with Corey around. "I should have bolted outside, put my fur away, and strolled back like nothing ever happened."

"You'd have been naked though, and that would have raised more questions. So this explains why my kitty's afraid of you." Corey sounded matter of fact about it. "You must smell wild to her."

"Yeah." Lon inspected the shampoo bottle for tooth-marks before restoring it to a tub ledge he could barely see through a wet haze. "Cats hate me. Dogs usually get over it, and if they don't, my teeth are sharper."

"If you keep coming around, Pumpkin will get used to you. She's pretty mellow."

Lon snorted. He'd yet to meet a cat that would let him touch it. Men, now…. That had to be Corey's hand at his waist.

"And now I know why you disappeared last week. Bears do all sorts of things in the woods, like play and eat. And it's why I never saw you and the otter at the same time. Except I did, I just didn't know it." A second hand at Lon's waist made him jump. Corey pulled him back again, to rest on strong thighs, wrapped in long arms. "Now I do. Is that so bad you have to run?"

"Bears are humorless fuckers. Gotta stay away from 'em." Three-inch claws had taught Lon the foolishness of teasing bears back when he was sixteen. Pulling away from

Corey's embrace would feel like the bear's lesson, but… "I don't want to be some curiosity to you."

"More like being a jerk." Corey squeezed Lon's middle, following it with a kiss between Lon's shoulder blades. "You weren't a curiosity last night or last weekend or this morning. Just the most copacetic man I've met in a long time, and I wanted to be with you just for that. Okay, I know something new and fascinating about you, but that doesn't change what went before."

Maybe—maybe it didn't. Lon allowed himself to relax a smidge. "Nobody outside my family's ever seen me take my fur off."

"Then I'm honored you let me see." Corey kissed Lon's backbone. "It doesn't hurt, does it?"

"No, it just tingles. Why would it hurt?"

"Because when you're a human, you're about five foot nine and one hundred fifty pounds, and when you're an otter, you're about so—" Corey unwrapped enough to measure out a four-foot span with his hands."—and maybe twenty or twenty-five pounds. Where does the rest go?" He cuddled around Lon's middle again, bringing warmth beyond what came from his skin.

"No idea. It's there when I need it and it goes away when I don't." Lon shrugged, and then twisted away to end on his feet. "See! I told you you'd have a million questions!"

"I was answering your question, I thought." Corey gazed up with hurt brown eyes. "Am I not allowed to be concerned for you?"

But—taking his fur on and off wasn't like doing a scorpion in the snow. Except—Corey didn't know that, any more than Lon knew if Corey'd been hurt until he asked. "Yeah. Okay. It wasn't idle curiosity." He put his hand out, braced to help Corey stand.

"I have more respect for you than that." Corey pulled lightly against Lon's hand on his way to his feet. "I do have questions, but you tell me what you want me to know, when you want me to know it, okay? I can figure some things out for myself, given some hints."

"Like what?" Lon went cold. He turned away again, busying himself with the wet floor and Corey's discarded towel.

"Well, why you have such thick, short hair, and why your pubes feel the same, and maybe why you don't want to shave down there. And maybe why your facial hair is just around your mouth, not all over your cheeks. It's a good look on you, by the way. You've probably never gone clean-shaven." Corey leaned against the door jamb, watching Lon dry the vanity doors. Lord, but he'd made a mess.

Nothing Corey said sounded like a question, but Lon answered anyway. "Yeah. I can't go clean shaven. I didn't get my fur until I was old enough to grow whiskers, and the one time I tried shaving, it hurt like hell and my fur wouldn't come out until the shaved spot grew back. Good thing I only got the middle of my upper lip. I was sick for weeks."

"Shaving hu—?" Corey chopped the word off.

Not asking any questions at all would probably make Corey pop like a crunched snail shell. Lon decided to let it go. "Hell, yeah, it hurt. I don't see how you do it every morning, except you just have whiskers. Mine are vibrissae, with all sorts of nerve endings attached. Dragging the razor against the grain got rid of the hair part, but really twanged everything else." He shuddered with remembered pain and smoothed the offended beard down the right way.

"I bet." Corey sounded thoughtful. "I was thinking you liked to shift about once a week, but if not shifting made you ill, then you probably need to shift."

"Yeah. It's a need." A like, too—Lon enjoyed his time in fur, with a thousand smells and the water for a friend. "I took my fur off as soon as I could today, but—" He yanked the toilet paper off its hook and made the shreds waggle. "—I need at least an hour. More than twelve hours and it's hard to remember how to talk and use tools. One to five

24

hours is about right. And not indoors if I can help it." He found another roll of tissue under the sink. Corey wasn't judging. He wasn't giddy or asking a thousand questions all at once.

"And I made you skip your fur time up in the mountains. Sorry." Corey took one end of the bathmat, and together they wrung a quart of water into the tub. "This is kind of my fault."

"You didn't know, and I was trying to keep you from knowing. I was going to say I fell asleep in the tub for an hour, but I forgot about turning the water off." He'd forgotten *how* to turn the water off, or maybe why it needed to be done.

"Now that I know, we can plan for it." Corey hung the damp mat on the shower curtain bar. "Anything special for the full moon?"

"No, that's the wolves."

"Wolves?" Corey rocked back on his heels.

"Why are you being so calm about me being an otter and then going all woo-woo about wolves? They aren't so careful about being seen and there's a lot more of them." Lon bared his teeth and raised his hands up in mocking claws. "They even get movies 'cause they so sexy!" Dropping his hands, Lon hoped the catch in his breath could be mistaken for residual growls. Stupid wolves. Sooner or later a wolf would want to star in one of those movies—Look! No special effects budget!— and they'd all be fucked.

"Hey, I believe you!" Corey patted the air, *stop stop.* "If anybody knows these things, it'd be you. Just give me a minute to assimilate this, okay?" Scrubbing one hand over his face, he swayed slightly, and then stood straight, and if not confidently, then at least not openly dubious. "Okay. There are wolves that shift with the full moon. Do you hang out together?"

"No!" Lon went still with the howling in his head. "I hate when the full moon falls on a weekend. I have to wear

25

my fur early and get home well before dark. They think I'm fair game."

"We can plan for that too." Corey opened his arms. "I don't want you getting eaten by anything."

Nearly diving into Corey's hug, Lon soaked up the promise of future refuge. "Then don't invite me to any faculty parties." He nuzzled into the base of Corey's neck, holding tight to more than promises in the warmth of Corey's skin.

"They're academics; they'll just bore you to death." A deep chuckle vibrated through Corey's chest.

"Your department chairman is not someone I want to meet during the full moon." In spite of himself, Lon shivered. "I don't want him to notice me ever."

"Huh. Guess that explains a lot about Melvin." Corey stopped laughing. "You really aren't joking."

Hell no, he wasn't joking. Lon growled against Corey's throat. "Don't ever let Melvin get close enough to do this, not with my scent on you."

Corey froze. "Erm, right.No faculty parties."

Oh shit. Corey might think "no Lon" would be safer. But he hadn't let go. And when he relaxed, Lon felt his own tension trickle away. With his vibrissae, he could feel every thud of Corey's pulse, which finally slowed to something approaching normal.

"There's no reason for the old fart to get that near—my field's not closely related." With some nuzzling of his own around Lon's ear, Corey suggested, "Let's get the kitchen."

Whoa. Lon had shaken more cereal around than he'd thought. "I'll get you another box of Cheerios."

"You were having fun." Corey crunched through the scattered bits to the broom closet.

"You can't tell me they don't feel funny when you squash them." Lon had to smile. They tasted fine when he'd licked off his paws.

"They do." Corey reached out a naked big toe to press a circle into powder. "Which is not the same as let's do it some more."

"You just did," Lon pointed out.

Corey offered the broom. "Can't help it, troutbreath."

Jerking the broom away, Lon started shoving cereal around the floor. "You ate just as much raw fish as I did the other night, and liked it just as much. What did you think *masu* is?" He swiped hard, sending half a cup of morsels under the fridge. Fuck the name calling, Corey could move his own damned fridge. "It's *trout*, the same fish I catch, only mine's lots fresher."

Flopping down in a kitchen chair and picking his feet out of sweeping range, Corey grimaced. "Yeah, I did. Sorry. It's too soon for teasing." He twisted away from the hearty whack Lon barely pulled from landing on Corey's shins. "Maybe some things will always be too soon for teasing. I just don't... Lon, I'm trying to keep calm here, but my whole worldview's been kind of turned upside down. 'My boyfriend is an otter' are words I never imagined stringing together."

Lon stopped sweeping. "If I'm not your boyfriend, you can keep on not imagining." He leaned heavily on the broom. "Since when am I your boyfriend, anyway?" Hadn't Corey said that when Lon had his fur on?

Corey set his feet down carefully in a Cheerio-free zone. "I'm not sure. Since you hand-fed me pieces of raw fish, or left a mountain you love because I was hurt? I've been practicing saying that since I saw you in the tub, because one part feels wonderful and the other part I need to wrap my mind around."

He was trying. Corey was really trying. Lon struggled to find the same openness for a secret he'd kept from the world, and certainly never shared with a lover. "What if I need to wrap my mind around the boyfriend part?"

Rising from the chair, Corey held out his arms. "I could keep repeating it until it sounds familiar?"

Lon swept a path through the cereal until he could reach Corey. The broom fell, forgotten, while Lon slid into the embrace that was starting to feel like home. "Good idea." He lifted his face for a kiss. "I've got tunabreath."

Corey smiled down with warm eyes. "I eat tuna."

Damned good thing too, because Lon opened his mouth under Corey's, and they stayed there a long time.

"Whahoo!" Corey launched his snowboard down the hill, swooping goofy-footed in huge curves. Lon bounded after him, catching up in two turns. He leaped onto the board, crouching between Corey's feet, letting his two-footed companion slide them down the hill. Before they reached bottom, Lon leaped away to belly-slide the rest of the way to the flat.

Hurr! Lon laughed, and Corey joined him, spinning to a stop before falling over. Once he hit the snow, Lon could bounce over to nuzzle his face. Corey chuckled, fending off Lon's whiskery caress, but who was quicker? Lon poked his nose under Corey's Sherpa hat, *whiffling* into his ear before yanking a tassel hard enough to steal the wooly headgear away.

"Give that back!" Corey twisted to grab his hat, and truth be told, Lon could have run away much faster with his booty. Tug of war was more fun though, and if he let go when he could have won, then the hat would survive for another game. This hat had blue tassels—Lon had learned the hard way.

He let Corey scoop him up in a warm, crackly hug. Gore-Tex would never match fur for softness or warmth, but it was the best Corey had, and it did let him play in the snow. Lon wriggled tight under Corey's chin, *chirring* his delight in the game. Corey was the best playmate ever!

His only two-foot playmate ever, but so good Lon couldn't imagine needing another. Not even when he put his

28

fur away and the games changed to what two men enjoyed, clothed or not. He nosed Corey's Adam's apple and chuffed along with his man.

"It's been about two hours. Do you want to board a couple of runs, or belly slide some more?" Corey rubbed Lon's flanks hard, fluffing his fur against the grain. "Or swim?"

Hmm—he'd had a great swim, and he'd munched down a brookie when Corey wasn't watching—the guy just didn't appreciate the best way to eat a fish. Lon didn't want to share his dinner if Corey was going to say, "Ick" again. But he might catch one for Corey to cook.

He'd had a good time in his fur, and he'd have a different good time in his skin. Lon *pushed*—his tail disappeared and his sides went bald. Bouncing up out of the snow, he looked frantically for his clothing. Some things were better with fur on!

"Under that juniper." Corey pointed. "Before you freeze off something I have plans for."

The wind chased Lon into his clothing almost faster than his fingers could pull, zip, or buckle. "It didn't feel that cold a moment ago." He popped his blue beanie hat over his thick brown pelt to cover his ears.

"Probably because you were down on the ground and your ears were little." Corey had stuck his snowboard upright into a drift, where it waved in the breeze. He now came to wrap long arms around Lon. "We can use the board for a windbreak for what I want next."

"Which would be…?" Hugging back and nuzzling along Corey's jaw line, Lon had a pretty good idea, but he liked hearing it.

"I'm going to suck your cock." Corey bore Lon backward into the snow, landing gently but insistently.

With his parka and pants to insulate him from the snow and Corey above him, Lon was sheltered from more than the elements. He opened his mouth under Corey's, to lick with his wide human tongue, and nibble with mobile human

29

lips. His vibrissae worked just fine, letting him feel Corey's weekend beard and smooth skin—he facestroked against Corey's nose and cheeks. Damn, but this man felt fine!

Corey pressed back, his mouth insistent, his body thrusting. "Had a good time?"

"Yeah. Did." And now with his cock filling within his long johns, Lon was ready for the next good time—with Corey.

"Don't know why I get so turned on watching you run naked in the snow." Straddling Lon, Corey removed one glove and scooted back until he could reach Lon's fly.

"I just tucked that away." Lon folded his own mittened hands behind his head, ready to watch, but also ready to retrieve his clothing if Corey uncovered too much.

"And now I'll untuck just enough." Grinning wickedly, Corey worked Lon's cock out and popped his mouth over the head. With one warm hand he covered what he couldn't engulf and worked up and down Lon's shaft, never giving the wind a chance to touch damp skin.

Corey chuckled around his mouthful when a flick of his tongue made Lon jump—and Lon chuckled too, for the soft voice of the wind in the pines, the evergreen tang of juniper, and a light dust of powder across his cheeks to go with the wonder of Corey's mouth. Brilliant blue Colorado sky turned to spangles when Corey coaxed the orgasm from deep within. Lon's *hrr* became "Ahh!" with each spasm and jet. Corey took him deeper, pinning his hips against the snow, until Lon settled back against the drift, his breath coming in choppy plumes.

With a quick slurp across the softening head, Corey flipped microfiber underwear over Lon's cock and zipped his waterproof boarding pants before the wind could get more than a taste. Grinning hugely, he jammed his hand back into his glove.

"Wow." Lon closed his eyes and lifted his hands to Corey, who snuggled back down with more kisses. "Best outdoor blowjob ever."

"That's what you said last week."

"Was true then too. They just get better." It felt funny but good to have his whiskers licked. He seized control of the kiss, rolling Corey to his back and scooting back into the shelter of the snowboard.

One mitten hit the snow, and Lon slipped his naked hand into Corey's pants, finding the hot column of flesh. Corey moaned into the kiss, his tongue matching the rhythm Lon set, and lay back to let Lon play as he would. Corey wouldn't undress even partially outdoors, crying cold, and although Lon suspected more reasons, he wouldn't press. Pull, though—he gripped Corey's hard cock, reveling in the slide of skin over firm core, gauging how close his lover was to coming.

Corey gargled, "Nggh!" and pulled his waistband down enough to let Lon aim his cock toward the side, shooting pale ribbons of come into the snow. Stroking the last shudders away, Lon pressed his mouth to Corey's jaw. In a moment, Corey released his grip on his clothing and turned to meet Lon's lips.

"Wonderful," he murmured. "Ready to head home?"

No, but Lon would be happy to go back to Corey's house. He'd solved the clothes/bus/get-to-work-on-Monday-mornings problem by packing work garb, and Corey dropped him off at the bank on the way to the university campus. "If you're done on the snow, or we could do another run or two on the boards."

"Nah, it's warming up—the snow's getting sticky." A slicker wax on the boards would improve the ride, but they should have thought about that before they left Boulder. Besides, they could have a leisurely shower when they returned, and Lon could luxuriate under shampoo and Corey's fingers. This time. He hadn't changed in the house in two months, not since the day he, Corey, and an ill-fated box of cereal met in the kitchen. Corey wouldn't take him away from fur time—now that he knew about fur time.

"'Kay. We can pick up a ride back to the truck."

On the way back to Boulder, Lon thought lazily of the future. "We're going to have to go farther into the mountains for good snow once it starts to warm up."

"Or find another place that's fun for you." Corey drummed his fingers against the steering wheel. "Do you ever swim in Boulder Creek?"

The stream that cut through town had a popular bicycling path running next to it, frequented by skaters, cyclists, runners, parents with running strollers, and the occasional homeless person. The water was an endless temptation and one reason Lon had come to Boulder, but it had some drawbacks. "I usually go upstream into the hills. Otherwise my clothes get stolen or some lunatic biologist tries to tag me."

"Tag you!" Corey took his too-wide eyes off the road for a moment. "Why?"

"River otters were nearly extinct in Colorado, but they've been making a comeback in the upper river basins, so I tend to draw some interest. I thought I was fast enough not to get caught, but once was enough. That tag hurt like a sonofoabitch to get off." Lon put a hand to the offended ear. He'd considered leaving it as jewelry to make a statement, but that could have led to some awkward conversations with Fish and Game officers, and besides, it pinched once he took his fur off.

"If I take my kayak out on the creek, I could fend off the biologists for you." Sounding like he'd whack them with his paddle if necessary, Corey reached over to pat Lon's knee. "Or spring their traps, or whatever. And I could certainly guard your clothes."

"Thanks. That would make warm weather shifts a lot easier—we could even go out to the rez." Lon liked Boulder Reservoir for a change of pace, but having to hitch home in a borrowed towel after his clothing and bus fare disappeared had sucked the joy out of his last trip. If Corey went along…. He placed his hand over Corey's. "Sounds like you're planning way into the future."

"Yeah, I am. Thinking about a lot of things, like how I still don't have a roommate, and you have more than you want, and if two people lived in a three bedroom house, we'd still have an office and we could otter-proof the third bedroom…." Corey squeezed Lon's knee. "Think it could work?"

"Everything but the otter-proofing, yeah." Lon wanted to grab Corey right there, and smooch the daylights out of him, but not on the highway. Guess they were almost home! "I get into about everything."

"Then we'll build you a koi pond in the back yard. It's big enough." Corey smiled, and the warmth in his brown eyes melted Lon into a puddle. "Move in with me, and we can start digging."

"I'd love that." Oh, how Lon wanted to add, "And I love you," but that should wait until he could follow the words with kisses. "I've never eaten a koi."

OTTER
Chaos

CHAPTER ONE

Guitars, fiddles and the skirl of the pipes begged Corey's toes to tap. The brewpub rang with a bouncy Irish tune. Corey wouldn't dance—he was no Michael Flatley, more of a Michael Flatfoot, but he couldn't stay still either.

Out of mercy to the group, he'd put down the wooden "bones" he'd been thunking along as a rhythm section, and retired from the circle of musicians to a stool at the bar. His lover Lon remained in the circle, picking the notes on his guitar. Lon's toes couldn't stay still either.

Corey knew the signs. Lon would be on his feet in three...two...one...

The session band was one guitarist short—a five foot nine, bearded dervish was up and prancing madly with his guitar. One hand on the neck, the other on the curve of the instrument's body, Lon held the guitar like a partner while his feet tapped and scurried. He wouldn't be invited into the cast of Riverdance, but who cared, when he was having such a good time?

Lon whirled by with his six-string partner, the facial fur of his deep brown goatee split with his grin. Corey applauded but wouldn't get up to join him. They'd tried that once, and succeeded in kicking each others' shins.

"He'd be quite the dancer if he knew the steps," Hugh, the bartender and Lon and Corey's neighbor, commented.

"Does it matter?" Corey raised his voice to carry over the music, given that he'd rather watch the dancer's progress than turn around. He leaned back when Lon clattered by. So what if nothing happening at the end of Lon's legs was an actual stepdance step? The whole pub followed him with their eyes, because how could they not watch someone having that good of a time?

The fiddles and the pipes hit a last note, lost in the flurry of applause. Lon bowed grandly, right, left, and then more deeply to Corey. That performance merited a blown kiss and a "Bravo!"

Maybe it should have been a toast with his beer and a *Sláinte*, since they were in the most Irish-like pub in Boulder, but Lon soaked up the applause in any language. Then he plopped back into his seat in the circle, ready to debate choice of the next tune with Steven.

"You have to play my favorite!" Lon urged the man with the pipes. "We'll sing!"

"I'll drown you all out," Steven objected, and demonstrated with a blast of the drones.

"Okay, we'll yell." Lon wouldn't be deterred.

"It's not an Irish tune." Steven rolled his eyes. "Or even Scottish."

"You make it sound so good on the pipes."

"He does." Corey spoke aside to Hugh, who grinned for the praise for his lover. Everything Steven played on his pipes or his cello, or his guitar, sounded good—the man was a pro. Corey opened the windows to catch the strains of Steven practicing at home, and Lon would slip next door to pick out a reel or a jig when the sounds of the Irish wafted across the way.

"How about—" Steven objected, but Corey deflected his suggestion.

"Make Lon happy, Steven." No other tune would do if Lon wanted this one. Not that Corey was sure which song Lon was begging for. Last week it was The Hills of

Connemara, which had everyone roaring along about the "mountain tay," and the week before that it was The Lilting Banshee. "Play it for him."

"Oh, all right." Steven smoothed his kilt, adjusted something on his pipes, and played notes that made Lon bounce in his seat and half the other musicians grin. He launched into "The Lion Sleeps Tonight," which stunned the revelers in the pub first into silence and then into gales of laughter.

Lon strummed along, and Corey helped yodel through the chorus, because this doofy song did sound good on the pipes.

"Emily, you pick!" Lon awarded the next choice to a young woman with a golden voice. No one minded Lon directing them—they were as much under the spell of his delight as Corey was. Well, maybe not that much—they didn't get to go home with him, but everyone enjoyed what Lon enjoyed, because Lon was so good at enjoying himself. Corey never imagined sitting in on a session until his lover suggested it. He was an economist, not a musician.

"How about Black is the Color of My True Love's Hair?" she suggested, but the group muttered apologies for not knowing the tune.

"You know it, Steven!" Lon offered his guitar. "Play!"

"Okay." Steven unhitched himself from the pipes and settled the guitar into his lap. Together he and the singer poured out a love song. Hugh leaned his elbows on the bar and drank in his lover's music. Steven had to be playing as much for him as for Emily. Having a committed gay couple for neighbors was a nice addition to the social life.

Lon turned to meet Corey's eyes, mouthing the words. *I love the ground on which he goes.*

Corey's heart hitched in his chest. Lon, sweet, quicksilver, exuberant Lon, had chosen to stay with him when he could have faded away into the woods. Yes, Corey begged him to stay, because Lon's secret wasn't anything Corey would ever turn him away for. "I love you too," he whispered, and puckered ever so slightly into a kiss.

The shimmering notes faded away. Lon held himself still until the clapping died away, bursting out with "You have to teach me that, Steven. Please?"

"Sure, Lon." Steven chuckled and handed back the guitar. "Come over. We'll work on it." He strapped himself back into the complicated tubing and canvas.

Two more tunes went by. Lon had to be getting dry. Corey flagged down Hugh for another glass of Coca Cola. The bubbles made Lon smile.

Out of the corner of his eye, Corey spotted a familiar figure in a group of recent arrivals. He'd go say hello to his department head in a few minutes. Not that he'd introduce Melvin Vadas to Lon, who had some strong but fantastic notions about the chairman of the Economics department at the University of Colorado, but Corey wanted to be polite.

Threading his way between the tables to reach the group, Corey intended to set the glass down on the small table in their center without interrupting the flow. Maybe he didn't really need to steady himself on Lon's shoulder, but it was a good excuse to touch his boyfriend, get a little squeeze and a promise for later in at the same time. "Bet you need to wet your whistle."

Lon jerked up hard enough to jostle Corey's arm. Brown liquid slopped over the rim of the glass. At least he missed Lon's instrument, but what—?

"No. Sorry. But no." Lon twisted under the strap of his guitar. "We need to leave. Now."

"Wha—?" Corey all but dropped the glass. "Why?"

"Now. Please." Lon was up and sidling toward his guitar case.

Corey followed. What else could he do? The man who'd been gleefully leading fiddles and mandolins had cased his instrument and bolted out the side door. Lon barely waited on the porch of the old house turned brewpub, dashing to the passenger side of the RAV4 before Corey was quite outside in the chill spring night.

"Go, go, go," Lon begged. "Quick."

"Okay." Corey tucked his long legs under the steering wheel and peeled out of the parking lot. "Want to explain the sudden need to be elsewhere?"

Lon's knuckles practically glowed with their white-ness—if the armrest of the passenger seat breathed, Lon would have choked the life out of it three blocks back. "I smelled wolf."

That again. "I did see Melvin come into the pub." Corey aimed the truck toward south Boulder, because Lon had that trembly look where his dark brown hair and beard seemed to puff out bigger. Absolutely no reason to stress him, and every reason to take him home and pet him into exhausted, sweaty peace.

"Can you get a job at Harvard or Stanford or somewhere far, far away from CU?" Lon whimpered. "Or decide you don't like me anymore?"

"No and no." Corey gave his lover a stern look on the turn into the driveway. "I'm headed for tenure here and I love you. I don't want to change either one of those things." He pulled Lon across the console to plant a kiss in short, sleek, hair. "Let's go look at the koi one last time, and then last one into bed is a rotten egg."

"Rotten egg! Ick!" But Lon was diverted enough to scamper to the back yard, not too fast to be caught.

CHAPTER TWO

The other side of the bed was empty. Still warm—Corey Levigne patted the dented pillow. Saturday morning, no particular place to be, and no special time to be there—and no Lon to snuggle on.

Maybe he got up to use the can. Or wanted coffee. Or some cereal, in a bowl with some milk, to be eaten with a spoon—this time. Though why, on their first lazy morning all week, had Lon left the bed? Corey pulled the comforter up to his nose. Five minutes from now, if he hadn't fallen asleep again or if Lon hadn't returned, he'd venture into the chill air. Spring came in fits and starts in Boulder, Colorado, and the furnace worked to bring the house up to daytime temperatures. Why heat the house when two of them warmed the bed up cozy as could be? Even if the covers fell to the floor, Corey didn't mind. Lon always seemed to run warm, and plastering against him beat the hell out of central heating.

The furnace clicked silent, its job accomplished for the moment. No sounds of a man moving through the house took the place of rushing warm air. Nor sounds of an animal—Pumpkin nestled into the curve of Corey's legs.

Lon had to have been out of bed for a while. The skittish orange cat consented to be in the same room with him now, instead of hissing and turning tail as she had in the early

42

days, but her calm didn't extend to sitting on any piece of furniture Lon occupied. Like she still expected to be eaten instead of played with. Lon might shoot a rubber band for her to retrieve, but she always brought it back to Corey. Pumpkin's cuddling on their bed had become stranger than her playing fetch. Her fuzzy presence would be even nicer if it didn't mean Lon's absence.

One day they'd come to a more complete accommodation, Corey hoped. He loved Pumpkin but he loved Lon more.

Comfort warred with curiosity. Corey and Lon hadn't been living together so long that idle mornings could or should be filled with anything except sex. Unless there was snow. Then they'd go snowboarding. After the sex. Except by May, snow was a rarity, and found mostly rushing down the canyons in melted form. Time to get out the kayak.

The weatherman had promised snow for today, but the weatherman had promised a lot of snow that never materialized, which still didn't make it warm enough to go hiking. Lon had a lot of energy to burn off, and Corey had learned to not keep him cooped indoors. How the guy managed working in a bank was a mystery. Lon would play outside alone in a blizzard, for which Corey was profoundly grateful. Gore-Tex and microfiber only went so far.

Shoveling burned up a lot of Lon's excess liveliness, which was how the koi pond in the back yard got to be five feet deep and about fourteen feet across in record time. The fill dirt made a hill for the waterfall they hadn't installed yet, but the liner was in, and lettuce-y floating plants that should survive any late freezes. Even without snow, the temperature had promised to drop today. Lon wouldn't mind. He'd make jokes about his fur coat keeping him warm, and then he'd tenderly wrap another length of pashmina scarf around Corey's neck. That and kisses heated Corey enough to romp naked in the snow. Almost.

43

The fish should be okay, even in the cold snap. He'd promised Lon a koi pond, and though work remained to be done, Corey had already fulfilled his promise. One pond, filled with thousands of gallons of municipal water dechlorinated with force and time, and pails and pails of little fish shimmering orange, white, and black.

A dollar an inch, the economist in Corey muttered. Four inch fish at four dollars a pop, twenty fish to a five gallon pail, enough pails to carry two at a time from the back of his RAV4 to the backyard in two trips each. And liners and pumps and pipes and electric lines and… and… and….

If he'd known what starting from scratch would entail, he might not have promised Lon a koi pond, but once he'd promised, he wouldn't go back, even if some of the features they wanted wouldn't get installed until next fall. But just the suggestion had made Lon so happy, and he had done the bulk of the digging, starting an hour before Corey joined him, and matching him shovel for shovel after. No, they didn't need to rent a Bobcat, Lon argued, not when they had shovels and strong backs, and Corey was grateful for one expense avoided. Would have been two expenses, but Corey didn't have a gym membership to cancel. His professorship, even the assistant sort without tenure, gave him access to top notch athletic facilities on the University of Colorado campus. So what if his upper body was a little overdeveloped relative to his legs? All that shoveling worked his arms, back and core.

Worked Lon's, too, and didn't that just make for some dandy times in bed? Or it would, if Lon would get his ass back into the bed, which was the perfect nest on the one occupied side.

But no, no Lon, and no sleep, and no anything but wanting to find out what dragged Corey's lover away from his side. Pumpkin mrrped sleepily when Corey slid to his feet.

Fleece athletic pants and a hoodie kept the still-nippy air off his body in his search for delectable. Corey found some in the kitchen, where coffee steamed in the carafe. He poured a cup and went searching for the maker. But Lon didn't answer his halloo, and their three bedroom house wasn't so big his call didn't carry.

The ground outside glittered white in the morning sun. Snow would lure Lon outside for sure. The pristine surface of the new fall showed every critter's passage. The delicate scratching of birds clustered around the feeder, where a solitary cedar waxwing picked at the seeds. Whatever made the big honking bird-marks wasn't there for the millet or sunflower seed. Those tracks marched along the water's edge. The two large, two small indentations of rabbit feet drew lines across the ground. The cloven tiptoes of deer led from the back fence to the pond. Corey tried not to call them "rats with antlers" where Lon could hear, but the damned things had no predators inside the city limits and ate the gerbera daisies and geraniums from planters like they'd been set out as a buffet. Now that he'd effectively built them a bar with deer-margaritas on tap, Corey didn't expect to get a single apple off his tree that he didn't scale a ladder to pick. Or that Lon didn't climb for.

Another set of tracks marked the snow. Five clawed toes around a heart-shaped main pad made clusters with all four paws and a long tail drag between. Yup, straight from the back door to the pond. The aerator shot a circular ripple into the water's surface, and a V of wake followed in the passage of a swimmer. A black nose broke surface and disappeared again. Orange, white and black flashes scattered, diving at the edges of the pond.

The black nose surfaced again, followed by a flat head with tiny ears, water streaming down the deep brown fur. An orange and white body thrashed, trapped by teeth of sharpness Corey knew only too well. He jammed his feet into the first pair of shoes by the back door, and hobbled outside.

"Hey!"

45

An otter emerged from the pond, its sleek lines glistening. The fish stopped thrashing when the otter ripped it in two, swallowing half in two quick bites, and chomping the tail end down before Corey reached him.

"Damn it! We talked about this!" Corey stabbed his finger at the pond. "For swimming! And playing! It's not an 'all you can eat' buffet!"

Except it was. To Lon.

Corey should have recognized the signs yesterday at the koi farm. His boyfriend had peered into every blue plastic tank, all but humping the PVC when the fish swam up to his dangling fingertips. "Feed us!" their gaping mouths demanded, and their barbels waved into the air with their excitement. Lon hadn't managed to close his mouth, breathing harder with each new discovery, demanding that Corey "Come here! Look at this kind!" The bigger the fish, the more he'd panted, and only the price tags kept them from bringing home bigger buckets containing fewer fish.

"They live a long time," Corey crooned, rubbing the back of Lon's neck and just incidentally steering him away from tanks marked 16-18" and 20-22", or "Premium" or "Select." Two or three of those older, larger, and more desirably marked specimens would have devoured their entire fish budget. "They'll grow. Fast. We'll get little ones. A year from now they'll be a foot long. A couple of years more and they'll be twice that." Would Lon stick around to see his fish grow?

No matter how big they got, they'd still look like prey. A tank of twenty-two inch fish with lipstick markings brought a thin *hurr* from Lon's throat, and Corey had to slap the reaching hand that had gone webbed and brown. "Don't!" Corey hissed, and Lon wiped his mouth quickly with long, neatly manicured fingers.

Close. Too close. If Corey could afford $200 lunches, they would be sitting in Ocean Prime or Mizuna, and they'd both get to eat.

The netter herded the wiggling hordes into buckets, twice as many as Corey planned on. Shouldn't their first foray into koi-raising be on a smaller scale? They could lose the whole school from some newbie mistake like improper chemical balance in the water, but when Lon whipped out his credit card and pointed at a tank marked "*Utsurimono*" there was no denying him.

Only the boldest of the fish remained at the surface when Corey and Lon released scaly treasures into their new abode, but the dark water showed flashes of color here and there. Lon had turned to Corey, the bucket falling from his hand, and kissed him with spirit that felt drawn from every new life they'd brought home. They'd frotted and rubbed each other into ecstasy, shadowed by the newly budding shrubbery, and taken their excitement inside, leaving clothing behind.

Lon had been quicksilver in bed, writhing and streaming and oh so ardent, leaving Corey in no doubt of his joy in their efforts. Worth it, every back-breaking shovelful.

What had been theoretical last night was a real problem now. Lon licked a shining scale from his rubbery black nose and spat it away. His ears lay close to his head, his whiskers went flat to his cheeks, and his eyes narrowed.

"Don't look at me in that tone of voice, dude." Corey became conscious of the light breeze whipping the snow into his exposed face and hands. Much too tall and not nearly furry enough to be as immune to the weather as Lon, he did his best to suppress the shiver that wanted to steal the impact of his righteous indignation. "We agreed this wasn't a feeding trough." Hadn't they?

Lon huffed at him and dove back into the pond. He disappeared completely, surfaced to slap the shining dome of water from the aerator, and disappeared again. Long minutes passed without a glimpse of underwater otter, leaving the wind and cold to play with Corey. Dressed like this, he couldn't outwait the fellow in the fur coat, and damned if he was going to go back in for his boarding clothes just to lurk with a scolding. Besides, he needed the two-footed, talking version of his boyfriend in order to discuss anything complicated. He hadn't realized the koi pond would be one of those complicated things.

Which was stupid. When Corey offered to build a koi pond in the back yard for Lon's once a week shifts into otter form, he'd been thinking outside. And once in a while. Not home spa for mustelids. Or sushi for breakfast.

Lon hadn't lied to him either. He'd accepted the offer with wonder in his eyes and a bit of drool. "I've never eaten a koi," Lon said, and moved in.

Well, now Lon had eaten his koi, and if there were 159 fish left, or 158, or, agh, 150, he didn't need to do it again.

CHAPTER THREE

Spoilsport. Big, dumb, two-foot spoilsport. Lon dove deep and didn't come up for a long time. What was he supposed to do with a koi pond? Stand on the bank and look at it like a human? The water called to him, begging him to put on his fur and swim, and the darting fish needed to be chased. Not eaten, not all of them, or most of them. Only a few, he was a little hungry. Two were enough. And Corey thought he shouldn't have any fish. He knew that look. It went with 'don't pounce with claws' and 'don't shake water on me' and 'don't don't don't.' Now it was 'don't eat the fish.' Lon would explain when he had his words back.

Other creatures wanted to eat his fish. *His fish!*

He used to think there was enough fish for everybody, but these fish were his. Not to share. The raccoons would like his fish. Have to nip at the raccoons. Dangerous. Raccoons nipped too.

Birds were harder to nip. They flew away. Some of the big ones liked fish. The tall ones really liked fish. And they came back. Dumb birds.

He swam past a group of bright fish, stealthily. Scare them, they'd be harder to catch when he wanted one. He wouldn't want one too often, these were bony. But tasty. And fun to chase. He did a U-turn in the water and the fish

49

scattered. More fun to chase than to eat right now. They were fish. They'd forget.

He surfaced. Corey wasn't there. Tracks back to the house showed where he went. Corey was mad. Why would Corey be mad about Lon's fish? Corey wasn't going to eat them. He usually said "Yuck" when Lon caught brookies or rainbows and tried to share. Thought they should be cooked. Made it hot and changed and not like a real fish anymore. Ick.

Sometimes Lon liked fish cooked. When he wasn't wearing his fur.

Lon swam, investigating the bottom of the pond, patting the drain and pipe outlets. Needed some rocks and a log, give the fish places to hide from the nasty birds and the bad raccoons. But Lon could still find them. If he wanted.

Lon swam off his mad, twisting and turning in the water. More fun to play with his fish than be mad at Corey. Mad could wait until he had more words.

When he got out of the water at last, the sun had melted most of the snow, leaving glop on the brown grass where only hints of green poked through. Lon bounced to the back door and yanked the latch open with one clawed foot. Cat door, hah. Pumpkin didn't know how to open the latch. And she wasn't supposed to go outside. Snooty cat wouldn't play with him. Swatted him. And he never nipped her, not even once.

Lon shook, head to tail, droplets flying off him. His fur went fluffy. Corey didn't like drippy. Drippy made messes for two-foots to clean up, and sometimes Lon was a two-foot. Besides, shaking felt good. Get him dry enough to only make a little mess.

He nosed open the flap and slithered into the kitchen. He pushed, and everything changed. His tail disappeared, his fur went away, claws became fingernails and his whiskers shortened to form a smooth brown goatee around his mouth. Kneeling on the floor put his nose too close to the shoes—

50

why didn't he ever remember to go farther into the house to put his fur away? At least he'd remembered to leave a towel by the back door. He'd dropped it in his haste to get outside, just as he'd shifted inside his clothing and had to nose his way out of his T-shirt.

Upright, dry and dressed again, Lon toweled his hair and wiped up the dampness he'd tracked in. Pitching the towel toward the basket on the washing machine in the alcove was almost a success: he mostly hit it. Really, Corey didn't have that much to complain about. Lon wasn't a slob or inconsiderate, and he really, really tried to keep his otterness under control indoors. Okay, so an occasional Cheerio from that one glorious tussle still surfaced. And he'd better do something about the roll of toilet paper he'd attacked inside the cupboard. The roll was completely subdued—and useless for the intended purpose. Oh well, he'd buy another four-pack before Corey noticed.

Most of the coffee remained: Lon poured a cup. Steam wisped from the surface, dwindling with the splash of milk and a teaspoon of sugar. The hot liquid sizzled down his esophagus. Funny how the cold felt different when he was a two-foot. He wrapped his hands around the mug and soaked up every degree.

He didn't turn at the sound of Corey's footsteps, though he did push the sugar bowl closer when Corey reached to the coffee pot. "Good morning."

"Morning."

Nope, nothing good in that greeting. Lon turned. "You're mad about the koi."

"We just bought a hundred and sixty fish to stock the pond yesterday and we're already down at least one." Corey lifted his mug to his lips but didn't take a sip: hot liquid splashed over the rim and on to his skin. He flinched and all but dropped the mug.

Lon handed him a dishtowel without comment. "We're down two, actually, possibly more, but I didn't smell any

51

raccoons. Yet. And yeah, I did have breakfast out there, but if I hadn't we could be down a hundred fish."

"What? Why?" Corey mopped his hand.

"Heron. It landed at water's edge. I put my fur on and chased it away." Lon topped off Corey's cup. "But it'll be back. This is nesting season, and it has babies to feed, or will soon. What a heron can do to a stocked pond is pretty grim."

Corey paused in mid-wipe. "You couldn't scare it away just by—?" He flapped his empty hand over his head.

"You can try, but I doubt it would see you as a threat. It wasn't too concerned about me until I was almost on top of it." Lon pointed out the window to the floating blue-grey plume he'd forgotten to bring to shore. "Pulling a feather out might have irritated it into not coming back for a while, but it won't avoid a food source this good forever."

"So, we're ninety-eight fish better off than we could be, and I should ignore the two we lost to a predator that should know better?"

"We didn't 'lose' anything. I ate a couple, yeah, but Corey, those are my fish too." Lon turned to look his boyfriend in the eye. "Aren't they?"

"Yeah, but…" Corey shifted from foot to foot. "They're not food fish."

"Sure they are. I just ate some, didn't I?" Pretty was fine, but crunchy was the point. "They're bonier than trout or panfish, so I wouldn't want them for a steady diet, but they're not half bad."

"They're supposed to be ornamental. We bought the prettiest colors, didn't we?" Corey protested.

"Yeah, it makes them easier to catch." Lon licked his lips.

"You aren't supposed to catch them!"

"Why not? You plant gardens for pretty, but didn't I just help you put in two dozen flowering kales, not to mention purple string beans and Red Sails lettuce mixed with the green kind? You plan to eat it all. Eventually." Lon ate salad as a two-foot and didn't grumble at it. "I don't see the difference."

"It's… it's…" Corey sputtered.

"It isn't. Fish are food. Not friends." Were all humans this squeamish about links in the food chain they didn't like? "Every raccoon and heron in Boulder will agree with me. We're going to be Pelican Central, too, if we don't put up some kind of netting. We should have bought a couple rolls yesterday at the koi store."

"Pelicans? In Colorado?" Corey goggled at him.

"Lots of pelicans. You've seen the huge white birds out at the reservoir, flying slow in twos and threes. The big black ones are cormorants, and they like fish too." Lon would call around for netting in Boulder, some place he could get to on his bike, because he didn't want to drive to Denver and back with Corey. "They find our pond and they'll be in heaven. Of course, the netting won't keep the raccoons away, but that's why we made the pond so deep. The fish can escape. We'll need to put in some underwater ledges and stuff so they have hiding places. Which will let them hide from me, but that's okay. I like a challenge."

"What will protect them from you?" Corey demanded.

"Nothing. They're my fish, to play with or eat. Unless they're not." Lon threw out the challenge he'd known would come one day. "I'm an otter, Corey. I can't stop being an otter. I can avoid shifting in the house, but I can't avoid shifting at all, you know that."

"Yeah. You've been really good about that." The admission sounded pulled from Corey with pliers.

"And I don't drip on the floor, much, and I clean up after myself, and all the animal hair around here is your cat's. I don't shed." Indoors, at least, because he didn't usually wear his fur indoors, and his pelt was season-appropriate when he shifted. "You wouldn't have bothered building a koi pond at all if I wasn't an otter, would you?"

"No…." That, too, sounded extracted with tools.

"So now that we have this koi pond, I have to stop being an otter?" Anything that sounded too good to be true probably was. Lon should have red-lighted this project the moment Corey suggested digging. He should have nixed moving in and everything smacking of a permanence that was going to be so prickly it would end up not being permanent after all.

"I didn't say that!"

"Yeah, you kinda did. How exactly do you suppose an otter sees a koi pond? Hint, it's not an aquarium." How had they managed to be on such different pages all this time? Every doubt Lon ever had about exposing his true self to Corey came back in a rush. He should have disappeared the minute his secret was out and left Corey to think he'd imagined the otter swimming in his bathtub and shaking cereal all over the floor.

"I... Lon, I guess I never thought about it. It was more 'digging a really big hole in the back yard is making you happy' and 'you can swim at home' and 'the fish are so pretty.' You didn't hide what you thought. I... didn't listen." The admission had Corey drooping. "I can't ask you not to be who you are. I wouldn't. I respect you more than that."

"I just can't be myself at home?" If home was where the fish were more important than he was, it wasn't much of a home.

"I didn't say that either, Lon. Don't put words in my mouth." Corey reached out both hands to Lon but pulled them back as if he feared to be bitten.

"I'm not trying to put words in your mouth." And here Lon thought words would make communication easier. "I'm trying to interpret the words you already said. You want me to have a koi pond but you don't want me to enjoy it. Or only enjoy it the way you enjoy it. Except, I'm not like you." No, he wasn't like Corey, he had to put on his fur once a week and leave words behind for an hour or two, or three, and the world was a lot simpler. Things to chase, things to eat, things to avoid, and the water for a friend. Maybe Corey's life had never been so simple that he could

54

see how complicated things were around him. "I'm going to get in the water and swim, and now and again I might get hungry. And now and again I'm going to do it at home, if home has a koi pond. I thought that was the point."

Corey slumped, one hip against the counter. The coffee sloshed behind him but didn't escape the cup. "It was. The swimming at home part. I don't think of fish the way you do. I need to get over it. Sorry."

Lon softened. "They are pretty, I do see that. And koi have twice as many bones as any other fish, so they aren't real attractive as snacks. I won't eat all of them, or even half. I just don't want you to be angry if I do eat one or two. Or have you blame me if some other predator gets a few."

"I guess we need to get a net for the herons and pelicans." Corey straightened and lifted his arms to Lon.

Was that enough words to be sure they agreed? It sounded like Corey understood, and wouldn't be mad. Lon stepped into his embrace, glad to look up the few inches into his lover's face and seal their understanding lip to lip.

But Corey turned his face to one side, giving Lon only his cheek. "You have to brush your teeth between fishes and kisses."

Fuck it all.

CHAPTER FOUR

Working together to string the strong, fine netting over the koi pond helped settle some issues, and brought a few others to the surface. Corey knelt at the side of the pond, measuring the distance under the nearly invisible barrier. They'd installed it at an otter-friendly height in spite of his misgivings. *They were Lon's fish too, they were Lon's fish too.*

Lon gave voice to more of Corey's doubts. "Your heart's going to bleed for any bird that gets entangled and can't get out, isn't it?"

"Probably. I don't want to cause anything suffering." Could the birds see the netting and avoid it? Corey really hadn't thought this through, and he knew Boulder was an urban wildlife Mecca, with deer and cougars and raccoons and all. Why had he not considered birds?

His doubts didn't shrink when Lon rested a hand on his shoulder. "Going hungry will make them suffer."

"There's other things for them to eat. Right?" Why else would cormorants and pelicans hang around? The landscape around Boulder was splashed with the blue of reservoirs and ponds.

"There are, but it might be farther away, or those fish might be harder to catch, or the territory belongs to someone else." Lon sat back on his heels and continued his interrogation. "You don't have an aisle staked out at the grocery store, so it might look different to you."

"It does, Lon." There was no way to win this argument. Would agreeing at least end it gracefully? He took Lon's hand, hoping a kiss would change the subject. Although a kiss had fucked things up yesterday and he'd had to apologize again for his humanity and squeamishness. "I've been working on the economic impact of endangered species conservation, so I'm not entirely ignorant of competing interests."

"It's just different when it's in your face, right?" Lon let Corey leverage himself to upright, which was a victory right there. Yesterday he might have taken Corey's hand in order to torque him into the water. Apparently Corey was in less trouble today.

"Yeah, it is." He pulled Lon against his chest, feeling the tension in his lover's body. Wanting to be honest and still get Lon more pliable made Corey pick his words carefully. "I want the birds to have what they need, but not if they take it from our resources, which is ungracious"—get his acknowledgement of frailty out there first—"but, I think, understandable. And I don't want to hurt them."

Lon softened against Corey's chest, so he hadn't stepped in the poop pile yet.

"You know otters are endangered, right?"

Corey nodded. "Think they counted any otters like you in the last survey?"

The chuckle against his chest was answer in itself. "I know they counted Mom and Dad and my big brother. We went up to Cabin Creek and got cautioned by the biologists not to bother the otters. Except we were the only ones up there. They got really excited about us." The sigh deflated Lon to about half his previous size. "Which means the numbers are worse than everybody thinks. That was years ago. I was just a kid. Maybe it's gotten better since then."

Corey tried to recall the numbers from his data, but he'd been working on water use relative to fish. Most of the protected habitat in his study was along the Colorado River, a perennial bone of contention among the five dry states scuffling for its water. "I think it has. There was talk of moving otters from endangered to protected status. Someone even got a picture of an otter in downtown Boulder a couple of years ago. First one in a century."

The swat on Corey's butt said everything. "That was me. I got careless."

"And you were adorable." Rescue this any way possible. "Cute and fuzzy makes everyone more willing to make the effort. It's harder to sell people on the need to protect humpbacked chubs and Colorado pikeminnows." Oh damn, there he'd gone, telling Lon not to eat again.

That irony didn't seem lost on his boyfriend. "What would you say if the sad, hungry otter had nothing else to catch but pikeminnows?"

"If the sad, hungry otter was you, I'd say shift back and I'll make you a sandwich. If it was an otter otter, well..." How was he supposed to resolve this moral dilemma? "I'm trying to see it from the otter's perspective, but I sort of see the fish's perspective too. And I also see from the perspective of a human who's going to tell a lot of other humans they can't have what they want because the otter and the pikeminnow need the resources."

"Ignore the humans. They take what they want anyway." Lon dropped his arms to his sides and his deep brown eyes were solemn. "What do you tell the otter?"

Corey still hadn't said what he'd tell the otter when he dropped Lon off at the Chautauqua Bank Monday morning. He'd clearly been wrestling with the question, though, so Lon didn't pester. Corey once said Lon would expand his horizons, so Lon figured he'd yanked hard on the western edge of Corey's thinking. Their goodbye kiss was full on and minty fresh on both sides.

"Happy macroeconomicking." Lon wanted another kiss but his desk waited on the far side of the double glass doors.

"Banking, saving, and investing for today. You could probably teach this section with your eyes shut." Corey drew his fingers along the edge of Lon's beard. He had no idea how erotic that felt, but Corey's whiskers were just whiskers, not vibrissae. Now with a simple goodbye, Corey was starting something and didn't even know it. Lon tried not to moan.

"Save it for tonight, okay?" Guess Corey did know, or figured it out fast. He withdrew his hand.

Lon chased that hand with his face and only stopped because the seatbelt caught him. He straightened up and unlatched. "I have a couple of complicated loans to work out. That'll kill the mood."

"I know how to bring it back." Corey's smile would do it, especially if he kept from making any more species-ist comments. "Pick you up at five?"

"My turn to make dinner." Lon jumped to the next thought. "Sweet potato kale curry okay?"

"Isn't that vegetarian?" Corey asked.

"Yes." Lon had noticed how Corey filled his dish selectively some nights. The nights the pot didn't contain a lot of meat and he'd made the excuse "there was a predator to feed." Which didn't explain the eggplant parmesan in restaurants. "Unless you want something else."

"No, that sounds really good." He smiled, and Lon stole a last kiss.

Vegetarian dinner wasn't a problem. Lunch in Boulder Creek might be a problem, but if he slipped out the back of the bank.... Or he could walk down the Pearl Street Mall for a burger.

A little compromise, and then maybe Corey would figure out what to tell the otter.

The pile on his desk killed the residual mood. Lon picked up the stack of papers detailing the property on which a group dubbed "The Full Moon Conservancy" intended to build something they described as a "lodge."

The current lending atmosphere was easier than it had been when Lon started at the bank, when he'd had to fight his way into a teller's slot suddenly desirable to loan originators who had no loans to work. Survival of the fittest—they'd moved on, he'd stayed, and worked into a desk where he didn't get as much exercise but did get paid better. The lending atmosphere wasn't so improved and easy that such a sketchy outfit could get a "no documents" loan from Chautauqua Bank.

Lon read, making tick marks and notes. The more he read, the more questions he had. Some were even related to the loan.

The walls of his office were mostly glass, but he scented danger before he saw it. The earthy, musky scent of fur carried over the familiar bank odors of popcorn packets in the new-accounts desk, spare shoes in the auto loan guy's bottom drawer, the head teller's grapefruity cologne, and machine oil from the safety deposit box vault.

Canine, male, not neutered. More than one. Unmistakably pheromonal scent of alpha. Nothing of fear. They frightened the receptionist though: her fearstink wafted at Lon. The three men speaking to her must have shepherds or huskies with them. Hope they were leashed.

Fuck, the last thing he needed was to be treed on his file cabinet with some rabid mongrel barking and slavering to take a chunk out of him. Possibly succeeding. Nothing like being targeted by someone with a nose sharper than Lon's in two-foot form, and if Lon was aware of them, they had to be aware of Lon. Otter had a tang that carried into human shape. He once had to choose between hopping on the desk or kicking the shit out of a Chihuahua when a client's purse-dog got brave, because growling it into submission would raise too many questions. His loan clients would be

60

here any minute and he refused to greet them from such an undignified position.

Closing the door would keep the humiliation down, though the barking would still bring attention. Lon got up to ward off the four-footed problem.

The three men headed to his door. No dogs, just two men in dress slacks and sweaters, a third in a suit. They caught him with his hand on the knob, more anxious than ever to slam the door between himself and trouble.

Alpha in the suit put his hand out, a twitch of his lips threatening to become a smile. "Lon Ewing? I'm Melvin Vadas, with Whit Bailey and Jack Schwimmer from the Full Moon Conservancy."

Lon put out his hand and told the lump in his throat to go away, no swallowing permitted. "Good to meet you," he lied. "Gentlemen. Come in."

Lon shut his office door with the danger inside. He knew exactly who Dr. Melvin Vadas was. Respected professor of economics. Chair of Corey's department.

Werewolf.

"So, gentlemen"—Lon edged his foot next to the panic button under his desk. If they rushed him, shifted or not, he'd summon reinforcements before joining the battle. "Tell me more about the Full Moon Conservancy. What do you conserve?"

"Ah, wildlife," Bailey finally offered into a silence that stretched entirely too long.

"Fascinating." Lon put on his best "Spock with the money" attitude, steepling his fingers before his face. "What kind?"

"Cougars." Vadas didn't miss a beat. "Delightful. Must be preserved."

Of course he'd want to preserve worldly, elegant women for boinking with silver-templed, smooth talking, distinguished professors of the University of Colorado. No doubt Dr. Vadas was the hit of the faculty parties Lon once begged Corey never to have him attend.

"I didn't see licensing paperwork for a big cat sanctuary amongst the documentation. Is the USDA still processing your application?"

"We didn't apply. They're wild animals." Bailey shrugged the question aside when Vadas didn't volunteer more information.

"So they are. With ranges that extend a hundred miles or more." Lon had learned to determine ages of scents early in his shifting life, about a week after he'd grown enough whiskers to make his fur come out. Knowing where the apex predators were had kept him alive this far. The older the scent, the farther away danger padded, until suddenly it was right behind. Or across the desk. "Your group preserves them how?"

"Is that pertinent to our loan application, Mr. Ewing?" Dr. Vadas took over the conversation. "We own no animals. Our blueprints include nothing specific to animal keeping."

"I noticed that. You do understand that these questions apply to determining your group's creditworthiness? If the bank can't ascertain what you're doing or how you plan to fund your repayment, we can't make the loan." Lon's mouth went dry with the words. "The Full Moon Conservancy has no credit rating, no Internet presence, no listing in the phone book. You're asking for approximately three hundred thousand dollars on behalf of a group that doesn't clearly exist."

"We exist." Dr. Vadas' words were clipped and precise. "We're nonprofit. We spend no extraneous money."

"That's commendable, but are you telling me you're a nonprofit organization?" Why didn't they just call themselves "Society for the Preservation and Enjoyment of Werewolves"?

"Yes." In triplicate.

"Then do you have copies of your 501(c)(3) paperwork? Or the forms for application, if that hasn't been finalized?" Lon wanted to loosen his collar, but he couldn't let them see him rattled. If he let his alpha status as purveyor of money slip, even for an instant, they'd be on him.

"We don't do business. Such things aren't necessary." If Lon didn't know what he faced, he'd be swayed to agree with Dr. Vadas' cultured tones and complete assurance.

"You're trying to borrow three hundred thousand dollars. They're necessary. Nonprofit doesn't mean no money." Lon tapped the stack of papers.

"You'll loan us the money." Bailey, or maybe it was Schwimmer, spoke with a low growl that demanded obedience Lon would not give.

His upper lip lifted slightly, twitching to show his teeth, and his beard stood out from his skin, making him larger. "These show no income stream, and your group as you've explained it has no obvious need for a building with ten bedrooms, a locker room, and a commercial kitchen. The need"—he showed his teeth, his puny human teeth that could become ripping fangs, to keep the trio from interrupting—"may well be there, but the means to repay is not."

He'd issued a challenge: they'd have to respond. The three men exchanged glances. Lon let the silence grow, waiting for the perfect moment of understanding, and then he could usher them out without having explicitly said the words that would set them upon him.

Dr. Vadas finally spoke. "We have the means, individually. And the land we want to build on has equity."

Something, yes, that would keep Lon from throwing down the definitive challenge of no. "We'd have to structure the loan differently if you're guarantors. The bank will need your individual documents. I'll give you the paperwork, and we can set up another meeting." With a different bank officer. Lon would pass this on to someone who didn't tremble with the need to shift and dive beneath the water.

To someone who would fall under the charisma of the alpha wolf and do what he wanted. Damn. Lon was stuck with this one.

"And, ah, the land you propose building on is in the Whiskey Creek drainage basin, correct?" Lon could read the topographical map, but wasn't sure his would-be borrowers could, or had, or understood his reasons for asking.

"This is important why?" Schwimmer, or possibly Bailey, sneered.

"Because the Whiskey Creek Basin is home to some of the last remaining silverscale dace left in Colorado." Lon's heart sank as he broke more bad news. "Before we can approve a loan to build in critical habitats for endangered species, borrowers need a population survey and an impact assessment."

"Population's zero," said Bailey, or perhaps it was Schwimmer.

"How do you know?" Lon persisted. "Was the count done by anyone who can reliably recognize a silverscale dace?"

"Toss a stick of dynamite in the creek, population's zer—" The rest of that statement exploded into "Oof!" as Vadas' elbow met not-Vadas' solar plexus.

"We'll have the population survey for you," Vadas finished smoothly. "Is there anything else we should know about the necessary paperwork?"

"I think that will be all." Lon hoped to hell he hadn't missed a document, because he didn't want to contact any of this group for any reason.

"We'll be back." Dr Vadas rose and took the stack of papers that should keep him busy and elsewhere, at least for a while. He sniffed, just enough to be obvious. "Do you perchance keep ferrets, Mr. Ewing?"

"No." No more than Vadas kept huskies.

"Odd. You have the scent of a small, fierce predator about you." He smiled, if the baring of his teeth could be called a smile because he walked on two legs. "The sort that tackles opponents much larger and stronger, and hasn't the sense to back off."

"Ah, the quick, bendy, mean sort." Lon wouldn't leave the description unadorned.

"The sort that makes lovely coats." Vadas and his companions stalked out, and the air didn't clear of their scent.

Shit. He'd never wanted Melvin Vadas to take notice of him, and now… He'd have to warn Corey.

CHAPTER FIVE

Thirty-two seconds after Corey dismissed his macro-economics class, his phone buzzed against his hip.

"Corey, you gotta stay away from Melvin Vadas!" came blurting through the airwaves.

"Lon, it's okay. We don't have much to do with each other." Corey tried to soothe the panic out of Lon. "Shouldn't be hard."

"I don't mean sit on the other end of the table at department meetings, I mean you see him and you run the other way, or get a brick wall between you. Corey, I'm not joking."

"Wait, what happened?" Lon had warned Corey away from his department head before, and the casual evasions had been enough to keep Lon calm. Lacking tenure and hoping for it would bring him into close proximity with his department head at the moment of truth, but until then, it wasn't much of a problem.

"I just spent half an hour with him in my office, explaining why I couldn't give him and his stupid Full Moon Conservancy a construction loan," Lon sobbed.

"You have to say no to loans all the time. Don't you?" Corey paused in mid-sentence, nearly getting run over by the hordes of students escaping his Power Point slides and bullet points.

"That's not the point. Maybe a little. But I could have said, 'yes, here's half a million bucks you never have to repay' and it would be the same problem." Corey could picture Lon tugging at his short, otter brown hair that never needed cutting but might have some bald patches if he was tugging as hard as he was urging. "Corey, he sat in the office with me. He knows what I am, he all but said so. And if he could smell me, he could smell you on me. And he already knows what you smell like—you've been in the same department for how many years?"

"Three," the pedant in Corey answered before the reality caught up with him. "He knows? You're sure?" The shock nearly kept him from shooing away the overeager student in the plaid poncho who danced from foot to foot with notebooks crushed to her chest. "Office hours at two," he mouthed, and turned his back to her and the stadium style seating that had been filled with economics majors a few minutes before.

"Absolutely sure," Lon wailed. "He all but took a bite out of me at the bank. I don't want him to hurt you."

"I really don't think he will." Corey tried for rational. "Faculty damage to each other is supposed to be limited to figurative daggers between ribs. And poached research budgets."

"Most faculty aren't werewolves!"

"Are you sure he's a werewolf?" When in doubt, ask more questions. Finding his boyfriend as an otter, seeing him shift from two-foot to four-foot, playing with the lithe, bouncy, furry bundle of happiness that was Lon as an otter convinced Corey otter shifters were real. Not the same as believing in werewolves.

"Werewolf? Kewl!"

Corey whirled to face the student in the oversized gray hoodie and the saggy jeans. "We're discussing Halloween costumes," he told the eavesdropper. "Office hours at two." He fled the auditorium, phone plastered to his ear, before the student could point out Halloween was six months away.

"Yes, I'm sure he's a werewolf! And so were the guys he had with him, Bailey and Schwimmer. Corey, if they want to build a lodge with ten bedrooms all at least fourteen by eighteen, there's more wolves in this pack than I thought."

"And they'll be up there and we'll be somewhere else. It will be okay." Could he say anything that would get that edge of panic out of Lon's voice?

"That's what I thought until I had Vadas in my office suggesting I would make a lovely fur coat."

"That son of a bitch would get a silver bullet for hurting you," Corey growled. "And he needs a smack upside the head for making the suggestion." His long legs chewed up the hallways back to his office, barely more than a cubby under the stairs, but it had a window. And a door that shut, to keep the world from hearing the rest of this conversation.

"A regular bullet would do, but Corey, you're not the one to smack him. Don't even," Lon begged. "You're prey to him. So am I. It doesn't matter that otters don't play stupid dominance games the way humans and wolves do. And you can't match him from either aspect. Can you?"

Not without a time-travelling miracle to let Corey fast-forward to the day he was head of department and Vadas was professor so very *emeritus* that he'd forgotten supply/demand curves. "I can put a leash on him."

"If you can lift a logging chain. Corey, you have to stay away from him!" Every trace of fun-loving Lon had evaporated.

Almost there. "Okay, okay, Lon. I'll stay away from him." Corey jammed the key into the lock on his office door. Could he talk Lon out of the trees if he mumbled some sweet nothings, lascivious promises for the evening? That kind of talk needed privacy. The lock offered no resistance, and Corey would have sworn he'd twisted the button. He swung open the door.

Dr. Melvin Vadas sat at Corey's desk, perusing an unrolled map. "Hello, Dr. Levigne." Bastard didn't even look up; no, he traced some feature on the topographical squiggles covering the paper. "I understand you're working on regional impact modeling for endangered species."

Corey fought the urge to slam the door and bolt. Lon's terror was contagious, but—this was his department head and colleague. Who didn't look inclined to—or capable of—eating him in any literal sense. "Yes, I am."

"Do you have any maps of the Whiskey Creek Basin?" Now Vadas did look up, and his eyes had gone icy blue.

Corey didn't want to see his teeth. "Later. Gotta go." He also didn't want Lon to hear his last screams. Or let Vadas hear "I love you," which would make better last words but tell a predator more than he should know. Corey shoved the phone in his pocket. "Next map down. Any particular reason?" Vadas' field was so far from his own. What would a labor economist need with maps of remote watersheds in the mountains?

"I've developed a sudden interest in the natural history of the silverscale dace." Vadas extracted the map and rolled it without a further glance. "You don't need it back anytime soon, do you?"

"No, you can keep it." He suspected Vadas might chew off any hand he'd reach out to recover his property. The US Geological Service had lots more. It wouldn't take him but an hour to re-limn the affected areas on a new copy.

"Thank you." Vadas rose, far more gracefully than anyone but a dancer should be able to do. He passed Corey on his way out. He sniffed. "Do you perchance keep ferrets, Dr. Levigne?"

"No." He backed up a step, not wanting his superior one centimeter closer than necessary, and not because he'd promised Lon.

"Funny, I would have sworn you did." With a smile full of too many teeth, Vadas disappeared.

Lon slid into the passenger seat of the blue RAV4, his eyes wide and his nostrils flaring. Corey pulled him close for a moment, resting cheek to cheek with his still-spooked lover. The normality of the embrace and Corey's obviously intact hide should calm him. "It's okay, Lon," he whispered. "We're okay."

"For now." Lon rubbed his beard against Corey's cheek, and the tension drained from his muscles.

What kind of information beyond "here" was he getting through his whiskers? Corey found Lon's goatee attractive, and these days it was stylish, though when the fashion changed, his facial hair would not. Part of being an otter, he'd said.

"Let's go home," Corey suggested. "I have a surprise for you."

"You're going to throw me on the bed and make mad, passionate love to me?" The twinkle was back in Lon's eye. Good.

Corey let go and put the little SUV into gear. "Not sure that will come as a surprise, but yeah, that too." He found a break in traffic and eased out onto 14th Street. Once he was on Broadway he could take his hand off the gearshift and squeeze Lon's knee for a block at a time. "I found something on Craigslist for the pond."

"Great! What?" Lon's sunny self was back—he was all but bouncing in his seat.

Sweet guy, he never stayed down for long. Maybe it was his essential otteriness, but definitely one of the things Corey loved about him.

"Don't peek in the back," Corey said, just to make him wiggle with anticipation and think about anything besides close encounters with werewolves.

They reached the tidy brick ranch-style house in the southern end of Boulder without Lon going pop with anticipation, but only barely. Corey's admonition of "some assembly required" got him out of his crisp cotton dress shirt and black trousers and into jeans. Corey found him at the RAV4, his nose pressed against the glass.

"What is it?" he asked again, but Corey sprang the hatch and started handing Lon planks of well-oiled hardwood.

"Take these out to the pond. We might as well build it where it will stand." The shaped pieces would give away the secret, but Lon was off like a shot with his burden. Corey followed with his arms full of wrought iron and a bag of hardware. Made it hard to wave at the neighbor kids playing in the next yard, but their shrieks of "Watch this, Corey!" meant he had to acknowledge or they'd sail completely off the swings to get his attention.

"Oh wow!" Lon started fitting the wood into the end pieces, and in a few minutes they had a garden bench with iron hummingbirds flitting between oak slats. "Perfect!"

They had to test sit their creation, with Lon tucked into Corey's armpit. His extra four inches of height always put him as top arm in the cuddles, with Lon's head on his shoulder, which was fine with Corey. They sat quietly in the cool spring evening, gazing out over their pond, where bright flashes of color flickered below the water's surface. A black feather floated near the aerator, caught in the water's churn.

"This is beautiful," Corey murmured, filling his nostrils with the clean, slightly animal scent that was Lon's pelt as a "two-foot". His other patch of pelt had a muskier odor, which Corey would explore. In a bit. Inside.

"It is." Lon drew his fingers up and down Corey's belly in a slow, sensuous motion. "And I like sitting here with you."

"I was imagining watching you swim when I bought this." And offering tangible proof of how he wanted Lon to enjoy their new pond. "And the fish, but mostly you."

"Thanks." Lon's hand moved lower. "Did you ever decide what to tell the otter?"

"Still thinking." And no closer to a conclusion. Furry and cute shouldn't mean "automatically wins over scaly and finny." Even though it kind of did. Especially when "going to be cute and furry" was squeezing his rapidly hardening cock.

Lon let go. "I'll get the feathers out of the pond." Eeling out from under Corey's arm, he stood to pull his shirt off.

"Guess we got the netting up just in time." Corey rose to rest his hand on Lon's shoulder. "I really am trying to see it your way about the fish."

"It would be easier to do if you had to kill your own dinner every night." Lon reached to his fly.

"Probably." Corey stopped him from unzipping. "Might not want to peel down in full view of the kids." The neighbors were friendly, and would probably stay that way if their children didn't get full frontal views of the gay guys next door.

"Oh, um, yeah." Lon grinned sheepishly and retreated into the shrubbery.

The honeysuckles were there when Corey bought the house, six feet high already and taller now. The pink flowers would come out in a few weeks, and would give way to red berries as the season advanced. They were pretty and the birds fed on them through the winter. Pumpkin spent many an hour on the windowsill chattering at the activity in the bushes. And they shielded the yard on that side. Maybe he'd add more around the perimeter of the yard, and then Lon could peel down as he pleased.

Corey sat back down on the bench, listening to the rustle of imminent otter. Lon bounded out of the bushes, his fur standing out lightly from his body. Raising up on his hind feet and balancing against his thick, muscular tail, he rested his webbed forefeet against Corey's thigh. "I love your fur," Corey told him, working his fingers into his lover's thick pelt, slightly oily with natural water repellent. Lon shrugged deeper into Corey's hands, and with a hop, landed on the bench at his side. He wanted lap—Corey let Lon nestle against his chest, his flat head tucked against Corey's neck. One tiny lick against his skin and a big sigh said he was comfy in Corey's arms.

Yeah. Corey never imagined this kind of contentment, where his lover had so many facets to his personality and was such a joy in all of them. Well, most of them. And he was warm and cuddly and was currently dry and without fish breath. Which might change in a minute.

But for right now all was still and perfect. Corey held his otter love in their backyard wilderness and wanted this forever, or until Lon needed to change back, when Corey would hold his lithe and muscular human body even closer.

A rubbery wet nose poked into Corey's ear—a whiffle made him pull back and let go. Lon hopped to the ground and, with a mischievous thrash of his tail, turned to bound the few feet to water's edge. With barely a splash, he slid in.

Corey never tired of watching Lon as an otter. He'd seen his future lover long before he'd known Lon as a man, playing in an icy creek up by the snowboarding hill. Corey had paused in his own athletics, charmed by the long brown shape dashing up the hill to come belly-sliding down the packed ramp he'd flattened with his body, to land splashing in the water and run to do it all over again. Part of the magic of the mountains, and now that magic was part of his life. He'd brought the cute guy who'd rescued an escaped snowboard home to thank him with pizza, which had become sex, long nights and lazy days, and about two months ago, moving boxes in a trailer his RAV4 struggled to pull across town.

Lon seized the black feather in his mouth, pulling it across the surface with a trail of ripples. Looked like the fisher-birds had found their koi. The soggy cormorant feather joined the heron plume on the bank. A few more souvenirs of thwarted raiders and Corey could build an effigy to scare them away. The netting wasn't very attractive, but Lon had been right—better the net than a heron buffet.

Lon spun in the water and disappeared, only to reappear as a speeding torpedo in pursuit of a red and black fish. He bumped it with his nose, no doubt inducing a piscine heart attack, not to mention some choking on land. *They're Lon's fish too! They're Lon's fish too!* Corey waved when Lon poked his head above water, snorting his nostrils clear and demonstrating his empty jaws. Then he disappeared below the surface.

Corey relaxed. Why couldn't he see it from the otter's point of view? Because the otter walked on two feet most of the time and ate purchased fish while sitting at a table, using a fork? He was going to break his brain at this rate. What Lon ate had nothing to do with the endangered species Corey had spent the last several months tracking. Along with the human activity in their habitats. No wonder the fishes' ranges had shrunk. "Humans take what they want," Lon said. Corey was trying not to be one of those humans. Harder than it looked.

Lon needed at least an hour outside. Corey would get the sweet potatoes started, even though Lon had offered to cook. Extracting abandoned jeans from under the honeysuckle and pointing toward the house, Corey explained his intentions to an otter who waved one webbed foot with understanding. Hmm, they should leave a stack of towels by the back door. Corey draped Lon's clothes over the back of a kitchen chair on his way to the linen closet.

About an hour later, the aroma and sizzle of sautéing onions drew Corey back into the kitchen. "Smells good." With his arms around Lon's waist and his chin on Lon's shoulder, Corey supervised peeling and chopping. "I love ginger."

"Me, too." Lon twisted to reach Corey's mouth. With one hand on the side of Corey's head, he planted a very deliberate and kind of sloppy kiss directly on target. Okay, he'd made his point about the toothpaste. Corey caught Lon's upper lip and sucked, knowing that made Lon a little crazy. And then he stopped, because too crazy and they'd leave dinner on the stove to burn. Or ginger fingers would make his ass burn. He broke the kiss with a squeeze to show he wasn't going far.

"This will be ready in about twenty minutes." Lon dropped the ginger into the pan.

"Mmm, 'kay." Corey nuzzled Lon's ear from behind. Just to keep certain ideas sizzling. "No appetizer?"

"I didn't eat any koi, if that's what you meant." Lon sampled a square of red pepper and handed one over his shoulder to Corey, who almost let it fall from his mouth. "Didn't want to spoil my appetite for the curry."

"I meant those frozen wontons in the bag, actually." The koi question had already been answered with that kiss. He chewed twice and swallowed. "Did anyone else get any koi today?"

"I didn't count." Lon took a knife to the sweet potato, which steamed when he broke it open.

"Um, Lon?" Asking about otter abilities was somewhat ticklish. Corey usually waited for Lon to volunteer information. "You'll have a thousand questions I don't want to answer" had been one of Lon's stated reasons for disappearing after that first shift in the bathroom. Corey tried to pay attention to dropped tidbits rather than ask, but this might overlap one of his research needs. "Can you count? When you're an otter?"

The thwack of the knife into the unresisting sweet potato followed by an answer told him Lon wasn't pleased to be asked, but wouldn't tell him off or run away. Today. "Some."

"'Kay." *Now just listen, dodohead.* Corey waited silently for elaboration that might not come.

Lon stayed silent for the dissection of half the sweet potato. "It's not important then. So mostly one, two, three, four, five, six, seven, eight, many, lots, and oh my goodness!"

"So do we have lots or oh my goodness in the pond?"

"Ah, Corey, when I'm shifted, I can't tell the difference between oh my goodness what we put into the water and oh my goodness less five the cormorant got." He attacked the second half of the sweet potato. "Besides, they don't hold still."

"Gotcha." With a kiss to the back of Lon's head, Corey decided to set the table. Helpful might bring more details.

"But we have oh my goodness. For now." Dumping a heap of orange cubes and big handfuls of green leaves into the pan, Lon swept everything from his cutting board into the mixture. Three thorough stirs, and he put the lid on. "Dinner in ten."

Ten minutes was enough for plates, forks, napkins, and some smooching. Corey rushed through the first to get to the last.

Corey hadn't asked more questions than the one—Lon could live with that. He'd come to terms with changing skill sets years ago, when it bothered him not to be able to tell time accurately enough to know when he was pushing his boundaries. He'd become adept in reading the slant of the sun in the spring and the angle of the shadows in the fall, but mostly he hadn't taken chances with butting up against his limits. Either he could change back or he couldn't, which meant more than an hour or less than an hour, and the sun went down to tell him "Put your fur away." He never started at dawn, and losing the light meant a firm deadline.

Besides, he liked getting back to opposable thumbs. They made it so much easier to do some things.

Possible to do certain things—Lon liked cuddling against Corey's chest, but he had no interest in Corey's body until after he'd put his fur away. Probably just as well. He had all that interest for now.

The futon in the living room slid to flat when Lon surprised Corey mid-movie. Who wanted witty dialogue? Lon did, which made it much easier to ignore the movie, and Corey didn't clamor to see how it ended. That's what the back button was for, in the unlikely case either of them cared that much. Time for clothes to come off.

Start with a stealth attack. Lon managed to ooze to his knees on the zig-zaggy kilim rug without Corey commenting, but that twitch at the corner of his mouth probably meant *busted*. So did his assistance in untucking his T-shirt. Just made it easier for Lon to nuzzle into Corey's belly. A firm touch kept the whiskers from tickling.

All pretenses dissolved when Corey started running his fingers through Lon's hair. Corey could stroke his head endlessly, never losing his wonder at the softness and the undercoat, just like his entire body when he shifted. His head did shed, a little, but Lon used the kind of brush that kept it from being a problem. The only thing Corey liked better than playing with Lon's head hair was playing with his pubes, which had the same texture. And the only thing Corey liked better than playing with Lon's pubes was playing with parts close to the pubes. And oh, he liked that a lot.

But he stayed upright, letting Lon have his way up his body, which meant treasure trail in reverse. Poor Corey, his hair was so coarse. No amount of conditioner ever got it as soft as Lon's, but he could grow it a lot longer. Right now it curled over his ears, making a shiny brown cloud whisping to bronze with the light behind him. Looking up from between Corey's knees made him look like an angel with a halo, although that might be the smile. Lon loved to make Corey smile, and getting him naked would make him smile a lot. And gasp. And cry out and call Lon's name, now that those pesky britches were down, and then whump, he'd unlatched the futon and it had obligingly shifted into a bed.

Lon climbed out of his jeans and over Corey, to rest chest to chest. He leaned into Corey's face to kiss him with lips that tasted only of the same vegetables and sauce that scented his lover's breath. He was trying so hard to see things Lon's way. Lon wanted to try just as hard, but… Eating kale was a small sacrifice.

Still a sacrifice—and if he didn't want Corey to give him grief about trout breath, he couldn't really make jibes about eating weeds.

And he was going to get some nice warm man into his mouth any second now, if he could tear himself out of those long, strong arms with their sparse coat of half-assed fur that didn't do much for protection.

Nope, not leaving that shelter. Lon brushed his lips over Corey's, reveling in every small movement of his lips that Lon could feel with the sensitivity of his goatee. Not tearing loose, not when Corey held him tight, and lifting his hips an inch and backing away, only to come closer. Their erections rubbed together, Lon's uncut length against Corey's smooth exposed shaft. Soft and hard all at once—Lon didn't think he could ever get enough of that either, because so much else called to him. He wanted to rub, but he wanted to taste—except tasting meant letting go, unless…

Lon flipped around, barely leaving Corey's embrace, and found out he could have it all. Corey clutched him even more tightly, almost too tight to move. He loosened up again when Lon took his hard cock between his lips, making a wet pad of his human-thick tongue to slide up and down, and around the crown, and to tease at Corey's slit, where precum grew in a salty pearl.

With one of Corey's muscular buttocks in each hand, Lon played with his prize, taking that stiff cock deeply as he could. He had to come up for enough air to moan—Corey returned the favor, and he was enough taller that his target wasn't the same.

Oh, geez, oh, man, oh fuck—no book had enough words to describe the feel of Corey's tongue between his cheeks. Soft but firm, wet, darting, Lon whimpered around his mouthful and spread his thighs more widely. Oh hell to the yes, let Corey probe and lick all he ever wanted. Lon stilled, his lips around Corey's glans and not able to do more than flicker his tongue on the velvet skin.

Oh fuck, if Corey kept doing that—Lon was a ball of want, want right now. Hafta have, but that meant letting go again, just long enough to—did they have any lube in the living room? Corey thought ahead for human stuff better than Lon did.

Maybe if he could stay still, well, not bounce up out of reach, Corey could lick him wet enough, but—that would mean doing different. Whatever Corey did to him, Lon wanted to last forever, if it could just happen at the same time as everything else he wanted to do. Oh. Ohhh…

But Corey wasn't getting anything now—Lon flicked away with what was left of his sanity. Sounds behind him, of *Guh* and *ah* and *yes* urged him on, and that heated laving tried to bring him to a standstill.

And where was some lube, damn it!

Lon bobbed his head, traveling down Corey's throbbing shaft, swallowing as many inches as he could, still not all the inches Corey had, but when a guy wanted everything, a challenge was good. Good for Corey—he pulsed and coated the back of Lon's throat with his creamy spunk, thick and salty and proof that Lon had given Corey all he could take. The motion at his backside stopped, but if Corey could still lick during his climax, Lon would have to improve his technique. And Corey seemed to like this just fine, the way he mumbled, "Oh fu… Lon… Lon, oh…."

His words vibrated against Lon's hole, bringing another moan to rumble against Corey's cock. Lon's own cock danced with the doubletime beat of his heart, rubbing the tip against Corey's chest. Good, not enough to find his climax, but like vibrissae against balls, so damned fine.

Corey flopped flat, leaving Lon's wet crack to be licked with air. The chill made him whimper, but not let go of his softening mouthful. Corey needed a minute. And maybe for Lon to get off his chest so he could breathe.

"Swing around, Lon," Corey offered. "Let me suck you some more. Wanna suck your cock."

Oh yeah. And straddling Corey's head let Lon run his fingers through Corey's hair, and thrust into his hot cave of a mouth. Corey could use that tongue equally well on his cock, and if Lon's hole felt neglected now, here came a questing finger to tickle at his pucker and find its way in. Corey breached him and sucked him. Lon didn't know if he should yell or fall or go catatonic. All of those at once— Corey pushed through Lon's tight ring and all the way to that wonderful spot inside.

Oh, man, he wouldn't last, not with fucking Corey's mouth, sliding between palate and tongue and firm, full lips, and being fucked with a long, knowing finger. Corey stroked against Lon's gland with every thrust, until Lon needed to brace himself with both hands just to keep from collapsing.

With desperate *hurrs* squeaking from his lips, Lon rocked faster, until he couldn't rock at all and froze deep inside Corey's mouth, spurting and pulsing and everything gone incandescent in his climax.

And after that, it was back to lying against Corey's side, touching body to body and held in his long arms again. Lon sighed—contentment and knowledge that moving to the bed would let Corey stretch out his legs pushed the breath out of him. His beard moved with the rise and fall of Corey's chest, sending wonderful signals of life and nearness through his vibrissae. Their mouths tasted alike now, curry and come.

And happiness. This had to be what happiness tasted like. Curry and come and Corey.

CHAPTER SIX

Corey joined Lon on the water's edge next morning. Together they sprinkled damp food pellets on the surface of the water. Masses of four inch fish came to seize the tidbits, hoovering them down and flicking away, only to surface again for another mouthful.

"This pond will be massively overstocked if they all grow up," Lon observed.

"I know." Corey flipped more fish food to the edge of the seething mass.

"We figured on some losses along the way," Lon said. Corey hadn't mentioned the otter vs. pikeminnow problem, and he didn't want the subject to swim away into obscurity.

"We did." He lowered kernels of food on his palm into the water, and let two of the bolder, hungrier koi feed from his hand.

"We had a visitor in the night." Lon had already skimmed the feathers out of the water, leaving them in the mesh basket of his long handled net. Had Corey noticed? "A hungry one."

"How many do you think he got?" Corey wiped his hand on his sweatpants and went back to tossing the pellets out to the koi.

"Don't know. The fish don't hold still." Even as a two-foot,

Lon liked watching the bright forms dart through the water. They'd get bigger and slower.

"How big do they have to get before they're too big to be heron chow?" The pan of fish food was almost empty. Corey shook the last morsels into the water.

"Pretty big," Lon admitted. "I've seen a heron swallow a two foot long trout."

"Wow." Corey rocked back on his heels, balancing himself with a hand on Lon's knee. "That's the size of a four or five year old koi. I'd be pissed with that heron."

"I was. I caught that trout first." Bastard bird stabbed him in the thigh *and* stole his lunch.

"Sucks." Corey turned to look at Lon, and Lon did not like that look. Like he was measuring the size of Lon's teeth and whether in four years' time he'd be snacking on one of the fish they'd just fed.

I hope you'll be used to it by then almost burbled out of Lon's throat, but Corey said something even worse than *Paws off the koi, bucko.*

"We need to go. Hope I don't find Melvin in my office again today."

Lon pressed the back of his hand against his lips, trying not to blurt out all his horror. "Again? Corey, didn't you hear what I was saying?"

Corey stood up and pulled Lon to his feet. "I heard you, but I didn't have a lot of control over the situation. That's why I hung up so abruptly yesterday. I opened a locked door and there he was, reading my maps."

"In your locked office." Lon started to tremble. "I didn't think werewolves could do the smoke under the door trick."

"I don't think they can either, based on prior plausibility and no data whatsoever." Corey rested his hand on Lon's shoulder, and for the first time, Lon got no comfort from it. "But the head of the department can get a key."

A key. Okay. Made sense.

"Erm, Lon, what can do the smoke under the door trick?" Corey's hand tightened.

"Vampires."

"Otter shifters, check." Corey swallowed hard. "Werewolves, check. Now vampires?"

"Only in movies." Lon disengaged Corey's hand from where it had started fusing into his shoulder, and led him to the house. "I've never encountered a real one." Though he'd heard stories... Not the time to mention it. "Maps, huh." Better to bring Corey's attention back to the real problem. "Let me guess. The Whiskey Creek area."

Corey let go long enough to drop some dry kibble and wet food into Pumpkin's dish. "Yeah. How'd you know?"

"That's where his Full Moon Conservancy wants to build. It'd be a great place for a werewolf social club, if they wanted some wilderness place with amenities for two-foots. Except..." He should shut up, let the pikeminnows and dace take their own chances, and not drag Corey into this.

"Except what, Lon?" That tawny brown gaze bored into Lon like a claw.

"You have that map because there's endangered fish in that stream, or in that drainage basin, don't you?"

"Silverscale dace, yeah." Corey stepped away from the meeping cat who brushed him on the way to her dish.

"There's about to be a lot fewer dace in the world." Lon gulped. "I asked for population counts and they mentioned tossing dynamite in the stream."

"Shit." Corey headed to the bedroom. "We really have to get going. I have to talk to Vadas, explain why that habitat is crucial."

Lon chased after him. "Corey, don't!"

"Why? We want to preserve the fish." Corey paused half in, half out of a polo shirt.

"I want to preserve you." Lon tugged at the hem, and snatched his hand back faster than if fabric could burn. "And my scent's on you, and he knows me, and he's ready to fight because I'm telling him no. And you want to tell him no too. He'll be angry with both of us, and these guys do not play around."

"Melvin Vadas will want to do what's right." Corey sat down to pull on khakis.

"He's a wolf. He'll want to do what he wants to do. And Corey, he'll hate you twice as much for smelling of me." Damn, but this couldn't get much worse. "Oh Lord, I've just gotten you into so much trouble."

He might have just gotten his lover killed.

CHAPTER SEVEN

All the way north to downtown Boulder, Lon worked on a stonewalling Corey. "You can't talk to him because you're admitting to knowledge you shouldn't even have. I'm not supposed to talk about clients' business to anyone outside the bank, and the more you admit to knowing, the more danger you're in. Smelling of me and knowing what you shouldn't—they have plenty of wilderness to hide your body. I might not be able to find you. Please, please don't talk to Vadas about this!"

"I can't just allow him to extirpate an endangered population because it's not convenient, Lon." Boy that sounded reasonable in human terms, but Corey did so not know what he was dealing with. "And I've known Melvin for a couple years. He's not a bad guy."

"He's probably a truly lovely personality *for a werewolf!*" Lon was ready to cry for the sheer frustration. "He doesn't think like you do!"

"Well, no," Corey admitted. "I can't even begin to follow some of his arguments. He's damned good at what he does. Kind of missing in human terms, but his numbers always crunch…"

"Kind of missing in human terms is precisely my point!" Lon yanked the "oh shit" handle almost hard enough to pull it off the little truck. Why couldn't he get Corey to listen?

85

"You think my thought processes are strange sometimes? I think mine are a lot closer to yours than they are to his. I at least understand doing things for other people who aren't otters. Do you think he sees not-wolves as something besides help, hindrance, or dinner?"

Finally, he'd gotten Corey to look at him like he was considering the merits of what Lon was saying. Finally. "You really think he'd kill me over this?"

"If you get in his way, and he can't get you out any other way, yeah. I do. Especially if he finds out you know what he is." Was this headway? "And if you're clearly connected to me, you don't have any plausible deniability on knowing he's a werewolf."

Corey pulled up in front of the Chautauqua Bank. "Maybe that's my secret weapon for getting tenure?"

"First you have to live that long." Oh damn it all! They were back to square one. "Don't kiss me. You don't know if you'll run into him and you mustn't get any more of my scent on you. Maybe you only smelled like we met casually. You did shower, and your soap is kind of overwhelming…."

"I'll get some unscented. You should have said."

"No! You're going to use the smelly kind twice a day, and you're going to wash all your clothes, even the clean ones, and I'll sleep on the futon tonight, or somewhere else, and you'll launder the bedding, and maybe we can de-otter you and the house enough—once I move out my scent should fade." Where to move to was the least of Lon's problems. His old roommates might let him come back, and there were always students needing a third or a fourth, he'd just have to not live with economics majors….

"Whoa. My colleague is not going to kill me and you are not going to move out." Corey grabbed Lon's hand, and Lon was weak enough to let him hold it for two seconds too long. He jerked away, but Corey kept reaching. "And I am going to kiss you, because I always kiss my boyfriend when I drop him off at work. Quit arguing, kiss me, and then motor or you'll be late."

"Why won't you believe me?" Lon opened the truck door. "And I should move out, I'm endangering you."

"If you move out, there'll be no one to play with the fish."

Two could make lunatic arguments. "How about I eat a dozen of them and you'll be mad enough to throw me out?"

"You aren't leaving." Corey leaned across the seat, but Lon had already put both feet on the pavement. "For any reason. The fish are a separate issue."

A couple of boxes should be enough for Lon's clothes and his few other possessions. He didn't have much beyond his snowboard and wardrobe. Corey ignored his request to stop at the liquor store for some cartons and drove straight home instead.

"You moving out isn't going to solve the problem, Lon." Corey pulled into the driveway. "Vadas asked me if I kept ferrets yesterday. He sounded like his tongue was firmly in his cheek."

"But that isn't certain." He wouldn't bank Corey's life on such slender evidence. If he made piles of clothes, he could see how many boxes he needed... Lon dashed into the house and didn't bother changing out of his business clothes. He yanked his shirt drawer open.

Corey came to stand in the doorway. "Today he asked again about the ferrets, and when I said no, he winked and said, 'Then something else that fucks like a mink.' Lon, he wouldn't say that unless he was quite sure about us. If he brings it up again I'll mention sexual harassment, because he's way out of line, but there isn't any real question about him knowing, is there?"

Lon sat heavily among the T-shirts. "No."

"Then there's no point to you moving out. The horse is already out of the barn you're locking." Corey shoved a pile of jersey to one side and sat thigh to thigh with Lon. "And I don't want you to move out. It won't solve anything and it would make me unhappy."

"It would make me unhappy too." Lon had drooped all day, to the point of the new accounts woman asking if she should drive him home. He snuggled against Corey's side. "But not nearly as unhappy as finding you spread across the forest floor as wolf scat."

"It's not going to come to that." Corey shouldn't sound so exasperated when he was talking out of his ass.

"Human pride."

"Yeah, human pride." Corey kissed the side of Lon's head. "Wolves are endangered species because of human predation."

"Vadas can use just as many tools as you can and shift too." If he couldn't protect Corey, Lon would keep reminding him to be vigilant.

"And he keeps missing the human factor." Corey squeezed. "I'll out-think him."

"You can try." Lon squeezed back. "I'll help."

"So you're staying?" Corey tipped Lon's face up to gaze all the way into the bottom of Lon's soul. "I had one more argument for getting you to stay."

So hard to maintain eye contact—could he bear to have Corey see his every secret? "Really? What?"

Corey stretched out one long leg, the better to dig in his front pocket. "This." He slid to the floor, kneeling between Lon's thighs, and took his left hand. "This means as much as you want it to mean. If you want me to put it on you in front of witnesses and with a lot of promises, I will. If you want to wear it just to feel close to me, that's fine." He slipped a silver ring onto Lon's third finger. "Just so you wear it."

A ring! A silver ring.

Silver.

The world went hushed, and all the smells went away. Corey's blue shirt screamed against the blond wood of the dresser behind him, and every garment in the open drawer beat against Lon's eyes.

Oh shit!

"I can't, Corey." Lon clawed the awful circlet off his hand. He didn't even want to touch it. Corey wasn't holding out his hand, no, he was kneeling with the kind of pole-axed look that greeted news of an IRS audit. "I'm sorry. I can't."

How could Corey even offer a silver ring?

Lon dropped the ring on the bed. Too close, but he couldn't hand it back and he wouldn't throw it.

"Oh. I thought… I thought you cared enough that…" Corey stared down at his rejected token.

"I do, Corey! I do, but…" Lon scrabbled for words. "I'd wear your ring. But that one's silver."

"What's wrong with silver?" Corey shook his head slightly, like a new idea needed room, or an old one had to go. "I thought it was pretty standard for guys like us."

"For guys like you." Lon had forgotten, but so had Corey. "Not guys like me."

"Tell me how I screwed up this time." Corey plopped backward to sit on his heels, and his scent went bitter under the fragrance of his soap.

"It's silver."

"You said a bullet wouldn't have to be silver. So I thought maybe everything else I learned about shifters from movies was wrong."

"It's not a killing thing. Silver severs the link between otter me and two-foot me. I couldn't smell you. And I wouldn't be able to shift if I wore it." He'd been half of himself with the band on his finger. "I saw more colors just now, but I couldn't smell you, even though you're right here. I was so scared." He slid down from the mattress, trying to hold onto the man who was slipping away with every revelation. "Corey, please. I want to wear a ring you gave me, but it has to be some other material." He should have denied that Corey screwed up, but he'd lost his otterness.

89

"So gold? Or copper?" Corey lifted Lon's hand, examining it as if it were some new creature. "Rings wouldn't stay on your paws anyway."

"Or hematite or onyx or jade or pot metal even, and anything under twenty-four karat gold has enough silver in it to be a problem." Lon shivered in spite of himself, and in spite of sitting on Corey's warm legs and trying to wrap himself in long arms. "Any ring except silver is good. Even the paper band off a stinky old cigar, if you gave it to me."

"Okay. We'll get some other kind. Can you come into a store with silver merchandise and help me pick it out?" Leaning into Lon's chest made it feel like Corey was relaxing, but his scent stayed bitter.

"I never tried. We can try. I think it has to be on me, in some encircling way, to interfere." Lon rubbed his chin against the side of Corey's head. "I know you didn't mean to scare me. And I didn't mean to scare you either."

"I was trying to convince you how much I care for you," Corey mumbled, sending the words vibrating up Lon's sensitive whiskers. "And instead I mess you up. How many more times are we going to find stuff out the hard way?"

"I don't know." Lon couldn't even guess, but what if it turned out to be one time too many?

CHAPTER EIGHT

Corey squeezed Lon's hand, not daring to let go. The koi pond tested his lover's resolve. The Denver Aquarium would test him further. They were about to walk into a building with a million gallons of tanks and habitats, housing untold thousands of delicious inhabitants.

"Are you sure about this?" Corey paused at a discreet distance from the ticket booths. The laughter and shrieking of toddlers riding the merry-go-round on the piazza nearly drowned his words.

"Oh, yes." Lon shook himself, settling his surety like a cloak, and, Corey feared, as easily shed. "How else am I going to know what a silverscale dace looks like?"

"Pictures?" They'd examined books from the university's excellent library, but Lon hadn't claimed expertise once he'd flipped through the pages, and demanded a first-paw look.

"Pictures don't move, they don't have a flavor, and what I see as a two-foot doesn't look the same as when..." Lon trailed off with commendable delicacy.

"You aren't going to lick the exhibits!" Corey didn't know how to take that "flavor" comment.

"No, but...." Lon whipped out his credit card. "Two, please." His grin at treating Corey was delight unto itself, but there was that matter of licking. "It's kind of taste, and kind of smell, and a bit of vibrissae-feeling that you may not have any reference for. Since, you, poor thing, have whiskers that only stick out and get sliced off and aren't good for anything but decoration."

"Just wait until I rub my morning chin across your butt," Corey grumbled. This expedition had huge possibilities for disaster. If Lon hadn't been genuinely shaken about the silver ring, Corey would have suggested wearing it as insurance. And then Lon would have only the senses of a two-foot. Which wouldn't have been an improvement over looking in books. They mounted the stairs into the aquarium.

What had been a municipal structure had been taken over by a seafood restaurant chain since Corey's last visit, and the exhibits had been streamlined into a one-way traffic flow. They could stop and look at anything that caught their interest, but going back to look again was definitely discouraged. "I hope we don't sail past the right tank. I really hope there is a right tank."

"Oh, they're all right tanks." Lon licked his lips. "One of them ought to have dace."

Corey squeezed Lon's hand harder.

The first section of exhibits was set up as examples from the headwaters of the Colorado River, and would change to show habitat and life as the river wound through its length, all the way to tropical reefs in the Gulf of California. Silverscale dace lived in the mountain streams—they'd find their target in the first group of tanks. The glass walls rose a few feet above the water line. Not far enough. Lon pressed his nose against the glass. Dozens of foot-long rainbow trout swam past his—snout?

"Lon!" Corey yanked on his lover. "Don't!" Oh, this was just too dangerous. They could end up owing the restaurant chain for the world's most expensive fish dinner. And then Lon's secret would be out. He might never get away from poking and prodding and the thousand questions he didn't want to answer. "Lon, chill!"

"Oh, okay." Lon stepped back, and his nose went pale again. "But gee, those look nice!"

"Look. Don't drool." One tank successfully passed. Ninety-nine to go.

"Not this one," Lon decided from looking at the fish and Corey from reading the placard, and "Not this one either," at the next tank.

Lon stopped short and shook out of Corey's grip. With both hands flat to the glass and his forehead touching as well, Lon leaned to watch the otters swim. Sleek, dark shapes flashed past, communicating with their observer, though their audience was large and squealing about the cuteness.

Lon watched the otters for long minutes. Shudders ran through his frame, and Corey didn't know what to make of them, imminent shifting or sorrow. He stood close behind Lon, one hand at the small of his back and leg pressed to leg. "They seem happy, but I'm just a dumb two-foot. Are they?"

"Mostly. Making the best of a bad situation." Lon sniffled. "They have everything, but it's a miniature world. Three of them, in a 'habitat' smaller than our back yard."

An otter swooped by, propelled by its tail, taking a good long look at them on its way by. Another paddled by more slowly, putting on a burst of speed to catch and tussle with its companion. The third, on land, sat upright and waved both forepaws. Lon waved back.

"They can smell me. Us. And they can smell freedom and a thousand fish they can't catch." Lon stood upright, leaning into Corey's side. He scritched his fingers against the glass. A passing otter paused to pat the glass from the other side. "And there's nothing I can do for them."

"Sorry, babe." When he walked in, Corey thought the aquarium was a good thing, preserving the creatures. Now he wasn't so sure. Still, better than being pelts in a coat. And if he had to reach that far for a comparison, he should hang up humanity as any example of goodness. He couldn't comfort Lon because he had no comfort for himself. Humans salved their consciences by keeping these animals in a pretty prison. His own work took on a cast far beyond the economics of sharing the world. "I'm trying to make sure they have good habitat in the wild."

"I know." Lon looked up with the weariest smile. "Be persuasive, okay?"

He left the otters behind, head bowed. Corey kept him from walking into anyone, all the while frantically scanning the placards, desperate not to miss the silverscale dace, if they were there. "Whoa, Lon. Look!"

Lon's head came up, his eyes wide. "Oh, yeah!" On his knees, his face to the glass where a shallow "stream" ran, he watched the three inch long fish fin themselves stationary.

Thoroughly unremarkable fish, to Corey's eyes. The barely metallic gray scales and boned fins didn't shout "important" or "unique" to him. Perhaps these fish were the quintessential example of why man had to be reined in, because the poor things were so unexceptional and unlikely to be savored for themselves. If their qualities weren't obvious, that only meant he should look harder.

Lon was looking really hard. Too hard.

"Tell me what's so unique here, Lon." Making his brain engage might keep Lon from taking a more furry interest.

"They're prey fish for cutthroat trout, and they like the running water more than the pools, not all the fish go for that microhabitat…" Lon gulped. "And they're—"

Whatever else the fish were got lost in a soft snuffle.

Corey glanced to his right? What? Where was… "Lon? Lon!" Holy fuck! Clothes wriggled on the floor. A brown head stuck out. "Lon!"

Shit, shit, shit! Corey glanced right and left, reaching down to arrange the clothes over a squirming mass of otter. Lon popped up on his hind legs. His vibrating excitement shook the T-shirt down his sleek sides.

Lon rested webby paws on the glass, his nose working a mile a minute. His claws scraped the protective barrier. The fish swam a few inches to the right. Lon hopped after it.

"No!" Wait!" Corey lunged, and closed his fist on air.

Lon's nose left wet marks on the glass. Oh Lord, how to disguise this? Corey shielded Lon best he could. His legs would have to rival an elephant's to be a good screen. The passers-by coming from behind him had their eyes on the tanks, not the floor. "Hold still!" Corey hissed, and scooped up shoes, jeans and shirt. Could he dangle them around Lon and not attract attention?

He hoped. He stood at the tank, trying to look at the fish and not at the upright otter at his feet. How far did Lon's tail stick out?

No hue and cry yet...

Until the fish swam six inches in the other direction, and Lon followed. Corey sidestepped too, trying to cover fur with denim, while a black rubber nose kept poking out.

If Corey's heart pounded any harder, his ribs would splinter outward. Don't look down, he implored the universe, and forgot that the aquarium was Rugrat Central.

"Mommy, look at the otter!" some little girl shrieked. Was she far enough away to be talking about the captives in the exhibit?

"Oh, my goodness, it's out!" Mommy shredded that forlorn hope. "There's an otter out!"

"No need to fear, ma'am," Corey tried booming out in his best teaching voice. "He's gentle and when he's through looking—which is right now," he hissed downward—"I'll put him back."

Put him back where? was another question. Lon needed another forty-five minutes, maybe longer, before he could shift.

Cries of "Ooh, he's so cute!" and "I want to pet him! Mister, can we pet him?" rang out. No and no, that was the quickest route to official attention.

"Don't touch him, please. Let's not frighten him. He's just interested in the fish." Corey stepped between Lon and the crowd, but he couldn't cover Lon's three exposed sides.

Caught between Corey, the glass, and the overly friendly people, Lon had nowhere to go but up. And up he went—stabby claws jabbed into Corey's flesh, right through his clothing. Four feet of muscle and fur wrapped around Corey's neck, and one webbed paw rested on the top of his head. Lon fretted in squeaks and hisses.

Official attention could be aquarium staff—or cops and sirens.

Corey held his hand out, trying to make a circle of space around him. "Step back, folks, I like my ear right where it is." With the other he stroked Lon, more to comfort the squealing children than to keep his lover from damaging him. He really had to get them out of there. Fucking big "there," and no good refuge. Corey started edging toward a dark alcove. Was that a men's room? Could he hide Lon in a stall? Could he keep a frisky critter quiet until Lon could shift back and get dressed? Damn the popularity of this place—a tide of people surged one way and he had to go the other.

"Easy there, Lon," Corey begged when hind feet scrabbled against his chest. "Let's get you out of here, okay?" Ripples of tension coursed through Lon's sleek sides. He might think his best getaway was into one of the tanks. The glass went up five feet, no jump at all from the shoulders of a six foot one man. "Stay right there, yeah, let's get out of the crowd." Corey kept up the patter for everyone's benefit, including his own. If someone started screaming about an otter-napping, things would go to hell. Further to hell.

A volunteer, a gray-haired man in a red vest, pushed through the crowd. "Scuse me, 'scuse me, folks. Hold still, young man." He wended his way through the staring throng, having an easier time of it than Corey had moving upstream. "Emmet, you naughty boy."

Emmet? What? Corey stopped, too far from shelter to run for it, and totally busted. "Easy, Lon, we'll figure this out." He hoped. Even if Lon made a break for it, getting outside meant going down two steep flights of cement stairs and somehow forcing his way through glass doors. The foyer couldn't have been designed as an otter trap, though that's what it would be.

The volunteer reached Corey's side. "Hope he didn't scare you. Emmet's a good guy, just kind of curious." He reached to Lon, who twisted around out of reach, rubbing his soft fur against Corey's nose.

He couldn't sneeze, not now. That would shake Lon right off his shoulders. "He's fine. Really."

"Now, now, we can't let this furry boy run loose. Liability, you know." The volunteer pursued Lon in a terrible ring a rosy around Corey, who helpfully turned to keep Lon away from those reaching hands. "Odds are of him getting in with the fish and providing a little too much nature show."

"He's fine, really." Corey pivoted another quarter circle.

"You can't carry him around, son. The aquarium folks won't like that at all." The man piled into Corey's personal space, forcing him against the glass of a trout-filled tank. Maybe Lon should escape into the water.

Yeah, and have staff with nets come scoop him out. Maybe tranquilize him. What would sleepy darts do to him? Make his fur go away? Or would he just fall over?

Lon stayed on Corey's shoulders, now with his nose against Corey's ear. He clung, chirruping advice or exclamations, but Corey couldn't translate anything from otter, besides *oh shit*, and he already knew that.

"Come on, you rascal." The volunteer got his hands onto Lon. Short of assaulting the old man, or claiming he'd brought an extraneous otter to a repository of fish, or worse, admitting Lon was an otter shifter, there wasn't a lot Corey could do.

The man lifted Lon away, holding him under his front legs, with his paws splayed out and his tail curved up under his body. *Ack!* radiated off him, and his thrashing wasn't making the man let go.

"Everything's fine, Emmet, just fine. Let's put you back, okay?" Four long steps brought them to the otter tank.

Corey cursed the designers of this fish-pit—open and airy and glass walls low enough for a basketball player to peek over meant—Oh shit.

The red-vested meddler lifted Lon up, not a huge task with a twenty-five pound burden, even a squirmy one, and got his front legs over the glass. "Get back in there, Emmet, and stay put." Another huge heave, and Lon splashed in with three curious otters who'd come to see the commotion at the front of their habitat. "Get on with you. Now we need to see about keeping you in there."

Corey followed, aghast. "But—" But what? "That's my otter?" or "That's my boyfriend?" Oh for pity's sake. He'd have to get Lon out of there somehow. Maybe in about an hour. He clutched the pile of clothing to his chest. "How do you know that was Emmet?"

The volunteer turned to him. "Edwin has a white stripe down one leg from a trapping accident, and Sally's smaller. That rascal Emmet's pure brown, and he's always checking out what people are doing. Didn't think he could escape, though."

He had to keep the man from noticing an extra. "He wasn't hurting anything."

"No, but he sure would have had a fancy dinner if he got into that habitat he was so interested in." The man turned back to the otters, but one had swum off and only three frolicked in the water close to the glass. Squeals of delight from the littlies at their feet cut through the ambient sounds of rushing water. "Those fish are endangered." He smiled fondly at his charges. "We've never had an escapee."

You still haven't, Corey wanted to tell him, but there was this issue of Lon's secret. No fair getting him splashed across the newspapers—again.

"Now, Sally and Edwin are great critters, but Emmet's something special." The man rested his hand against the glass. One of the otters swam over to nose at it, and Corey wouldn't swear it wasn't Lon. He'd never seen his boyfriend in fur and in the company of other otters. "You stay in there, fella."

That's what Corey was afraid of. How was he going to bust Lon out of jail?

The volunteer left, and with any luck, no one else would come along who would notice the aquarium now had 33 percent more otters on display than it had ten minutes earlier.

Corey leaned his forehead against the glass and ignored the small children who jostled for best viewing positions. Of course the otters would attract a crowd now: one kept scraping his paws against the glass.

"Sorry about that," Corey mouthed. His voice wouldn't carry through the noise and then underwater. "I'll get you out of there."

Lon licked his front leg. Yeah, time. He wouldn't shift back for close to an hour. Corey looked at his watch. "I'll be back when you can shift again, okay?" He didn't want to attract more attention to himself and the bundle of clothes he carried.

Lon floated on his back on the surface, waving his paws and making his audience squeal. One of the other otters tackled him, and they were off and rolling. Lon's whiskers pushed forward—he was happy with this, and no one was biting. The crowd at the otter exhibit grew thicker.

Reluctantly giving up his prime viewing spot, Corey backed away. He waved at Lon, Lon waved back, and returned to tussling with his new friend. Someone was going to have a good time for the next hour.

Corey could too. He'd paid to see the denizens of the deep, and he could go have a look.

He wandered through the dark hallways, pausing to look at desert pupfish and sunfish, largemouth bass and a seven foot long carp, fascinated in spite of his worries. Corey spent the next hour traveling back and forth from the other exhibits to the dace, memorizing fishy features until he was quite sure he knew every species to be found in the Colorado River watershed.

Had Lon found a vulnerability he could exploit for his escape? Corey meandered against the flow of people, back to the otter tank.

Lon, the big hambone, left off grooming Emmet or Sally or Edwin, coming to turn circles underwater to the delight of the throngs. He paused on the surface, his flat head swishing from side to side when Corey mimed up and over with one lifted hand.

Yeah. Too many people. Corey left to look at sergeant majors, conger eels, and manta rays.

Another trip back, earning him the beady eye of a staffer who disapproved of anyone not following the prescribed path through the exhibits. Yeah, this place was set up for maximum extraction of cash from pockets. Their idea of proper second looks at the first tanks was to circle around and buy another ticket. Not happening. But Lon still couldn't escape—the otter exhibit had become the bottleneck for the tourists, who ooh'ed and ah'ed over mustelid antics. Lon was adorable with his fur on, but just this once, it would be nice if he shifted into a skunk or a snake or something with a heavier ick factor. How was Corey going to get Mr. Fuzzy out of there unseen?

Go take a nap! Corey mouthed, but Edwin, Emmet, and Sally had him pinned in a group grooming session. "Oh, they're so cute!" was the consensus among the two-foots.

Another hour of sharks, groupers, and jellyfish, and still Lon was trapped under the scrutiny of too many visitors. Corey went to look at seahorses.

Every half hour Corey came back to see if the crowds had thinned to the point of permitting a jail break. Every half hour he went off to look at sharks or lionfish or manta rays. Lon had upped the attractiveness factor of the otter exhibit by a lot more than 33 percent. Corey had lunch in the aquarium's restaurant, hoping that when the otters got their chow, Lon had the sense to stay out of sight of people who knew how many mouths they planned to feed. Did otters have enough sense of community that they'd share? They'd been in the aquarium more than five hours now. Lon had to be hungry.

Three hours later, Corey was no closer to getting Lon out of the exhibit and was unhappily sure there was no chair whatsoever in the entire enormous building that wasn't pulled up to a table with the expectation of a meal. Nine hours after they'd entered, he snarled at an employee who tried to shoo him to the exit. "I paid to look at fish, and I am going to look at fish, damn it." Or otters. Otter. An hour after that, he was looking for places to hide after closing, and discovered that the staff was alert to him. He had company in three different men's rooms. He returned the beady eye.

Half an hour before closing, Corey sat on the floor across from the otter habitat, his long legs stretched out in front of him.

"We need you to head out, sir," a young woman told him. "We'll be closing soon."

"In a bit," Corey responded. "I still have some time, and I like looking at the otters."

"They are cute," she agreed, "but you need to leave now. Maybe come back another day?"

Not again in this lifetime, if he could help it. "I have twenty minutes. I can get out of here before closing."

"We stopped letting people in, sir."

He fixed her with his best "aggrieved professor" look, a good trick from three feet below eye level. "I noticed." What he'd really noticed was that she was the only impediment to a rescue. "I'll be out of here shortly."

That was enough to make her quit annoying him. "Okay." Damned if she didn't press her nose to the otter tank for a moment, but only three animals bounced, rolled,

101

or swam where they could be seen. One went into the den, and the other two disappeared behind some logs.

Lon had to be more than ready to shift back by now. Corey watched the young woman disappear and was on his feet. "Lon! Quick!"

An otter dove into the water, arrowing to the glass. Before impact he shifted, flailing with a human hand to grab the edge of glass that was still two feet beyond his grasp. Lon sank to the bottom, gathering his legs beneath him for a grand leap, and managed to hook two fingers over the top of the tank wall. With excruciating slowness, he gained more purchase on the edge, and then every muscle in his arms and magnificently nude torso flexed to heave him upward. He hooked one foot over the lip of the tank, and rolled up and over, flashing his bare ass to any security camera that might have been looking.

Corey shook out Lon's clothing, holding out the shirt to let him dive in, and offering the jeans for him to struggle into with his wet limbs. Underwear was a silly formality when speed was this important. Covered, finally, Lon jammed his feet into his shoes without untying them, and once shod, he stood up to face Corey. A hurried toss of his head and his hair fluffed out, nearly dry.

"Are you okay?" Corey took his arm to guide Lon out of the dark serpentine paths that he'd come to know entirely too well. They hurried past the dace with a quick glance, and wound past coral reefs and mangrove swamp where bright bodies flickered at the water's surface.

"Kind of." Lon leaned on Corey's arm, paying no attention to the stares of the staff who'd grown accustomed to Corey's face that day. He said nothing more until they'd escaped from the building. "I'm hungry."

"I bet you are." Corey unlocked the blue RAV4. "What would you like?" Food of every description could be had along the highway corridor that would take them from downtown Denver back to Boulder.

"Sushi—no. Not sushi." Lon licked his lips. "People food. Meat. Not fish. And fast."

"Larkburger's on the way home." Corey was equally ready for one of the drippy, thick patties on a toasted bun. He'd ordered from the appetizer menu earlier, more as rent for the seat than because he wanted it, and picked at the bits of breaded seafood. "Did you get anything at all?"

"Little bit." He yawned, and his teeth flashed in the headlight punctuated darkness of I-25 North.

"You looked like you were enjoying yourself, aside from the matter of getting seen." Corey dodged an eighteen-wheeler to make the curve onto Highway 36.

"Was." Lon leaned back with his eyes closed. "They're nice." Corey glanced over to see his smile. His whiskers usually lay flat in a proper goatee. Maybe they'd dried that way, but Corey was sure every hair pushed forward in an otter's smile. "Good time."

"Too tired to use more than two words at a time?" Corey teased. "Swimming all day?"

"Can't." Lon scrubbed his face with both hands. "Too hard."

A few minutes later they pulled into the burger joint, and Lon was still speaking cryptically. He managed to order his own meal, but if the cashier hadn't asked yes or no questions, he might still be waiting to get fed. Once he got his hands on the juicy burger and a few bites into his stomach, his sentences grew longer and his descriptions more vivid. By the time every fry disappeared and the hamburger was reduced to a memory and streaks of ketchup, he'd left Hemingway sentences behind and was closing in on Faulkner.

"I'm really confident that I can recognize the dace whether I'm shifted or on two feet," he assured Corey. Lon sounded like his usual self, bubbly and happy, and not at all tired. "That was a really good idea, to go look at the actual fish in something approaching their natural habitat. The composition of the stream bed apparently matters, and so does the location of the fastest flowing water. I could tell what flow speeds the fish preferred, just from watching the specimens in the tank. No wonder they're endangered if they're that finicky about water conditions. Perhaps they're overly specialized, but those rayed fins would only be a problem in still water, and faster water would overwhelm them, given their musculature relative to their body size."

That one speech lasted them from the burger joint to Boulder, and man, was Corey glad for the waterfall of words. "Okay, okay, Mr. Ichthyologist!" Corey hadn't picked up on the more subtle details when he watched the dace, but he'd noted body shape and fin angles. "I think we're both able to recognize those poor endangered fishies. Uh…" He risked a sideways glance once they were in the driveway. "Did you notice all of that when you were furry or not?"

"Some of both." Lon grinned happily. "I didn't have words for some of it while I had my fur on, but I knew it." He lost some of his happiness. "Actually, I didn't have a lot of words at all until after I'd eaten."

"I could tell. You must have been really hungry." Was food the trigger for escalating Lon's return to his usual self? Corey stopped asking daring questions and hoped Lon would understand his need to know more.

"All I got was the tail end of something that probably died in one of the other exhibits, and then only because—" He chopped off, his brows wrinkled. "Male, young."

"Emmet or Edwin," Corey prompted.

"Huh. Still can't tell you who. The name I know him by is more of a smell. Anyway, he chomped his fish in two and I grabbed the part he dropped." Lon wrinkled his nose. "Dead food. But no, hunger was only part of it." He led Corey to the back yard, bypassing the house, to measure out fish pellets. He remained silent, throwing bits in for the swarming, colorful school of koi. Corey rested his hand on Lon's shoulder silently, pressed a kiss to the side of his head, and helped him fling pellets for their fish.

When the food had all been scattered, Lon grabbed Corey's hand to all but run into the house. Once inside, he threw himself into Corey's arms. "Can you feed the fish tomorrow? Without me?"

"Sure." What a strange request, but something about the pond was upsetting Lon. Too much time spent wet today? Was there such a thing as too much time spent wet for an otter?

"Good." Lon shrank a little but didn't let go. "I want to stay away from the water for a while. It's…calling."

"Tell me what you think I should know." Nine hundred seventy-eight of the thousand unwelcome questions still lurked unasked and unanswered, but maybe this would do for a workaround.

"Back when you first found out I had fur, I told you I needed at least an hour, remember?"

Working his fingers into the tension of Lon's back, Corey agreed. "You said one to five hours was about right."

"How long did I have my fur on today?" Lon snuggled harder into his embrace.

"We got there around ten thirty, and you put your fur on not long after that." Corey consulted his shaky memory. "And they tried to throw me out about nine, which means you took your fur off a little after that. So about ten hours, maybe a bit more."

Lon shuddered hard enough to rock Corey. "I stayed shifted for twelve hours once when I was seventeen, and it was hard to remember how to talk and use tools. This… was like then. Not quite as bad. My words didn't go all the way away. I couldn't have eaten with a fork though. And the water wants me to put my fur back on and come play."

What the…? Dear God, what had Corey gotten himself into? Eight years of college didn't prepare him for this. Shifters ought to come with a manual. Lon had to answer Corey's questions. What other critical information had Lon forgotten to tell him?

"That sounds like a really bad idea right now." Corey would tackle him if Lon tried to go back outside, but he wasn't trying to escape.

"If... if I put my fur on now, I might not remember to take it off again." Lon turned his deep brown eyes up to Corey's, so solemn. "I like my life, sometimes with fur and sometimes without. Help me, Corey. Help me hold on to what's human about me."

"I love you, Lon. With fur and without." How could he stand to be without the joy of his lover? "Should we do something you can only do with two feet?"

"Yeah." Lon's beard rasped against Corey's shirt. His vibrissae. Not whiskers.

"I'm not about to get out the Scrabble board." Corey slid his hands under Lon's shirt, finding his lean flanks with the scars on one side. "Come to bed with me." He pulled the T-shirt over Lon's head. "Let me make you glad you're a man."

Only as a man was Lon tall enough to stand on his feet to kiss his human lover, and only as a man did he want to. Camaraderie and affection were all well and good, fine for when he wore his fur and played with the tall figure who wouldn't swim in the koi pond or the winter streams. But as a man, Lon could look at his lover and feel his heart swelling in his chest fit to burst.

Only as a man would he kiss Corey and take his caresses. Only as a man could he lie next to human strength and sinew and touch him as an equal. If Corey wanted Lon to be a man to embrace, to rut with, to enjoy, he would stay on two feet.

He let Corey steer him to the bedroom, leaving a trail of discarded clothing. He walked out of his shoes and left jeans lying where they dropped from his ankles, to be nude and human with Corey. If Corey couldn't match the softness of

Lon's body hair, he had the same furry patches at chest, armpits and groin, the same light sprinkling on arms and legs, the same barely-there fuzz on buttocks. Once through the bedroom door, Corey grabbed Lon's butt, squeezing the big muscles and lifting him enough to make Lon look down into the drowning pools of Corey's brown eyes.

Their water called to him but not like the streams or the lakes—no, these pools invited him to dive to the bottom of Corey's soul, where only human dwelled.

Oh but he loved this man, and only as a man could he love. Skin to skin, with his erection pressed tight to Corey's belly, Lon had no interest in the ponds or creeks. He wouldn't go where Corey couldn't follow. The call of the water faded in his ears.

"Stay with me," Corey asked, and dropped them both to the bed. Lon writhed under Corey's weight, wanting to thrust his cock against the bare skin of his man. Working his way up Lon's chest, Corey drew lazy trails on Lon's skin, tonguing one nipple and inching upward to the dip of his collarbone.

To hold Corey he needed hands, not little clawed, webby paws—no, he needed long human fingers to grip the diameter of Corey's upper arms. How else could he pull Corey up into kissing range, or keep him there to slip his tongue into Corey's mouth, a tongue broad and mobile as Corey's own?

Mouth to mouth, chest to chest, cock to cock. Lon moaned, the same sound his lover made, through a throat that could form the words *I love you*. He could still feel every motion of Corey's face through his whiskers, details that Corey would never know, but tonight that made Lon human and more than human, because those movements meant smiles and gasps and want. The same want he had. To never let go and to fly apart with his orgasm and to stay on the peak until Corey came and then fall all the way down, shedding sparks.

The chill on his chest when Corey sat up to straddle Lon's thighs was nothing to the wonder of being encircled by that big hand with short-clipped, buffed nails. Not just encircled, but clasped in the same grip with Corey's own cock, the same long columnar shape with the same bulbous head, with reddish skin pulling up and sliding back, covering and revealing. Hard enough to ache, held stiff by engorgement alone—Corey might never have heard of a baculum and wouldn't believe Lon sometimes had a bone in his penis. But not tonight. Tonight he was like Corey all over, and Corey was all over him.

"Do you like this, Lon?" Corey asked the question, but he knew, he had to know. Lon's heart bucked in his chest— his cock jumped with every earthquake beat.

"Yes, oh yes," Lon whispered, his words answering as much as the harshness of his breath, but not as permanent as the rise and fall of his hips. "Oh, Corey." What should he to do with his hands? He'd wanted them back so bad. Should he grab Corey's thighs? Stroke his face and jaw? Pinch his nipples until his sharp intake of breath said *enough*?

Hands. He had to keep his hands to touch this amazing man whose every caress was heaven.

"Do me, Lon," Corey murmured. "Be inside me."

That request alone was almost enough to steal his mind, but Lon could not let go that much. Anything for Corey. Anything this wonderful for them both. He gripped Corey's thighs and hissed when the chill lube hit his bare skin, to warm under the friction of his lover's hands. "Make you slick. Make you ready to enter me. Make you come inside me." Corey lifted up to point Lon's cock to his hole. "I can only do this with a man. The only man I want to do it with is you. You'll stay a man for me."

"I will," Lon gasped. "I am. For you." His world had the dimensions of a king-sized bed and the only other citizen was Corey.

The tightness that was Corey's ass engulfed him—his cock slipping inside that hot passage, gripped with muscles that eased just enough to let him inside. Lon groaned deep in his throat, not a growl, for men didn't growl and he was a man. But what Corey did, sliding down the slick, full human shaft jutting upward from Lon's groin, was enough to make an animal of any man. Even himself—the deep moan of pleasure trickling from Corey's throat couldn't have been written in words.

Ass to groin and now hand to hand: Corey twined his fingers into Lon's, balancing himself on the axis of Lon's cock, rising and falling in the tides of their desire. All but crushing Corey's fingers, Lon steadied him, lifting his hips and falling away, never loosening his grip nor taking his eyes from Corey's.

His lover rode him slowly, exquisitely. Lon followed Corey's speed, savoring the deliberation of their coupling. Some other night they would pound each other in a frenzy: tonight was for feeling every nuance a man could enjoy. Corey gave him a lot of nuances and kept his attention on every one.

Until they all coalesced and became a pulsing and throbbing, starting in his depths and roiling outward. Lying flat, he couldn't fall from the glory of his climax. Wanting to sail to the heavens on this rocket Corey detonated in him, all he could do was curl up to press his face into Corey's chest, swept up into an embrace that couldn't contain this much pleasure. An eon of gratification still ended too soon, dwindling into harsh panting and memories.

Lon lay flat to the mattress again, chasing the last of the pulsations. Corey flexed around him, forcing another shudder and spasm.

"Touch me," Corey whispered. "Wrap your fingers around my cock and stroke me."

Those words were as good as another climax. He seized with a last pulsation, juddering against the pleasure and unable to stay still, and why would he want to do anything but writhe under his lover's touch? Corey brought their joined hands to the stiff cock jutting out over Lon's belly and transferred Lon's grip.

"Won't take much," Corey gasped, his hand cupped around Lon's.

Lon could do wonderful things with his hands: write, make music, and bring his beloved to shattering climax. Stroking at the same slow speed Corey tormented him with, Lon lifted and dropped his hand, pumping Corey into a hip thrusting frenzy. Yet he wouldn't cede control—Corey had to go with the long smooth distances Lon traveled against his shaft, until control disappeared. Corey thrust his hips forward into Lon's grip, losing penetration but demanding his fist. Thick white ribbons spurted from him, dampening Lon's skin with the product of joy. He shot again onto Lon's belly, the white gel dripping and catching in the soft hairs.

Corey opened his eyes at last. "You are an amazing, amazing man."

Perhaps Lon was. He'd have to take Corey's word for that. The water's call dropped into the background hum of his world, not loud enough to lure him from the bed. Spooned into the curve of his lover's body, Lon knew himself for a man who would dream the dreams of men this night.

CHAPTER NINE

Now that he'd finished teaching his macroeconomics class, Corey intended to spend some serious time working on the Whiskey Creek Basin section of his research. After yesterday's adventure in the aquarium, dropping Lon off at the bank seemed like leaving him in the safest, driest environment around.

The dace probably hadn't come to any grief while Lon and Corey were doing their research. Vadas' henchmen, henchwolves, whatever, might have been at work with blasting caps, but then again, they might have as little idea of where to obtain such things as Corey did. Vadas himself had been held captive in a classroom listening to two PhD candidates.

Not that defending dissertations wasn't nature red in tooth and claw in and of itself—Corey had been one of them not so long ago and had to snap and struggle for his position in the department. Both of these two would love to replace him, just as he wanted Vadas' chair one day. He was in no position to challenge the alpha economist. Yet.

Challenging the wolf had to be done on another level. Corey extracted reports from the Game and Fish Department, intending to plot dace sightings against topological maps that he'd just incidentally marked with property lines. Quite a lot of land in the mountains belonged to the government, one way or the other, but land could be leased, and even national parks and forests had a certain amount of human activity.

Unwilling to be disturbed, Corey locked himself into his office and surrounded himself with maps, reports, rulers, and colored pencils.

About halfway through the slender Game and Fish population survey detailing "Whiskey Creek: three adult females, two adult males, seven unsexed juveniles located between confluence of Little Jug Creek and confluence of Wochita Creek," Corey had blue dots all over his map and a sinking feeling about the probability of a successful building loan.

He didn't care one way or the other about midnight romps in the forest: the wolves could have all the fun they liked under the full moon. He and Lon wouldn't be anywhere near that particular creek, or even that particular mountain, if they knew that's where the fangs would be concentrated. But five of the pitiful twelve dace counted in a three mile stretch of prime habitat were clustered within the property lines of the proposed Full Moon Conservancy.

Perhaps those juveniles had grown up, or perhaps they'd been eaten by hungry trout. Perhaps for every fish counted there'd been three or eight or twelve that had not. Perhaps...

His office door swung open.

Corey jerked upright, the hair on his arms standing to attention. Melvin Vadas stood, still twisting the key in the lock, fully framed in the doorway.

Defending his territory against physical intrusion came instinctively to Corey—at least Vadas required a key. He might not have faced smoke coming under the door with such ferocity.

"Is there something you need, Melvin?" Corey wouldn't dignify the intruder with his title. "I'm very busy here."

"Ah, yes, as a matter of fact...." Not cowering, but certainly taken aback, Vadas stumbled over his words.

Nothing like catching him red handed to improve the balance of power. Before, Corey shrank away from Vadas. Today he set his forearms protectively on top of his maps and reports. "Something you need badly enough to raid my office to get?"

"Ah...." Vadas didn't form a coherent sentence after that.

"Something you needed so badly you didn't bother to knock?"

"You weren't here yesterday, Levigne, and I anticipated you'd be out ill another day." Vadas recovered enough to say.

"I wasn't ill, thank you. I was out doing field work." Corey tapped his pencil against the map. "Which of my research materials did you abscond with yesterday?" Righteous indignation was a position of weakness, territoriality was not. Corey went with the stronger mode.

"I would not abscond with your materials." Vadas stood taller, his shoulders somehow broader. "Looking harms nothing, and you gave me that map, if you'll recall."

"And now I should give you everything else I'm working on?" Corey challenged him. "I think not. My project, my grant, and no, you will not be putting your name on the resulting paper." Accusing Vadas of intellectual poaching ought to tweak his pride. If he had human pride.

"I intended no such thing, you imbecile. And if you value your position in the department, you'll watch your accusations." Oops, Vadas had that kind of pride.

"Then what exactly prompts you to sneak into a locked office for a second time?" After seeing Melvin with a key, Corey trusted his memory of a locked door enough to issue the challenge.

"If you must know, your research overlaps information I need." Vadas' eyes went hard, but not blue. This time. "That ferret-faced little loan officer wants population studies on some damned kind of fish in a creek on my land before he'll approve the money. As if he has the right to a say in anything I choose to do."

That might be a wolf sentiment, or a purely human thought undisguised with social conventions. "Since you can't be troubled to ask first, you can go download your own information." Corey laid his hands protectively flat on his papers.

"You'll tell me what I need. And where it is." With both hands on the door jambs, Vadas blocked the exit.

"Fish and Game website. As for the rest"—Corey bared his teeth without lifting the corners of his mouth—"you can hunt for it. Same as I did."

Vadas backed out of the doorway, not turning, and not shutting the door behind him, either. "No problem," he gruffed out, and disappeared.

No problem? Wrong, oh wrong. Corey let his head tip forward into his hands.

"It's a quarter moon tonight," Lon said happily. "We shouldn't be overrun with wolves."

Steering the little SUV around a cattle truck growling its way up I-70, Corey didn't have a glance to spare for the rock layers exposed on either side of the highway cut through the ridge. Feeling like he was pushing the vehicle uphill at speed with his own tension, he counted the hours until dark. Too few. "Two seems like enough for 'overrunning.' One, if it's aggressive."

"Obviously I don't know all that much about the ways wolves think, but they probably retain a lot of human understanding, like I do. Just without as many words, and simpler concepts." Lon pressed his nose against the glass until they passed the point of geological interest. "A philosophical discussion of otter needs versus pikeminnow needs would probably be beyond them."

That again. "I suspect they'd know wolf needs just fine." A little farther and Corey could relax his white-knuckled grip on the steering wheel. Maybe.

"Wolf needs mean they wouldn't tackle you unless you're helpless and they're hungry, or they're hungry enough to have gone totally stupid, or you've cornered them and they feel threatened." Lon sniffed appreciatively at the odors around the Evergreen exit. "We'll assume they don't know the extent of your interest in their affairs, which makes a totally different problem."

Corey sniffed too. The Goose Egg must be doing a booming business in steaks this evening. Maybe they'd stop at the rustic log restaurant on the way back down for a bite to eat. Red meat ought to reinforce Lon's ability to stay on two feet.

Because they were about to take some chances.

"I think if we get face to face, I'm going to feel threatened."

"Ooh, we do not want to be in that situation." Lon quit admiring the scenery to stare at Corey. "Too bad you can't smell them."

"I'm not sure how much they can smell in human form." Not looking at the scenery here was the most absurd thing Lon could do—they were coming around the bend at the Chief Hosa exit, where the view stretched a hundred miles and three mountain ranges. Corey would stare at the view aside from the small matter of keeping the SUV pointing down the highway. "Vadas tried breaking into my office while I was inside, and by the way, he needed a key to do it."

"Why? What did you have that he wants?" Twisting his hands together, Lon squashed them against his mouth. "He already has your map!"

Corey could drive one handed—he covered both of Lon's with his own and made them still. "He wanted the population data. I think he's trying to do the right thing, maybe. He's such an arrogant ass it's hard to tell."

"Or maybe he just wants to know where to take his net!" Lon fretted silently past Idaho Springs and up the secondary road into more nameless regions. They turned again up a single track road and followed a stream.

115

Corey found a wide spot to pull off, where the brush didn't butt directly against the road. Lon's door scraped the mountain mahogany. He shut it again rather than forcing it, and hopped over the console to come out the driver's side. He unzipped his jacket, but didn't remove it yet—he'd feel the nip of the mountain air as much as Corey did when he was bare and on two feet. A jay called from the top of a pine tree, and a dozen other bird voices went silent. Corey didn't feel like that much of a threat.

"I guess this is where we find out how much we learned at the aquarium. Tell me what I need to know to keep you safe, Lon." Meaning *"How the hell do I convince you to change back if I have to?"*

"Talk to me. If I have to work hard to understand you, I'll pursue it into the form where it's easier." Lon smiled briefly, making his whiskers stand out. "Mind you, if you're reciting Milton or something, I might not find it that interesting." He paused to kiss Corey. "But we're only going to be out for two hours, tops."

"Right. We'll lose the light." With one last kiss that didn't calm his thumping heart, Corey let go. This next part, no matter how much it frightened him in a way it didn't a week ago, still fascinated him.

Shrugging his clothes off for someone with hands to gather and fold, Lon peeled away fabric with a shiver and put his warm fur coat on. He twisted, rippled, and became. One moment he was a man, the next, he blurred dark and smaller, and in a few seconds he was the familiar humped figure on four paws, with a rubbery bulb nose and a thousand whiskers standing out around his muzzle. He rose up on his hind feet, patting Corey's thigh.

It's okay, Corey translated from the sign language and hoped desperately that Lon was right. His otter friend bounced to the water's edge and slid in. Certain Lon wasn't paying attention to him now, Corey eased the nine millimeter Luger from his pack. He'd check the safety

116

one last time, making sure he could thumb it off with his gloves on. Perfect. He slid the gun into his jacket pocket. An unregistered relic of his grandfather's war, the pistol worked perfectly, if inclined to throw a trifle low and to the right. Any wolf Corey expected to meet would understand what he held, if matters grew dire enough for him to pull it out.

Willows and other vegetation grew up near the creek. Corey followed on the bank as best he could, staying near enough to see the water if he could. Whippy branches just beginning to show buds forced him away from the creek, putting him out of contact with the water more often than he liked. His sturdy Sorel boots were waterproof for most applications, but they weren't meant to be waders and his feet would be soaked in minutes if he tried walking in the stream. He wasn't even sure he could stay upright against the current, and he might not survive falling. He'd read his Jack London: if the running water didn't kill him, hypothermia might. He was smart enough to build a fire and dry out if he got soaked, but first he had to get out of the water. Mountain creeks flowed fast and hard this time of year, when snowmelt fed them endless drips. Even Lon might find the water too cold, though his happy chitters and *hurrs* suggested he was a long way from done with the weather.

When Corey could see Lon's sleek shape, he was a lot more confident in what they were doing. Three days after the aquarium incident, Lon insisted on doing a fish count of his own. Corey couldn't fault the wisdom of having their own accurate information, collected by the undisputed master of fish identification. But damn the timing. Lon was so sure he was ready for a brief stint in fur, but Corey wasn't sure he agreed.

So Corey hiked, and Lon swam, sometimes jumping up onto the big rocks in the middle of the water, sometimes leaving the stream entirely to gambol around Corey's feet. Hard to believe this wet otter was the same man he'd made love with this morning.

Lon bypassed the fastest flowing sections, choosing the path that grew suddenly steep instead. Which made sense. If his intended prey, and Lon had assured Corey his only interest was in counting—this time—liked mid-speed waters, no sense in trying to buck the current where no fish lurked.

Checking his GPS every hundred or so feet, Corey waited for the signal Lon had found dace. He found sticks and rocks and a few other fish. A trout sailed into the air, slapping back into the water to dart under a ledge. Lon did his whisker-grin: of course it was all a joke on the fish and the human. But not once did he rise up to slap his forefeet together. If Otter Lon knew his numbers up to eight, he most assuredly knew zero.

Were there any silverscale dace in this stream?

Half of a mile of slow going: Lon had to check all the right microhabitats. Checking the GPS again, Corey figured they were still a good mile and a quarter from the southern border of the land controlled by the Full Moon Conservancy.

Whiskey Creek babbled drunkenly with its meltwaters. If Corey hadn't been looking he might have missed the commotion. A second brown torpedo shot through the water, its flat head at the surface and aiming at Lon, who clung to a rock, looking in the wrong direction. It struck him at the hip, tumbling over and over in the water. Both otters disappeared and stayed gone long enough for Corey to panic. That might have been twenty seconds. But it might have been closer to three minutes. Prepared, Lon could stay underwater for just over five minutes, but he hadn't been expecting to submerge.

Two otters surfaced downstream, where Corey and Lon had already investigated, their muzzles sweeping against one another. One, and Corey couldn't decipher which one at this distance, clambered up onto a big rock in the middle of the stream. The second joined him. The orgy of sniffing and grooming and rubbing pushed Corey's heart out of his throat and back into his chest. He'd watched Lon greet new friends in a warmer environment just a few days earlier, and everything these two did was just as good-natured. Maybe no one should be rubbing Lon's muzzle but him if it looked that much like a smooch. Oh well, Lon had his fur on and the only thing that mattered was the wild otter's friendliness.

Very friendly: they tumbled back into the roaring waters and disappeared again. One reappeared with a fish in its mouth—too big to be one of the dace they sought. The fish flapped, its partial submersion giving it hope of escape. The otter swam upstream and didn't lose his prize. The second otter tried to steal the fish, but with every open mouth lunge, the triumphant fisher turned away enough to keep control of his prey. Lon's legs probably weren't long enough to throw a good elbow, but that was certainly the effect. Now Corey was quite sure that was Lon—the wild otter would have no reason to climb out on the bank and drop its prize at Corey's feet.

That stance always presaged something gory. He didn't want to watch but was too entranced to turn away. Lon ripped a long strip of flesh from what turned out to be a cutthroat trout, and backed away from the carcass. He hunkered down to nibble on his share. Corey took a few steps back, edging behind Lon. Lon chewed away at his fillet with his back teeth, for all the world unconcerned that there was a human standing close enough to touch. The other otter eyed them both thoughtfully before bouncing over to a ready meal.

The wild otter was noticeably smaller than Lon, so either a juvenile male or a female. Without an impertinent undercarriage check, something Corey wasn't about to risk his valuable hands on, he couldn't determine sex, and wasn't sure it mattered. Lon would explain later. Just finding a wild otter told him something about the health of the stream. And possibly about the dearth of dace.

119

Lon's new pal picked up the fish, pausing as if uncertain about taking it. Lon had ceased defending the trout, though, and gazed at the other otter with a shred of fish dangling from his mouth. *Go on, take it* was the message Corey got from the tilt of Lon's head, and in a skinny minute, both otter and fish splashed into the water. Corey watched its progress upstream, until it dove beneath the surface, headed sideways toward the bank.

"New pal, huh," Corey teased. Lon swallowed the rest of his share and wiped his mouth on Corey's pants leg. "Hey! Gross!"

Lon's *hurr, hurr, hurr* cut off when he splashed back into the stream.

"Brat." Corey didn't mind Lon laughing at him all that much, but there would be payback for the fish goosh.

Trudging upstream, Corey had his eyes down or on the water, though he managed to notice most of the willow branches before they slapped him across the face.

The sun was dropping ever lower in the sky, and the light was fading faster than he expected. He should have accounted for that, since they were on the eastern slope of the mountain. When Lon appeared next, he'd urge him to put his fur away in exchange for jeans and a waffle weave Henley, boots and a jacket. The trip back to the truck was all downhill, and without the need to stop for fish checks, it would go much faster. This section was relatively flat.

Had he missed an important signal? He peered between the whippy branches to see Lon standing up on another mid-stream boulder. He dropped to all fours and then into the creek, crossing the few feet of rushing water to stand on the bank some twenty feet ahead. He rose again to balance on his tail, patting his front paws together.

"You found a dace?" Corey yelled out. Yay! That was the first sign they'd had that Whiskey Creek still harbored a population of the endangered species.

Lon patted again, once, twice, three times.

120

"You found three?" Wah hoo! Corey fought his way through the thicket between him and the creek.

Lon patted, and patted, and patted. Corey, fighting with the willows, lost track of how many pats. It might have been eight, or many, or lots, and they hadn't established how many oh my goodness was in Arabic numerals. Finally he reached an open space and could cut across to chat with Lon. One-sidedly, but they did communicate across the species barrier. He checked his GPS, noted the coordinates with a quick poke of Save, and dropped to his knees to hug the best fish finder ever, no matter how wet he was.

Lon didn't hold still to be cuddled.

He dashed out into the woods, the "having fun here" message of his humpy gait totally lost in a fierce, guttural growl that Corey had never heard. His ears went flat to his head, his eyes narrowed, and he stopped four trees away. Humped and puffed, looking as big as it was possible for an otter to look, Lon challenged something in the woods.

They didn't have much to be afraid of out here. Maybe a bear. Or a cougar. Lon wouldn't challenge a skunk. Corey wasn't too sure about wolverines, and wolves that stayed wolves were few and far between, and mostly farther north. Wolves with PhDs had no business running around on a night with a quarter moon.

Corey pulled his gun loose. If Lon needed backup, he'd be there. He ran after his lover.

Lon needed backup.

Three wolves, hackles up, heads down, barely showed their teeth to him. One stalked sideways, looking to get behind Lon, who had his back to a pine that didn't offer anywhere near enough protection. Two mottled brown creatures, one white with gray markings around his jowls and across his back, all with fangs too long. They seemed interested, not angry.

"Back off!" Corey screamed. "Leave us alone!" Noise should be threatening, words should be worse. Did they understand? They had to—that white wolf sported the icy blue eyes Corey last saw across his desk. "I will shoot!" He aimed left of the wolves and at his shoulder level, knowing the bullet would travel to wolf chest height. "I don't want to, but I will if you take one step closer. You"—he growled at the sidling wolf—"you need to stay right there."

The wolf stopped, whether he thought Corey would shoot or at the low growl from the white wolf, but he stopped, and his interest melted into something more neutral, with his tongue hanging out sideways. Seriously dopey look for a wolf.

"We try negotiation first, and if negotiation doesn't work, we can do force." Corey motioned with his gun, held out in a two handed grip, his arms extended over the screeching otter at his feet. "Best case—you leave without bothering us, we leave without bothering you."

The white wolf let his lips relax, mostly covering those long teeth, and his head rose slightly. The second brown wolf let his ears swivel back, generating a growl where he'd been silent before. Corey didn't dare drop his attention to Lon, but if the sound effects meant a thing, Lon hadn't relaxed one iota. Everyone here outweighed him by at least a hundred pounds, couldn't blame him.

"Better." Corey had to force his voice to firmness. "Worst case, someone dies. Might not even be the right someone. Might be a lot of someones." His hands shook slightly, and if the gun was trained on the brown wolf to the left, he still might take out the white wolf in the center. Point blank, say, with a heavy furry body on top of him, he wouldn't miss. "And it doesn't have to be that way. You head off. We'll head off."

Dopey-faced wolf made a quick grab toward Lon, only to face the open end of Corey's pistol and a lightning fast slash at his tail from the white wolf. It yelped and dropped flat to the forest floor. The white wolf shook a wad of buff undercoat out of its mouth.

"My otter. Don't. Touch." Maybe they needed smaller words to be clear. Using Melvin's name would be clear, but also escalate the potential for violence. Plausible deniability was getting thinner and thinner—knowing the wolves could be communicated with was one thing, knowing names quite another. Probably worth the risk of killing the human and chasing down the otter at leisure.

"Everybody's just out for a nice hike in the woods. Go on." Corey motioned with the gun's muzzle. He'd never pointed it at anyone. His hand shook. "Enjoy your evening."

Nobody moved. Three wolves stared at Lon, who backed up far enough to bump into Corey's legs.

"My otter." Corey finally remembered to unlatch the safety. The click of the moving part sounded metallic against the organic growling down by his shins. He and Lon could be bloody shreds on the ground already, without a shot fired. Some protector he was. His guts roiled. He tightened his hand on the gun. It would fire. Now. He dug up some John Wayne courage. "Go on. Git."

Did wolves laugh? That lifting of lips looked so like a sneer. The white wolf poked his prostrate companion with his muzzle, bringing the would-be hunter to his feet. The chastened wolf turned away from Lon and Corey, shooting a glance over his shoulder that didn't look nearly cowed enough, but he followed the leader into the trees. The third wolf trailed the other two, and like wisps of smoke, they disappeared into the forest.

The woods went quiet. Lon stopped hissing and flopped to his belly. Corey scanned the woods for perfidious canids circling back around to take them out. "Are they really gone?"

Lon huffed a sigh that brought him low and flat as a pelt.

"Guess so." Corey flipped the safety back and replaced the pistol in his pocket. "Or you'd still be on alert." Kneeling next to the prostrate otter, Corey stroked him from head to tail, long firm strokes meant to reassure both of them. "Are you ready to

123

put your fur away? I brought your clothes. Because I'd really like to get out of here. We're losing the light."

Lon eeled out from beneath his hand. He didn't stay on all fours to become a crouching man as Corey'd witnessed so often, but rose to balance on his tail, waving his front paws up and down. Looked like get up. If he was wrong, Corey would go for translation number two. He rose.

Must have been right—Lon did that comical back-footed hop to come close enough to rest one forefoot on Corey's thigh. He lifted the other forefoot and his muzzle, craning upward.

"Pick you up?" Corey guessed and Lon chirred. Okay. He hoisted Lon to his shoulder, where his pal twined around his neck, partially resting on the back pack. "Yeah, let's leave that sharp nose in otter mode." If the wolves returned, the advance warning Lon could give might save their lives.

Corey headed downhill, his long legs eating up the distance back to the truck. What had taken them over an hour going up was less than ten minutes going back. Every stepped-on twig crackled Corey's nerves. Every shadow in the corner of his eye had fur and fangs. The jay's warning cut the air, but for danger real or imagined? Lon remained alert but cried no alarms. Corey kept one hand on the butt of the pistol, ready to flick the safety and shoot through his jacket. Nothing disturbed their passage. Corey's heartbeat dropped to something approximating heavy aerobic exercise rates by the time they reached the SUV.

Corey knelt to let Lon scamper to the ground, and started pulling clothing out of his pack. Lon growled at the back of the RAV4, his hackles up. Corey reached for the gun, but Lon remained pointed at the truck, where something liquid had dripped down the quarter panel.

"Let me guess." Corey laid Lon's clothes out for quick dressing. "Wolf piss."

CHAPTER TEN

The drive back to Boulder was quiet, and stopping for a burger at the Goose Egg had lost all its appeal. The scent mark on the truck bothered Lon into nibbling his cuticles rather than talking, and it wasn't until they passed the hogbacks on Highway 93, with only a few miles left on the way home, that he finally spoke up. "They could have just eaten us."

"They didn't try real hard." Corey flicked his high-beams on, hoping the dusk hadn't brought mule deer to stand in the middle of the three lane highway. "Maybe because they understood about the gun?" It had made a great bluff with the safety on, something he was trying not to kick himself about. He hadn't needed to fire, after all.

"I didn't know you had that." Lon took his hand out of his mouth. "It smelled like tools."

"Very useful tool." A solitary vehicle's headlights came toward them. Corey damped the high-beams again. Didn't get but a quarter of a mile at a time of good illumination with them anyway. "They backed off."

"I thought they wanted to hurt you at first, but they all concentrated on me." Lon rested his chewed-on hand against Corey's thigh. "I'm glad you were there. I mean, I'm sorry you were there, and I tried to protect you, but…"

"You did. We protected each other. You're fierce, but you against four hundred pounds of wolves isn't a fair match.

They didn't even seem to think you were a threat, which was weird. But I think we evened it out." Corey patted Lon's hand. "I was more worried about you liking the water too well, if you must know."

"It was fun." Lon slid his hand a little farther up Corey's thigh, like he was forgetting the danger and thinking of other things. "I think—I don't know what to call her. The other otter."

"Um, 'Other Otter' is awkward, and I can't pronounce a smell." Corey had a feeling he'd be hearing a lot about the only other wild otter Lon had met since they'd been together. "Maybe Terri? Or Lu?"

"Lu," Lon decided. "It would be fun to play with her more. Teach the babies to swim."

"Babies?" Corey slowed down: the highway had turned into Broadway now that they'd reached Boulder.

"Yeah!"

Baby otters were adorable by definition, but Lon sounded kind of parental. Was this another one of those thousand questions? Rings Corey'd thought about, but babies of either species hadn't crossed his mind. And hadn't Lon said he was a two-foot until he'd grown whiskers?

"She has two. That's why I shared the fish. Um, that and so she'd sniff you. Know you were one of the good guys."

"She's probably pretty clear on where wolves fit into her world." Corey made the light at Table Mesa Drive and started counting streets to 42nd Avenue.

"Maybe not, Corey. Aside from 'big' and 'new' and 'probably dangerous.' Wolves haven't been part of the ecosystem around here for seventy or eighty years." Lon wasn't so distracted that he failed to wave at Steven and Hugh, the next door neighbors, who were loading Steven's cello and guitar into the back of his Subaru. Steven had promised to teach Lon a new tune, but they'd missed the session on Tuesday. Lon was good, but Steven was a pro, and together they made Corey wish he could stepdance, play the fiddle, or flail around out of joy the way Lon had.

Shutting the door between home and the outside world left Corey feeling just a little safer. "Tell me about the dace," he prompted while loading leftover spaghetti onto plates. "I lost count of how many you found."

"Many!" Lon spun a fork into a shining silver pinwheel and caught it before it could bounce on the table. "All in that one area!"

Corey debated pouring a glass of red wine. "Does 'many' have a number now?"

"Noooo..." Lon considered. "But probably between fifteen and twenty!"

Corey needed the wine to toast that large a population. "That's more than they found in the entire stretch of creek last time." He lifted his glass to clink against Lon's water glass.

"I'm more efficient at spotting them," Lon reminded him, a strand of pasta dangling from his lips. "But still an improvement. And we haven't checked but a third of that section."

"A hell of a lot of the rest runs through the Full Moon Conservancy's property," Corey reminded him. "Not safe. Even the upper stretch from the Little Jug Creek down is pretty close. We weren't on their land tonight."

"Doesn't Melvin have a paper to give in Brisbane or Tokyo?" Lon asked. "Nominate him for something that gets him out of our hair."

"I think he's the brains of the operation." And maybe the only one of the bunch Corey could approach on some terms of equality. "That would leave us the muscle to deal with."

"Crap." Lon tossed back the rest of his water and poured wine into the empty glass.

The looming figure of Melvin Vadas blocked the doorway to Corey's office. Again.

"Yes?" Corey looked up from his map and printouts for the barest show of civility. He was unpleasantly certain he knew who had lifted his leg against the RAV4 and was inclined to piss back.

"Exactly how protected are the habitats of endangered species?" Vadas demanded.

"Depends on the species. You said you were interested in silverscale dace, which means mountain streams. The Whiskey Creek basin has old gold mining claims and tailing piles, which are nasty, toxic things. A lot of arsenic, lead, cadmium. If you're planning to disturb that stuff, you're going to get turned down in a heartbeat. Are you? " Corey would insist on some information in return.

"Doubt it."

"'Doubt it' won't get you past the planning stage. You have to know." Corey figured he'd drop the next bombshell. "And if you have to improve the roads to get your building materials in, that's part of your proposal."

"Why the hell does everyone want to make this project difficult?" Vadas barked, leaning over Corey's desk.

"You're picking a fight with the wrong guy, you know?" Corey barked back. "I'm trying to strike a balance between the creatures who can't speak for themselves and the ones that can, so everyone can have a share. Or would you prefer to live in a world where only the rats, roaches, and pine beetles live well?"

"You have a damned high opinion of yourself, Levigne," Vadas snarled, but he straightened, getting out of Corey's face.

"Do you want to know how to get what you want, or do you just want to scream at me?" Corey leaned back in his rolling chair, refusing to stand up and sacrifice his status as "he who was approached." "Because if venting is the only thing on your mind, I have work to do."

Slamming the door shut and dragging a guest chair up to the desk, Vadas made it clear he wasn't leaving. "I want to know what I need to do to get this project built."

"I can show you which agencies need what paperwork, and what will screw your project to a standstill. If you can lay off of me and the loan officer." He paused to let that sink in. "Some of this stuff isn't obvious."

Somehow or other, Corey was going to get Melvin Vadas and the rest of the wolves off his and Lon's backs.

"Little ferret-faced banker is trying to push me around," Vadas growled, rummaging through a stack from Corey's desk as if the right forms would glow violet when he located them.

Corey confiscated the entire pile. "His name is Lon Ewing, and he's trying to do right by his employer and the world," Corey reminded him. "Also, he's my boyfriend, so quit calling him Ferret Face."

That got Vadas' attention. "So, he's under your protection, am I hearing that right?"

"Damn right he is." Corey meant everything he'd said about rings and promises, and this was the real world application. Facing down an angry werewolf could definitely be filed under "for worse" and possibly under ill-health as well. "And since he's the one who can give you what you want, he should be under your protection too."

"All right, you got it. He's under my protection. Now show me how many thousands of pages of crap we have to fill out and for whom." Melvin threw up his hands at the mountains of paper on Corey's desk. "Still think Whit had the right idea to start with…"

"Which idea would that be?" Corey paused with a file drawer half open, not wanting to admit knowing about the dynamite.

"Never mind." He thumped the desk. "We're doing it the official way."

With any luck, Melvin could make that stick. Corey sorted out a handful of pages. "Everything starts with the survey. You probably got that when you bought the land…"

An hour later, Corey had a thin film of sweat on his brow and Vadas had sticky notes all over his copies of governmental forms.

"If this doesn't go through, we've already attracted so much attention we can't go back to plan A." Melvin confiscated a stray butterfly clip to confine his papers.

"As long as you aren't rerouting the stream or dumping sewage into it, which means a properly placed septic tank and leaching field plus composting toilets, you aren't going to have that big a problem." Corey double checked the list of projects he'd priced into his impact statement, not wanting to surprise the world's crankiest and most unwanted consultation client. "Get someone reliable to do the population survey."

"I suppose Ferret Boy's got a conflict of interest, being with the bank."

"Don't call him Ferret Boy either." Corey considered recommending the most expensive fish and game consultant he'd identified.

Vadas smiled, and it looked genuine. "Just checking."

If he was checking on whether Corey would push back on every shove, he was right. Corey would.

"I don't want anyone coming back months later when the lodge is half up and demanding a recount." Vadas rose and stretched, and somehow Corey didn't have much trouble imagining a fluffy gray and white plume sticking out behind. "Neither does your little buddy Lon. He has an interest in that count being accurate. If he wants to do an independent verification for all our protection, that's fine with me."

"I'll mention you suggested it." And Corey would follow it with his own recommendation to stay the hell off werewolf lands.

"So, Levigne, just what do you think I'm protecting him against?" Vadas smiled, with a lot more teeth than before.

"The sort of folks who pissed on my truck." Corey rose too. Eye level for equality and all.

130

"You got some cojones on you, Levigne." Melvin tucked his stack under his arm. "You don't have the slightest idea what you're getting into, but you've got a lot of balls."

"I suppose I do," Corey shot back. "Whiskey Creek's going to be beautiful under a full moon."

CHAPTER ELEVEN

Lon had his nose practically pressed to the map. "I think the road goes all the way to Little Jug Creek. Probably we should have started upstream and worked down, but I don't mind doing the lower creek again if Vadas makes his wolves leave us be."

"He said you were under his protection." Corey had his doubts about going back to Whiskey Creek without Vadas, but Lon was anxious to count fish before the official survey. Just in case somebody located a couple sticks of dynamite to finalize a local extinction. They wouldn't be headed back into the mountains this fine Saturday morning otherwise: they'd be in the canyons above Boulder with Corey's kayak and a picnic lunch.

Lon glanced up, his lip between his teeth. "Did he say anything about you being under his protection?"

That brought Corey up sharply. "No, not exactly." In fact, Corey felt distinctly left out of any shade Melvin's alpha umbrella might cast.

"I'm not so sure he didn't say something already," Lon considered. "Even though we washed the truck."

"You mean the piss mark?" Which stunk, and Corey had aimed the sprayer into the undercarriage as well as over the body work. He still wasn't convinced the RAV4 was decontaminated.

"Yeah. It could have been him being a smartass, but he could have been claiming you." Dropping the map and clutching the "oh shit" handle, Lon bounced with the little truck and its too-civilized suspension. "I'm pretty sure it was him."

"Joy," Corey muttered. "After getting a gun pulled on him, you think Melvin would claim me?" He spared a glance for the road making a T junction with their single track. A hand lettered sign marked "The Full Moon Conservancy," but the signpost probably smelled of wolf pee.

"You talked to him instead of just shooting, and you're part of his department. Maybe he doesn't want to interview candidates for your position?" A particularly deep rut dropped the truck into its gulch, making Lon's voice go high and squeaky with the surprise.

"Maybe it meant 'eat this one.' I don't know, Lon." Corey steered to the side of another deep spot that might have high centered the so-called sport utility vehicle. It was more of a mall utility vehicle, in spite of the roof rack. "I really think we should have waited to make sure he'd passed the word." That uncertainty led Corey to pack his grandfather's pistol. If Lon had noticed, he hadn't said anything.

"The fish can only wait so long, and I want to get back to Sat-fur-days." Lon started pulling his boots off. "I think we're here."

They were, if here meant "no more road." Two weathered picnic benches and a fire pit that looked long unused dotted the margins of what might have been a cul-de-sac. A creek tumbled down from a rocky gorge into the relatively tamer Whiskey Creek. Lon glowed like he'd been taken to Disneyland for otters. "Wah hoo!" he yodeled, flinging his jacket aside. "Last one in is a rotten egg!"

Corey would be the sulfurous one, because neither love nor money would get him into that frigid creek. Well, love maybe, but Lon was more likely to do the rescuing than to need rescuing. Corey gathered clothing while Lon put

133

his fur on, and followed the bounding otter to the stream's edge. "Dace, here you come!"

Lon pushed all his whiskers forward in his happiest otter smile. Pausing just long enough to accept a caress, he plunged into the rushing water.

Not a hundred feet below the confluence with Little Jug Creek, Lon circled around in the lee of a boulder, making dark streaks in the green-black depths. Corey hefted his phone, ready to poke the coordinates. But Lon left the boulder without clapping, to check a slower current to the side of the stream. He popped up, patting his paws together so many times he might have passed "many" and "lots" to reach "oh my goodness". Corey could hope. Another slow, shallow section got four pats, and a hundred fifty or so feet farther down made Lon pat and snort water all at the same time.

"Lots?" Corey shouted over the sound of the rushing water. Lon patted again and chased his tail for a moment.

The terrain grew steep enough for Lon to abandon the water—no fish there—and weave between Corey's feet. "Lots of dace!" Corey exulted. "The population is recovering!" He picked his way over the huge pieces of granite at the creek's edge. Lon led the way to a calmer stretch of water. He stopped to wipe a paw through his whiskers and cocked his head at Corey.

"No, I don't know how many fish will get them off the endangered list." He made a mental note to find out. "It might require recovery in several places in their range. Ready to find some more?"

Lon whuffled and chirred and slid back into the water. Corey eyed the next rock over, stretched out one leg to bridge the gap, and missed his footing. Doing the world's most dangerous splits, he grabbed sideways, finding enough handhold to keep from toppling between the boulders. Too close to going all the way down, he worked his legs back under him. If he bashed himself, help would be a long time coming.

Corey stayed hunkered on his haunches and steadied himself with both hands, his leather gloves catching against the rough stones. One monkey step at a time, he worked his way back to the bank. The leaves on the willow and mountain mahogany were slightly bigger than on their last expedition, but there was a break in the undergrowth and Corey wanted to get off the rocks. He was no mountain goat.

Once on firm ground, he checked for Lon. A brown head poked up out of the water about fifty feet downstream. No problem. He pursued Lon along the creek, recording another group of dace, only three this time. In less than an hour, they'd found three groups of fish, and they were still close to a mile from the conservancy's boundary.

The low growl made Corey turn slowly. Trapped with his back to the tumbled stones of the creek, and neither left nor right offering any kind of refuge, he'd have to stand his ground. He eased his hand into his pocket.

Safety off—click. His pistol was a puny thing against the two huge wolves. Neither sported a pale coat or a neutral attitude. Their bared canine teeth would look right at home on a *T. rex*, and the low rumbling from their throats didn't offer a lot of possibilities for negotiation.

Corey withdrew his gun, letting them see it. "You're supposed to leave us be," he informed them. Had their leader made his wishes clear? If his wishes included both of them. "Melvin Vadas said so." Bad time to consider that Melvin might not be the leader of the pack.

The wolf on the left, with a deep gray coat, lifted his lip a little higher, and didn't stop rumbling. His mottled brown companion took one step forward, head down, his yellow eyes never leaving Corey's.

"You leave me alone, I leave you alone."

God, where's Lon? Please let him be back in the water where the wolves wouldn't follow him. Corey didn't dare look around, keeping his stare and gun trained on the wolves. The brown wolf looked likeliest to charge—first shot for him.

135

"You're way outside of your territory." Words, words, use words until he had to use force.

Unfortunately, his backup, the Mighty Attack Otter, didn't have a lot of words. Lon appeared between Corey's feet, puffed up and his teeth bared, though silent. Damn the silence—Corey jumped. And landed on Lon's foot. Lon screeched and yanked. Corey fell, his gun pointing at the heavens.

The gray wolf pounced. Snatching Lon in jaws that could bite him in two, the wolf dangled a snapping, writhing otter by the middle. Paying no heed to Lon's struggles, the wolf bounded away to the south.

"Let go of my otter!" Corey screamed, directly into the muzzle of the brown wolf. His assailant loomed over him. One paw smashed down on his chest. Sharp teeth clamped Corey's wrist. He got his free hand on the wolf's ear. He twisted until a squeal erupted from his assailant's throat, but the wolf didn't let go. Corey tried to jerk his gun arm free. The wolf gripped him harder, though his fangs didn't push through the Gore-tex. Corey tried rolling them. The wolf remained upright. It did step on his groin with a saucer-sized clawed foot, forcing a scream of sufficient pitch to make the wolf pause.

Corey froze in his pain. The wolf froze with him. He let go of the wolf's ear, intending to start gouging eyes. The wolf relaxed its jaws and moved its fucking foot off Corey's soft parts. The pain cleared slowly. The wolf waited, holding Corey's forearm.

Think, think. The hellbeast hadn't tried to dismember him. Corey jerked away, only to meet serrated resistance. He froze, and the wolf relaxed. "You're not actually trying to kill me, are you?" Corey gasped. Those teeth would have broken through the thin protection of the fabric if the wolf wanted to get through.

The wolf lifted his upper lip ever so slightly.

"You just don't want me defending Lon." A quick yank

on his arm brought pressure enough to hurt this time. The wolf growled deep and low.

"He's my otter." This was not negotiating from a position of strength, damn it.

The wolf growled again and started a heavy pressure with its jaws. It leaned down, forcing Corey's gun hand to the ground. Resistance was futile—Corey could lower his hand slow or he could lower it fast, but his assailant had the upper paw and leaned the weight of a man against Corey's wrist. Biting hard enough to bring the threat of drawn blood, the wolf made its point.

Corey flicked the safety on and twisted, dropping the pistol next to his head. "See? No gun."

No wolf.

The creature released his arm and snatched up the pistol, bounding away in a blur of fur. Corey watched the damned thing drop his grandfather's Luger into the creek. With its tail curved high over its back, the wolf regarded him for an instant, lifting its lips in something that looked too much like a smile, and then whipped away. Running south. After his companion.

After Lon.

Upside down and flung around—Lon couldn't get his teeth on any part of this stupid werewolf! Once he bit a front leg and got kneed hard in the snout. He tried again and got shaken so hard he thought he'd break. The wolf ran and ran, shaking Lon all the way. Ow! And uh oh.

But those sharp teeth around his middle weren't chomping him. No big bites and ripping and blood. The wolf could hurt him. Or kill him. Or shake him hard, until his neck snapped. No, Lon was just dizzy and mad and getting farther away from Corey. If the other wolf hurt Corey, Lon would bite his nose off!

If this dumb werewolf ever put him down!

The wolf stayed near enough to the creek to hear the water laugh at him even through the bouncing. Near the creek meant Corey could find him. Corey would look for him, and that meant Corey would find the wolves. Oh bad.

Lon wanted to put his fur away and talk to this dumb wolf, find out what he wanted, but it wasn't time. If he could take his fur off, he'd be too big to carry. And naked and no match for a werewolf that wouldn't think he was an otter any more. Then Lon couldn't fight back or run away into tiny places or friendly waters.

The wolves didn't try to bring Corey. This wolf wanted something from an otter.

Smells of wolves, of cars, of metal and cut wood. Clang of metal, men shouting. Lon's head rang with *thud thud thud* from the upside down, nothing made sense. The wolf slowed—Lon could see. People. A fence. He twisted, and the wolf bit down harder, pushing teeth through thick fur to hurt.

Lon's middle hurt from the wolf's mouth. Couldn't breathe. Couldn't bite. Couldn't even screech. Just flop.

The wolf threw him down on the ground. His nasty nose stuck into Lon's face, snuffling nasty wolf snuffles. Yuck. Lon screeched and smacked. He needed the kitty's claws, hurt the wolf, slash him up. Dumb wolf licked him, ick ick ick. Slobbery tongue right across his face. ICK!

Rotten wolf nosed him across the middle where teeth grabbed. Hurt. Lon screeched.

The wolf left.

Get up. Flopped was vulnerable. Didn't smell anything sneaking up on him. Wolf was gone. But still.... He dragged to his feet, couldn't stand still, back and forth. Spread paws wide, that helped. He wiped his eyes on his front leg, that helped. Made his shaken head hurt.

Clang

Men laughed, not close. All on the other side of a tall fence. Wire with big holes, perfect to climb, just stick paws through. Straight up.

138

Not men. Wolves. In man shape. If he put his fur away, could he talk with them? It would be time soon. Pushing didn't make his fur come off. Yet. Soon.

One man was naked. The one laughing the loudest. "Little bastard squirmed the whole way here. Nearly dropped him three times, and he bit me."

"Aww, da big bad woof got an otter owie!" A man with clothes whacked Naked Guy on the shoulder. *Come on, Clothes Guy, hit him harder.* "If you want sushi tonight we'll know what happened."

"Yeah, only you gotta catch it yourself!" someone else razzed Naked Guy.

"Hell, no!" he laughed. "Damn thing bit me, he owes me dinner. I want silverscale dace, none of this trout shit. Nobody cares about the trout."

"You think dace taste okay?"

Dumbass man. Have to catch his own to find out.

"Doesn't matter. Otter gets hungry enough, he'll eat it." Naked Guy stuck his legs into pants. "He'll be in here long enough to catch every damned one."

One of the men turned. "There's Whit. Somebody let him and the boys in."

Whit? Lon knew that name. Knew that smell. Bad Whit, who thought booms would kill the fish. He felt a little better. His legs were steadier. He'd run out when they let Whit in. Oops, right into a crowd. How fast could he run?

Not fast enough—even right at the gate he got knocked aside by a wolf with big feet and an ugly growl. And something squirmy in his mouth.

Three mud-caked wolves slipped into the pen. With otters. Two babies, the ones who couldn't swim yet. Wolves spat them out plop on the ground. One baby squealed.

Whit stepped on Lon, like he was a rock. That hurt! His foot slipped off Lon's shiny coat. Lon bit his icky, muddy leg. Too bad it wasn't his balls! Still got him with sharp teeth.

Whit dropped his mouthful and turned on Lon. Head down and a horrible promise grumbling out of his throat, he advanced. Lon backed up, hissing and screeching.

Tear your head off translated from wolf to otter just fine. Lon would take a piece of wolf with him, and that translated to wolf just fine too. Nose to nose, they promised bloodshed.

An otter screeched from behind him. Lon would fight to keep the bad wolf away from the babies.

"Hey, asshole!" distracted Whit enough to turn his head. "Leave the otters alone. They have work to do!"

One fanged snap in front of Lon's nose and then Whit turned around. He ran to the gate where one of the men let him out. The gate clanged shut.

An otter chattered and chirred behind him. Lu! She had her babies in a den by the river. The wolves must have dug them out and brought them here. Lon turned to touch noses with her. They were safe. For now. She touched noses back and picked up one of her little ones. She stood with a brown bundle dangling, checking desperately for which way to go.

Rocks by the creek made tunnels and holes. They couldn't dig far enough to get a dry nest fast, but the rocks would be shelter. Lon picked up the other baby by the scruff and chased after Lu. They clambered over boulders close to the chuckling creek, looking for shelter. Lon found a narrow tunnel.

Some other otter lived here a long time ago. Faint traces still clung to the hollow where a few old grasses remained. It wasn't great, but it was dry enough, and it was under rocks much bigger than wolves. Lon dropped his burden and backed out to let Lu by. She squished in with the other baby, the end of her tail sticking out. Lon groomed it. Something normal in a day full of bad surprises. Three licks were enough. Lu stuck her head out for a nose touch and disappeared into the makeshift den.

Okay, babies safe, Lu safe. Lon was safe for now—everyone else was on the outside of the fence, screaming at one another. The breeze carried their smells. Some he knew, like Whit and Jack, more he didn't. He stood on the rocks, watching.

One voice he knew, with a smell he was afraid of. Melvin, screaming at the other wolves. The breeze carried words Lon could understand. "You idiots! What do you think you're doing?"

"We're taking care of the silverscale dace problem. No dace, no problem."

CHAPTER TWELVE

Whit and the other wolves ringed Melvin. They were out there, Lon was in here, with no one but Lu and the pups. Safe enough to sit on the rocks and watch. Listen. He could change back in a little bit and then he'd have hands and words and talk his way out of this pen. Or climb out now. He splashed into the stream. Let the wolves fight. He'd go check out the best way to escape.

Metal wire made a fence going a long way up and down the stream. Like catching the stream. Why did they want to catch the stream? The water ran away, through the wire. Could he swim under the wire?

Upstream first—Lon paddled against the current to the fence line. With a big breath he dove. Under the fence, out, and find Corey. And clothes. Then they'd come back and rescue Lu.

Lon smacked into the wire fence. Nasty wire all the way down to the bottom! And on the bottom—Lon tried to dig under it, but the wire went a long ways flat on the bottom. He could stick a paw through, and that was all. The holes were too small and the wire was too strong.

He surfaced. The wolves were still shouting.

"We file some papers, pay a couple of fees and no one ever bothers us again, you morons!" Melvin yelled louder than anyone.

"If this isn't dace habitat, they still don't bother us," Whit growled back.

"It's dace habitat for three miles we don't control up and down this creek, and there's too many interested parties already. They aren't going away. What do you think you're going to do about the Fish and Game people?" Melvin roared.

"We could chase them down and eat 'em." One of the wolves who'd put away his fur but hadn't dressed bristled like he'd put his fur back on.

"We don't just eat everyone who comes along. How do you maintain your day jobs?" Melvin shook his head.

"Fuck the day jobs, and fuck the humans, Melvin," Whit drawled. "We pay too much attention to 'em as is. We're predators, remember?"

"I remember just fine, Bailey. I also remember how to win at human. I like winning at both."

The other wolves made a ring around Whit and Melvin. Lon couldn't see them very well, even though he could hear them argue just fine. Not all the words made sense.

"You're too human for this pack, Vadas. Always trying to follow human rules. We're wolves. We're going to act like wolves."

Uh oh. Wolves were bad news for otters. These wolves wanted otters in a pen. That couldn't be good. Lon scurried to the fence on the far side of the stream. If he could climb the fence to freedom, so could Lu. They could take the babies out and bring them to Corey.

Where was Corey? Had the wolves hurt him? Lon bounded to the fence. Let the wolves argue. He could climb.

Reach and grab, all four feet. Careful, careful, up, up, up. Lon could climb a Corey height of this fence with its big holes, no problem. Easier than trees, nice grips.

And a shelf sticking backward over the pen. Lon flailed, scratching the wood. Just... a... bit... farther! If he could reach his claws to the edge, he could swing out...

Too far.

143

He pulled back, thinking. Maybe boing out, catch the edge with both front paws? He bunched up under the shelf and sprang out. His claws scrabbled on wood. Couldn't catch on!

Lon landed hard on the ground. No breath.

"Hey, that otter's trying to get out."

"Let him try."

Stupid werewolf. Lon would get out somehow. Even if he had to take his fur off. Hands would make this easier, but he wouldn't have hands for a while yet. And the wolves were all over on the other side of the long pen. If he waited too long, some would come over here.

Maybe hang on with back feet and boing out? Lon climbed the fence again. The fence was the easy part. Dumb shelf. He coiled and stretched.

Scrabble, scrabble, claw, claw, smack! He hung upside down on the fence. What went wrong? He could reach, but he couldn't get a grip on the edge. His claws found the edge and couldn't catch.

When he had hands again he'd be out of this cage so fast those wolves would barely see him run by. Lon held on and swung his body around, getting his tail pointed at the ground so he could climb down. Better take a look. Then he could try again.

From the ground he could see how the wood went around the whole pen. He could reach the edge of the wood, but then the edge pointed up and went twice as far as his claws. Somebody who didn't like otters made this cage.

Hmmph! There'd be a way out. Lon would find it.

The shouting got louder across the creek. The wolves shouted, and some of them growled. Maybe the fence was a good thing. Kept the wolves over there and the otters over here. Still trapped, but not near the wolves.

Some of the wolves had their fur on. One, two, three, four with fur on. Lon knew four. And others without fur. One, two, three, four, five, and a young one. Too many to know all at once, just many. A big circle of two-foot and furry bodies surrounded Melvin and Whit. They were still shouting at each other.

"We follow a couple of human rules, we get what we want and they leave us alone. What's so hard to understand about that?" Vadas snarled.

Whit circled around him, like he was looking for a good place to bite from behind. Lon knew that old wolf trick. Good way to get your underbelly ripped out. "And it'll cost us another fifty thousand dollars, and bring another dozen inspectors out here, and just in case you hadn't noticed, Vadas, wolves are an endangered species too! They start getting sightings and we really have humans crawling all over this project."

"We don't go wolf while someone's here to see, and then when they're gone, we have all kinds of fun." Vadas turned to keep his face to Whit. A wolf growled at his back. "It's called delayed gratification."

A gate was the easiest way out of a pen. Lon swam across the creek. If he could open the cat flap at home, he might be able to get this gate open too. The wolves weren't paying attention to anything except Melvin and Whit. A couple of them had tongues hanging out. The ones without fur probably couldn't smell him. The ones with fur had something to distract them.

Ooh, good! Just a latch! A little too high to reach standing on his back paws. Lon pushed, extending his front leg farther than it wanted to go, by tipping a little sideways and hanging onto the mesh. He got the latch moving. Up, up, little farther, it might go the rest of the way if he could reach a little farther…

He grabbed the fence with one back foot. A little more… Lon could see that latch about to let go of the pole, just a tiny bit more…

A heavy body crashed into the gate with a vicious snarl and a giant clang. The impact knocked Lon backward.

145

He twisted to land almost on his feet. The dark gray wolf showed huge canines and threatened pain if Lon came through that gate.

Lon growled back. Just wait until he had hands again!

And until then, the fence was a good idea.

"You're spending our money, Vadas, and you're making decisions we don't agree with." Whit had his fists up. "You're acting like some kind of king. Making alliances and committing our funds to unnecessary crap like 'environmental studies.'"

"I make those decisions because I am the leader, and because I'm looking out for the long term welfare of this pack." Vadas was almost as cool as an otter, just staring down Whit like he was some sort of bug. "If you don't like it, there's plenty of open space in Wyoming."

Some of the wolves growled. One crept closer to Vadas, sticking its snout into his butt and getting cuffed across the ear. It backed up, whimpering.

"I'm not the one leaving for Wyoming, Vadas." Whit wasn't cool at all, not if he was shouting. Lon backed up just a little all the same. "You can go catch yourself an antelope any time."

"You're challenging me?" Vadas dragged his shirt over his head and threw it to the ground.

"No, I'm telling you you're done." Whit leaped and before he struck, he shoved his fur out. A huge brown wolf tumbled the man Vadas to the ground, the circle of wolves opening to let them fall.

The man would have landed on his back, but Vadas' fur came out so fast Lon didn't even see it. A white wolf fell under the brown wolf, rising and snapping silently. He slashed at Whit, laying an open red line across his face. His huge white ruff made him twice as big as before.

Lon should run. He should hide. Let the water cover him and hide him from the wolves. Lu and the babies were safe in the rocks. She wouldn't let them out with the sound of battle raging. But there was a fence, and the fence made him safe. He could watch.

The wolves circled and snarled. Whit didn't leap at Vadas, and Vadas stalked him, forcing him backwards. Back one step and then two, until his rump nearly touched the gate.

One of the two-foot wolves jumped at the fence, slapping the latch up and letting the gate swing open. Whit's butt bumped it, and he never reacted, only took more steps back with his head lowered and his fangs showing. Vadas pursued, his icy eyes never leaving his retreating opponent.

Lon better retreat! Unless he could run through that opening really fast, but wolves on the far side snarled, their eyes on him.

Nope, not going to run down their throats. Lon backed away.

He huddled by the fence, safe from all the wolves, even the two now battling it out. The white wolf had the brown one down, but only for a moment, even with the weight of the giant smashing him at the shoulder. Whit's ear bled, but he wasn't surrendering.

More wolves rushed in, silently and fast. They piled onto the other wolves, their bodies shoving the fighters down to the ground. A two-foot rushed in, a shining loop in his hands. He reached into the heaving pile of bodies and came away with nothing. He ran for the gate, yelling, "I got him!"

What had he gotten? The lesser wolves peeled away from the battle, fleeing through the gate. The two were alone in the enclosure with the otters. Lon dared not move; he'd do nothing to make those fangs turn his way. He hid under a spruce tree, its low branches hiding him and its forest smell covering his own. The branches wouldn't be enough to keep the wolves away if they wanted him, but they snarled and fought on, paying no attention to anything except each other.

The gate clanged shut. Two wolves circled and growled, heads down. A ridge showed in Vadas' pale fur. That hadn't been there before. He ignored it, focused on his opponent.

He sprang, they clashed, and they went down in a tangle of legs and snarls.

"Is the rest of the pack going to be okay with Whit for leader?" someone on the other side of the fence had a voice to ask with. Young, male.

"Fight'll be over long before the rest get up here." Older voice, assured. Lon didn't take his eyes off the fighters. They might roll over this way into his tree. He didn't care who talked. Maybe he should. He'd listened back at the bank, and knew Whit and Vadas didn't agree, but up here, it was Vadas against everyone else. "Nobody in that bunch is foolish enough to challenge Whit."

"Do they have to fight to the death?"

Sounded that way from in here with the fight.

"Nah. Winner walks out of there on two feet. There ain't so many of us we can afford to kill each other for dominance." A short bark of laughter, no mirth. "After, though..."

"Dr. Vadas is gonna be mad at us if he wins."

"He ain't winning this one, son."

Lon watched the fighters, then he watched the watchers. Nobody looked like they cared about an otter. The wolves rolled away from Lon. Red streaked the white fur. Harder to see red against brown.

He ran, leaping and stretching and whipping over ground in bounds that didn't cover nearly enough distance. Faster! Faster! Lon splashed into the creek and across it with only the top of his head above water. He could leave the wolves to their battle and be out of here in a flash. Lu and her fuzzballs were safe where they were, and when he came back with Corey and reinforcements, they'd take her family back to her den by the creek. He angled through the trees and to the fence. The snarling and fighting went on behind him.

He peered up. Long ledge here too. Too long for this otter to grab. When he had paws. He'd had his fur on for more than enough time. That ledge wasn't too long for arms, and nobody was paying attention to him.

Lon pushed, expanding his body and disappearing his tail into the length of his back. His fur went away, all except the small patches that always stayed and never needed a trim. Long limbed, with opposable thumbs, a lot more words, not a stitch of clothing, and able to get the hell out of this trap. Six foot fence with two foot wide overhang? No problem, and the lip on the edge of the shelf would be a fine hand hold for a guy with fingers.

Hell, he might just bring this section down by hanging on it and that would be even simpler. In fact, he wouldn't even have to climb, just jump and swing. Noisy if it cracked, but oh well. Everyone else was over on the other side.

The sooner he got out of here and found Corey, the sooner he could have his britches back. Lon spat on his hands and reached up. Just high enough to get a purchase on the three inch lip. That would have been hopeless with claws. The ledge dipped under his weight but stayed intact. Swinging sideways, Lon got a foot up on the shelf. He hoisted, getting more of his leg up, and enough height on his upper body to grab the far end of the shelf. Easy peasy now, just the ridge of the lip to drag his chest over. And—ow!—his groin. Which hurt, but not nearly as bad as being a prisoner. From his vantage point lying flat on the top of the fence, he could see the combatants appearing for a second or two between the trees, and the audience on the far side of the fence. Of Lu he saw no sign.

Time to blow this pop stand. Just slide his legs over, catch the chain link with his toes, and away he'd go. One step left to the ground and freedom.

Snarling made Lon turn around. He went back up that fence a hell of a lot faster than he came down. Three milliseconds to the top, max, and that was almost one millisecond too long—wolf jaws snapped where his ass had been. A huge brown wolf glared up at him. A huge brown wolf he hadn't smelled coming, damn the wind.

A huge brown wolf that wouldn't have any trouble at all joining him on this nice wide ledge. Six feet up was climbing range for an otter, and nothing but a good stretch for the asshole standing right below him.

So far he was staying down there. Corey had negotiated. Worth a try.

"I'm just going to mosey on out of here," Lon suggested. "Looks like pack matters. Not my business, so I'll be on my way."

The wolf sat down, went silent, and didn't break eye contact. Okay. Lon reached one foot down. He yanked it back a lot faster. The wolf leaped and snapped. Not a sound did he utter, and he came way too close to taking Lon's leg off.

Lon tried sitting cross legged on the ledge, and hoped it wouldn't choose that moment to give and dump him on his back. He had a lot of bruises already from this adventure. Sitting with his butt half off would test the fence's construction to the max, and no way around that unless he stretched out centerfold style, making a nice long target, with his nads completely unprotected. At least if the ledge gave way it would drop him inside and not outside the fence, where he wasn't going until he'd come to an understanding with the wolf. Lon knew the scent—this one had been at the bank. If Whit Bailey was having it out with Melvin Vadas on the other side of the creek, this had to be Jack Schwimmer. Should he try using the name? "You sure? I'm just a nuisance around here."

The wolf was sure. He stood up on his hind legs, not quite tall enough to get his jaws on Lon, but too damned close to tender bits anyway. If he decided to jump—oh shit. Lon scooted backwards.

Schwimmer liked that. At least enough to sit back down and resume his silent staring.

"You don't want to catch me, and you're just sitting there when I'm sure there's a thousand things more fun to do." What could Lon offer? "There's a jackrabbit about fifty yards over that way."

Schwimmer didn't even follow Lon's pointing hand with his eyes.

Might have something to do with the fictitious nature of the jackrabbit.

"Deer? Do you like deer?" Maybe Schwimmer was hungry and could be tormented through his stomach. "Deer are so tasty. Raw haunches, yum. Gooey, mushy entrails, mmm, mmm, mmm. Do you ever get the liver on the kill?" Lon talked up the joys of newly slaughtered venison, gaining a slight queasiness and a fresh appreciation for Corey's point of view regarding trout, dace, or koi, but those were delicious and Lon had no desire to tackle a deer. "You could be out looking for game instead of staring at me. Wouldn't that be a lot more interesting? Go find some deer!"

Too late, Lon considered that his own liver might not taste appreciably different than a deer's. And here he was, no pesky jeans to rip through.

But Schwimmer wasn't taking that bait, or Lon's entrails. "Squirrel!" Lon's hand flashed out. And again he got no response. The wolf remained at the base of the fence, still and staring.

"What do you want? You don't need me. I'm just a two-foot"—Lon nearly choked making that claim—"and better out of your hair. Fur. Whatever. And nobody's going to believe a word I say ever again if I talk about wolves at Whiskey Creek. Everybody knows wolves are extinct in Colorado."

Oh, bad, bad thing to say. Schwimmer lifted his lip and a deep rumble trickled out. "And a damned shame too," Lon babbled. "The cougars have made a comeback with nothing to prey on them. You wolves used to keep them in check. You got along like cats and dogs and it worked great, nobody got too numerous. But now we have cougars all over the place. You can't hardly go to an office party without getting long, acrylic claws stuck into you...."

Sharp, white, bare teeth snapped inches from his leg.

"Yipes!" Lon pulled back, and he had no back to pull. He was already jammed against the lip of the ledge; flinching overbalanced him just the wrong amount. A quick grab behind and he caught on the ledge enough to do an Olympics-worthy flip over and back, letting go before he ripped his arms out of their sockets. He landed on his feet, still too close to an angry wolf, but with the fence between them. *Note to self: do not abandon day job for standup comedy.*

As if that mattered. Schwimmer flung himself against the chain link, which seemed to stretch with his weight. Lon turned to run, horribly certain that his top speed might be faster than Usain Bolt's for this one last sprint, and that it wouldn't make a damned bit of difference.

The fence rattled again behind him, with the scrabbling of paws against wood. Oh dear Lord of Creation, the wolf had come over the top.

Lon was faster as an otter than he was as a two-foot. Between one step and the next he threw out his fur and hit the ground running on four feet. Bound and stretch, bound and stretch, he tried desperately for that airborne moment to speed him through the air and still had one paw on the ground with every leap.

The wolf breathed down his neck for the seven paces to the water. Lon went in, certain he could stay under long enough to come up some place Schwimmer wasn't, even though he had nothing but a section of creek. He wouldn't let the wolf catch him at the far end of the enclosure, trying to escape where the water flowed and otters were stopped.

Heavy splashes followed Lon into the water, but he was in his element and the stupid wolf couldn't swim like he could. Dumb wolf, lost his chance. Lon surfaced on the far side of the creek, far enough from the fight that hadn't ended. The rocks on the bank made tunnels where wolves couldn't chase, and that was safe for Lon. He clambered up, slid down and watched the wolf get soaked.

Guess he didn't like that! Dumb wolf waded back out of the creek and shook his soppy fur. He lifted his head to watch across the creek. Watching the fighting wolves. Not Lon.

The wolf turned and ran back to the fence. Over he went, in one easy leap. He turned to look at Lon, with his tail over his back and his ears forward. His tongue lolled out and his whiskers pushed forward.

Bastard wolf was laughing.

CHAPTER THIRTEEN

Fucking werewolves! They took Lon! They took his Luger! Corey pulled himself off the ground. Where they'd gone wasn't much of a mystery. What the hell did the wolves want with Lon? If they hurt him, Corey would... He'd something, just let him find his gun. Or a ranger. Or the Fish and Game people. His gun was closer.

His pistol lay on the bottom of the creek, about two feet from the bank. Guess a wolf couldn't spit a two-pound gun all that far, especially if he wasn't willing to get his feet wet. A gray fishy form hovered near the dark gray metal, tantalizingly close to the surface. Corey found a dace all by himself. Fish, just get the hell away from the gun. Corey didn't want to touch it or otherwise molest it, plus the water was deeper than it looked. He stripped off his jacket and waffled Henley to keep them dry. He knelt at the water's edge. Submerged to the shoulder, he groped for his weapon. Lon swam in this stuff? And liked it? Without freezing his little otter balls off in water five degrees away from ice?

He retrieved the gun before his arm went totally numb. He dove into his clothing, cuddling his iced arm to his chest. Warming up hurt. His feet still worked—he could pursue and recover. It was only one sixth of him—he wouldn't take the time to build a fire.

He emptied as much water from the mechanisms as he could. The cartridges probably hadn't gotten too soaked to fire in the brief time they were underwater. Either Lon would be rescued or things would have gone completely to hell before anything in the interior rusted. The clip contained nine bullets for taking on God knew how many wolves. He couldn't spare one for a test fire.

Following the creek had to take him where he wanted to go, if the silverscale dace were the connection between the werewolves and Lon. Corey kept the burbling water to his right. His chilly arm worked again.

The chain link fence up ahead had to mean he was nearly at his goal. It cut across the creek, and looked like it dipped beneath the water. The mesh would let smaller fish go through, but nothing the size of an otter. The fencing went twenty yards at least to either side of the water, and who knew how far downstream it ran. The length of their property? Did these wolves think their building would only affect the habitat on their land? Did they not consider downstream?

How close did he dare come? One wet finger to the wind told him nothing the first time—Corey'd licked one of his barely thawed digits. The habit of right handedness wasn't serving him well. He could sense temperature on his left hand perfectly well. He tried again. The breeze brought him sounds from the east to chill his soul as much as his finger. Voices, urging someone named Whit to "Get him! Get him!" and curses for "that damned Vadas."

So, two-foots to deal with, who knew how many wolves, and the only wolf he could count as not an enemy was in the pen, fighting. White and brown rolled between the trees, with snarling and snapping. Where was Lon?

Lon had to be somewhere safe, he just had to. *Please don't let him be a casualty of fangs or misfortune!* They had to want him for something: they'd keep him alive and unhurt—mostly— if they needed him.

155

Corey never answered Lon about what he'd say to the otter if the choice were hunger or dace. This fence was the wolves' answer, and a no-blame way to be free of a species with the potential to cause them headaches. Except—hadn't he shown Melvin Vadas how to accommodate the fish and still have what he wanted?

Vadas—but not the rest, and a lot of voices were cheering this Whit on to bite the hell out of his department head.

Where was Lon? Corey didn't have line of sight on the whole creek, but one of the rocks seemed to move. "Lon?" He didn't dare yell, lest he be heard by any of the spectators to the fight. It moved again, turning to become an otter's head. A second otter bounced up and slid away. "Lon!"

With a glance toward the fight, the otter began a stealthy path to the end of the fence, always staying low among the rocks, picking out the dips and finally slipping into the stream to swim the rest of the way. Every foot he traveled had to be one foot closer to safety.

Finally he reached the fence, rising up on his back legs to grip the metal of his prison. "Lon, are you okay?" Corey knelt to reach through the mesh. The holes were wide enough to accommodate his open hands, too narrow for Lon to slip through. He stroked both sides of his otter lover's head, conscious of his wrists being trapped if something sneaked up behind. Too vulnerable! He withdrew one hand, knowing he should pull back both, but not willing to relinquish contact with Lon. "Can you put your fur away and get out of there?"

Even leaning into Corey's hand, Lon's headshake of *no* was unmistakable.

"Why? It's been more than an hour."

Lon dropped down to four feet. Tremors ran through him, the kind that usually presaged a pattable bare butt and the return of words and kisses. Nothing happened, though he shook with the effort.

Corey checked his watch. "Damn. Did you take your fur off for a while and restart the clock?"

Lon nodded, his whiskers flat against his cheeks.

Fuck, that could mean fur for a minute or an hour. "How long until you can take off your fur?" was a question they hadn't worked out a system for answering, and Corey usually knew anyway. "Can you climb out?"

Lon looked up. So did Corey. A wooden ledge stuck out, no doubt designed to prevent that very thing. "They really wanted to keep you in here. Forget that."

The ledge would be a nuisance for him, not a barrier. Corey could just climb in and boost Lon out. The mesh made good climbing—Corey went up that fence fast enough to make his monkey ancestors proud. And he didn't need to get all the way in, either. Lon climbed up the inside. Corey'd grab that long body, park him on the shelf, and get them both off the fence and out of here. He bent over the ledge, damn that lip for digging into his chest, but he had his hands on the other side of the fence, and his legs sticking out away from the fence for counterbalance. He couldn't quite reach, but Lon turned, tense and ready to spring across the gap.

A silent weight hit Corey's legs. He slid sideways across the shelf with the impact. Grabbing the ledge, he tried to hoist himself up and out of danger, but his assailant sank fangs into his calf. Sudden pain strengthened his grip. If he went down, they were both doomed. Kicking furiously with his free leg, Corey tried not to imagine the bloody tatters of his flesh, nor what would happen if he survived this attack. First, survive. He struck flesh with his boot, and struck again.

The wolf let go. Corey scrambled, desperate for the shelter of the fence—inside with Lon was safer than out here with fangs.

The wolf struck between Corey's legs. He chomped into a mouthful of ass and nads. "*Not that!*" Corey grabbed at his

157

vulnerable crotch. The wolf pulled him off the fence. He dropped six hard feet to unforgiving ground. Landing on his back drove every breath out. With an angry wolf's nose to his, Corey had no way to gain another.

The wolf straddled his chest. Thin lips exposed sharp teeth. Hot, rancid breath bathed his face. Barely breathing was almost a blessing—Corey still inhaled the scent of death. "You took my otter."

The wolf blew a foul gust into his face.

"I want him back."

The wolf huffed again.

Corey moved stealthily, one inch at a time. The wolf hadn't torn his face off yet. His hand crept to his pocket. Whiskey Creek's snowmelt flow hadn't stolen all movement. Corey could still make a credible threat.

He stared at his mortality in the brandy-colored eyes of the wolf above him. If he went, he wasn't going alone, and if the wolf could be faced down, he'd do it. He inched the gun out of his pocket, thumbing at the safety. He jammed the barrel into the wolf's ribs, poking a louder growl from his assailant.

"That's a gun. You understand what that is, don't you?" His thudding pulse would shake his hand and spoil his aim if they had any distance between them. Point blank meant no missing. "Yes, you do. I'm not kidding. I want my otter. Back off." He jammed the muzzle hard into the wolf's ribs. That thick coat wouldn't stop a 9mm slug.

The wolf backed up, understanding in its eyes. It didn't stop growling, but it did retreat over Corey. The farther the wolf went, the more Corey could sit up. He lifted himself with one elbow on the pine duff, holding the gun out straight with his right hand. The wolf was over his feet now—Corey gathered his legs under him and started to get up from the forest floor. His hand shook less, and he could almost feel what he was holding.

Millimeter by millimeter he rose. Something fell with a jangle. He'd retrieve it later. He was most of the way to upright, and the wolf was a good six feet away. Progress.

Lon screeched from within the fence. What was attacking him? One bullet for that threat—

Wrong threat. Another wolf struck Corey from behind, knocking him face first into the ground.

The gun flew from his hand, thudding into the dirt. A second wolf stood on his shoulders, rumbling against his neck, promising death, but not dealing it.

The gun lay three feet beyond his hand, and then it wasn't there anymore. The first wolf morphed into a middle aged man, stocky and nude, with a lot of body hair on a slight paunch. A man with hands to take Corey's weapon.

"You know, you're getting to be a total pain in the ass." The man examined the pistol. "I should have dropped this into faster water. Getting it out made you a little too cocky. Although shooting me with the safety on don't work so well." He flicked the lever back and forth a couple of times, and Corey couldn't swear which position he left it in.

Damn it, he was sure he'd taken off the safety, half-thawed hand or no. Corey had to spit a pine needle out of his mouth to answer. "I want my otter."

"And I want a million bucks and a red Corvette." The man grinned at him. "Your otter is now my otter, and he has work to do. Fish to catch, shouldn't be too hard for a little ferret face like him. He gets them all, and we might just let him go."

"You need to let him go now." Getting Lon out of that pen ranked ahead of getting out from under a wolf with big block feet.

"Nope, and I kinda hate letting you go. You keep coming back. That's annoying. And that's going to turn fatal any minute now." The man exchanged some kind of signal with the wolf standing on Corey. It snapped at his neck. But it didn't connect. And it got off his back.

159

Corey sat up, way too conscious of teeth at ear height. "A little weird that it hasn't already. Not that I want you to change that." He spat out another chunk of old pine parts. Glaring at the reddish wolf who'd knocked him down brought a growl. Corey growled back.

"Oh, I'd like to. That would solve all kinds of problems." His captor's smile turned ugly. "But you're under Melvin Vadas's protection, and right now—" He turned to the pen, his attention far beyond a crouching and blessedly silent otter. "Right now, Melvin's still alive."

Oh, fuck. "Then you can't touch me? Yet?" Corey leaped to his feet.

"Yet. Might give you a little escort though." The man jerked his thumb at Corey. "Stay with him as long as you like, Barbara. You can even make him run if you want to. Just don't kill him until we know Melvin's toast."

Barbara looked way too pleased with that idea. She lowered her head and approached. Corey held his ground. She lunged, all teeth aimed at Corey's junk. He jumped back and punched at her, dropping Lon's clothing.

"She'll take you if you don't get moving," the man spoke over her throaty rumble. "Not killing you don't mean not hurting you. Get him out of here, Barb."

"Hey!" Corey backed away from his not-yet attacker. "You chewed me up pretty good. Doesn't that mean I'm going to be one of you now?" Problem for later but question for now, because Vadas might not be around to answer.

Laughter was his only reply. Barbara lunged at him again, grabbing a mouthful of jacket this time. Corey turned and ran.

The wolf let him choose his path, hurrying him on his way with snapping jaws every time she decided he fled too slowly. For close to two miles he ran in boots that jarred his spine all the way to the top of his head with every step, all too conscious of the teeth tugging on the sag of his jeans. She grabbed fabric every time he slackened the pace. He tried not to slacken—his pursuer seemed like the humorous sort who'd pounce on him if he stumbled and explain the mauling with "Oops, I thought you guys took care of that pesky professor already."

Finally—the RAV4 waited ahead. Another hundred yards and he'd be in a position to roll right over the bitch that just nipped his ass again. "Knock it off!" he yelled, but she took out the seat of his jeans and connected with his buttock. "Damn it! Go find out who won, why don't you?"

Hah! First thing he'd said to her to get her off his back. Or on his face. She put on a burst of speed to dash around and in front of him. Corey couldn't stop—he went somersaulting over her groin height shoulders and skidded face first into the dirt. "Barbara! You are such a bitch!"

The big red wolf licked a nasty swipe across his face and trotted back the way she came, head held high and tail out straight. Corey watched her go.

Guess in her world that passed for a compliment.

He trudged the last paces to his SUV, hating every step that took him away from Lon. His only reassurance was in the werewolves' desire for Lon to clear the stream of silverscale dace. They wouldn't screw up his ability to hunt, not if they wanted the last of the endangered fish cleared out.

How hungry was Lon, and how many fish did they think he'd catch?

Maybe Lon didn't have as much time as the two-foot wolf made it seem.

Corey fell against the door, groping in his pocket for the keys. Nothing. Nothing in his jacket pocket. Nothing in his jeans pockets, neither front nor back, though one of the back pockets wasn't in any shape to hold anything, flapping as it was on three sides. Shit! An echo of the metallic splat when he was facing off the male wolf jingled through his mind. He could have those keys in his hand, he could be driving off to find the cavalry, but no. No keys. No way to make the RAV4 move. Damn it all to hell! Praying Vadas

161

stayed strong and Lon made the wolves think he was fishing, Corey turned back the way he came. Staying on the road this time, he set off on the three mile hike back to pavement. Maybe someone would come along to give him a lift for the last fifteen miles into Idaho Springs, because he had some wolves to report, and some dace to save.

And an otter to rescue. God, if they harmed Lon in any way…. Corey set one foot in front of the other and tried not to measure the height of the sun.

Chapter Fourteen

Stunned into silence, Lon watched Corey run. Corey had to run fast, he had to get away. Lon couldn't get away, but all the wolves wanted was for him to be an otter, and he could do that. He still wanted to get away, because he wasn't supposed to do what the wolves wanted.

The man who was a wolf turned to the pen. He had Corey's gun. That was bad. He wouldn't shoot Lon, but Corey couldn't shoot wolves. Except Corey hadn't shot any wolves when he had the gun.

"You, go catch some lunch." The man grinned at Lon, and it was a wolf's grin. "Have a great big buffet, you and your new girlfriend. Make some more baby otters and feed them too." The man shivered in the wind. Lon shivered too, but not for the same reason.

How come the wolves could put their fur on and take it off and put it on again so fast? What did they know that Lon didn't? The man became a wolf again. Wolves shouldn't be interested in man things like guns, but this wolf picked up the gun in his mouth and trotted away. Hope he liked the taste of the oil. *Pfeh.*

Lon didn't know what else to do—he wouldn't fish because the wolves wanted that. He couldn't escape, and he'd have fur for a while yet. He'd go check with Lu. Corey would rescue her too. When he came back.

The wolves had broken apart to glare and growl, panting hard. They'd been fighting for a long time. They still didn't like each other, and they had blood on their coats. The white wolf still had that weird ridge in his ruff. The brown wolf's fur lay smooth.

Lon slithered down between the rocks to Lu's new den. The babies squeaked but they didn't sound scared. Lon could imagine licking and nursing and cuddles on warm mama. That would make everything all right again. For them. They were too little to know anything else.

Lu knew. She stuck her head out of the den to sniff Lon, chittering low in her throat at the wolf and man smells clinging to his fur. Maybe the gun smell too, but she wouldn't know what that was, only that it was a man thing. Or maybe it smelled like traps to her. Lon hoped she'd never met a trap.

She nosed him, still chittering. Lon sniffed back, and groomed her, trying for "everything's okay, Corey will be back, he'll get us out of here," but those ideas were too fancy for not having words. Licking her ear only meant "I'm here and I like you." Which was better than nothing, and all they had right now.

He licked again and backed out of the den. He sat on the rock to watch the wolves. Lu came to sit near him. She chattered for a second and fell silent. Lon licked his stepped-on paw. Maybe he'd chew the laces on Corey's boots to get even for that.

Lon glanced up, away from the fighters. The sun was getting lower. Soon it would touch the mountain and the sky would get dark. He needed to take off his fur. It would get chilly for a guy with fur when the sun went down. It would be icky cold, maybe even killing cold, for a guy with no fur and no clothes and too big to get into the den with the otters.

If he stayed here. Once he took off his fur he could run away, if the wolves weren't paying attention. The two in here didn't care about him, and the ones outside had all put their fur away and were wearing jackets. Some of them weren't even watching the fight.

"Hey, we gotta get back to Denver," one called. "I'm supposed to go to work early. Tell Whit to call me, okay?" He and two others left the group by the fence, and in a little, Lon heard the sound of an engine.

Two others left. Lon wanted them all to go away so he could run to the fence and put his fur away. He counted again. One, two, three, four, five. Five wolves to run away from. Better chances than with many. Maybe four wolves, if the young one didn't have his fur yet.

The two wolves in here weren't fighting right now, but they might start at a twitch. Lon watched them, wishing they'd attack and give the others something to watch besides his escape.

The sun went lower. Lu went back into the den with the babies.

One of the two-foot wolves outside shouted, "Hey, Whit! Why don't you just shift and walk out of there? Then we can shoot Vadas and end this standoff."

What kind of nasty, scatty rules did wolves have? Lon hated wolves. They turned on each other.

The dark wolf edged toward the gate, followed by the white wolf. Close enough to touch the latch now, the dark wolf shifted and grabbed for the latch. Before he could lift the metal, the white wolf seized his arm and dragged him away from the gate. He threw the man down and stood over him, teeth to his throat. New blood ran down the man's arm.

Lying on his back, he changed back to wolf. The white wolf bit him again, and the fight was on. They rolled and snapped. If they rolled over here, Lon would hide in the rocks or the water.

The wolves had been fighting a long time. Weren't they tired? Or hungry? Lon was hungry, but the fish here...

Something about the fish here... He couldn't remember, but he was only a little hungry. He'd wait.

The sun went down.

Corey trudged the narrow road back to Idaho Springs. He'd put his thumb out if there'd been any traffic to flag down. The one vehicle he'd seen had been heading the other way. The driver had wished him luck but wouldn't turn around to backtrack to town. If Corey had known that would be the only vehicle he'd see, he would have begged harder for a lift, anniversary dinner or no.

What a fucking clown he was. Dr. Corey "Rescue All the Endangered Species Single Handedly" Levigne, now up the creek without boats, paddles, or webbed feet. "I'll outthink them" sure sounded good back in town. Thinking got him into this. Why hadn't he just shot?

Because he didn't have to be the one to turn it lethal. They were having fun with him, even bitch Barbara. So much for being the human in this drama.

But they hadn't hurt Lon. They didn't want to hurt Lon; no, they wanted him to do their dirty work. He'd be okay. He had to be okay, at least until Corey could get back up the mountain with reinforcements. Melvin, well, that could turn bloody. He didn't like the guy, but he didn't want him—how had Lon put it? Spread all over the forest floor as wolf scat.

How the hell did an armed man manage to get taken down? Twice. God, he was an idiot.

Someone did pick him up about five miles from town. He accepted Corey's explanation about lost keys and drove the length of the long narrow town to the Fish and Game station. "Unless a bear swallowed your keys, these guys won't be much help." With a pointed look at the bloody shreds of Corey's pant leg, his rescuer added, "Is that what got you?"

"No. Long story." Corey thanked his ride and wondered how he was going to explain to officials who thought wolves stayed wolves.

The ranger at the Fish and Game office took one look at Corey's leg and headed off for first aid supplies. "We need to get you in for a rabies series," he said, pouring hydrogen peroxide into the wounds. Corey hissed between clenched teeth, and was intensely grateful the crotch bite hadn't actually broken his skin.

"I don't think the wolf was rabid," he gasped. "Just territorial and I encroached."

"Wolf? Are you serious?" The ranger looked sideways at him. "We've had one wolf wander down from Yellowstone in the last twelve years, and she got killed by a car."

"It was a wolf. I don't know where these people got it, but they have at least one penned up, and they have a couple of otters penned up, and they have the stream blocked off so nothing can drink." Explaining about one wolf was a lot easier than heading off inquiries about where the rest of them went if the whole pack looked like people.

"Yeah. Problem. They can't be trapping endangered species." The ranger wrapped yards of gauze over Telfa pads, reducing Corey's leg to a medical curiosity instead of reason to scream."Are you sure you weren't bitten by a Husky?"

"I'm sure," Corey snapped, and immediately backed down. "Sorry, I just know it wasn't a dog. It was much too big, like about twice the size of a Husky. No mask markings either." Yay for all that time on the internet making sure he could distinguish one from the other. "And besides, wolf or not wolf, it's a danger to the otters."

"It was certainly a danger to you." The ranger finished his patch job. "Still think we need to get you in for rabies prophylaxis."

An unnecessary series of shots would only slow Corey up. "No. I'm really sure that's not the problem. It wasn't foaming at the mouth"—He held up a cautioning hand to

167

intercept an interruption—"not that it would, necessarily, but it was acting very, very deliberately. It wasn't flailing or wandering or acting impaired. It wanted a chunk of me, and that's what it got." Boy did it. "Can we please go rescue the otters?"

"Show me where they are." The ranger pulled out a map. "I'll round up a team and we'll go up in the morning."

Without him. No.

"We need to go tonight. I don't know if someone's going to feed that wolf. He might kill an otter." He could certainly kill a man, and if Lon wasn't an otter, would they have any use for him? If Vadas was dead, there'd be no mercy. Corey would beg. "Please, let's go now."

"Have you noticed that the sun is down?" the ranger pointed out. "Mark the map."

Hell yes, he'd noticed the sun was down. "I don't know where it is on the map. I can't read it," Corey lied. "I can take you back up there."

"In the dark?" the ranger scoffed. "You can't find it on a map, you sure won't find it in the dark. Not to mention we don't like walking into what could be an ambush situation. They have a wolf, they have otters, they could just as easily have guns. They won't want to give up the animals."

"They have at least one gun," Corey admitted, though he wouldn't claim it as his. *Sorry, Gramps.*

"My point exactly." The ranger threw a handful of bandage wrappers into the trash. Corey tugged down what remained of his jeans leg. "You're mustering the cavalry. You have to let us do it by the book."

The Book could get Lon killed. But the ranger wouldn't budge. Corey deflected with practical concerns, like, "I need a place to stay" and "When do we leave?"

The Fish and Game officer, whose name turned out to be Ray DeLuty, had a couple answers, like, "Since you're making it impossible to leave you behind, you get a sleeping bag on the couch at my place" and "It will be my pleasure to kick you out of bed around five a.m.." He was also good for a pizza at Beau Jo's, though Corey barely had an appetite for the prairie pie. Knowing that Lon would have to catch anything he ate, if he succeeded in catching anything with the commotion going on, added a sprinkle of guilt to each bite. That Lon's dinner could be exactly the fish that shouldn't get eaten was good for a side dish of shame. One beer wouldn't wash the away the taste of guilt.

Ray munched, firing off questions that wound here and there, away from otters and wolves, into knowing Corey as a person, and into dangerous territory Corey recognized too late. "Since you're looking at development impact, you need to know about the proposed projects and the species affected, right?"

Corey nodded, his eye on the thick edge of crust on his slice and his thoughts running to Beau Jo's offering honey and rebranding the crust as dessert being genius.

"Then I don't believe for a minute you can't read that map." Ray set down his glass of pop. "Why are you really so anxious to get back up there?"

Busted. Maybe. "My truck." Corey'd explained about hiking into town.

"Doesn't explain why you want a posse going up there to fetch it."

"The wolf bite isn't enough?" Would he end up confessing the very things Lon wanted kept secret?

"Not really." Ray destroyed three napkins getting the pepperoni grease off his hands. "Otherwise you'd let us do our jobs while keeping your professorial ass out of range, and come back later for your truck. So I ask you again, why do you, desk job economist Dr. Corey Levigne, need to be part of the team storming the ramparts?"

Corey set the crust down and picked his words very carefully. "My best friend is up there, and he can't get out. Not without your help. I have to go back for him."

"Now we're getting somewhere." Ray took a long swig through his straw, letting Corey stew over offering details.

"I have two Forest Service law enforcement officers, one sheriff, one deputy, and my partner on this team. Sounds like I should have called SWAT instead."

Maybe that wouldn't be the worst idea ever…. But the wolves had followed the rules as they understood them, and so far, no one had died, or even been hurt. Much. Corey wouldn't call certain death into their camp. "I think you have the right team."

"You are so full of shit. We have a hostage situation and a civilian thinking he can make the decisions. Hell, I'm not qualified to make these decisions. I rescue animals, not people. Dickhead." That last exploded out of Ray hard enough to make every person within earshot swivel around to stare.

"You are, though." Corey spoke softly, hoping all the disapproving mamas would turn around to pay attention to what their tots were doing with the honey bottles.

"And why would that be?" Ray dropped his voice. Guess he didn't want to attract the attention either.

"Because—" He chopped off the explanation. Not only would Ray call the SWAT team, he'd call the men in white coats to bring the straightjacket. "You'll think I'm delusional."

"You're trying to direct this rescue. I know you're delusional. So you might as well tell me, or you don't go tomorrow." Ray destroyed another napkin, this time with malice. "I can piece together a destination from what you've already said. Somewhere on Whiskey Creek."

Whoa. He should have seen that coming and anticipated that a Fish and Game officer would know his territory well enough to add up the details. Corey dropped his voice. "I know you're the right guy. Because…" Oh shit, how did he not reveal Lon's nature?

"Because why? Spit it out!"

In a whisper, Corey said, "Because my friend looks like one of the otters."

"Oh." Ray's righteous anger disappeared like smoke. "It's like that, huh."

"Like what?" Corey hadn't admitted to Lon being his lover because he wasn't going to cut through layers of resistance, disbelief, and homophobia too. The first two were barriers enough; he wouldn't take a chance on the one that could get Lon left for the wolves.

"Shifter." Ray dropped his voice to something nearly inaudible.

Of all the reactions Corey expected, the right reaction wasn't at the top of his probability list. He spoke at the same infinitesimal decibel level. "You believe in shifters?" *Oh please, don't let Ray interpret that as mockery!*

"Sounds weird, I know." The middle-aged man in the khaki shirt started wadding up the napkin shreds into little balls, his eyes trained on the task. "But there was this girl once, see…." He looked up to Corey's face.

Glory be. "Her name wasn't Barbara, was it?"

"No, that was her sister." Ray chuckled, and then his eyes grew wide. "You've met Barbara?"

"In a manner of speaking. She chewed my ass, you might say." The officer had seen the remains of the seat of Corey's britches.

"Oh, man. I am so sorry." Ray laughed, and his voice was back to conversational levels. "She can be such a bitch."

Chapter Fifteen

The penned wolves settled a little. They weren't knocking each other down or snarling all the time. If one moved the other growled. Otherwise, they stared at each other, two steps apart, lying on the ground. They'd flopped down, their tongues hanging out. The sun went away and the sky was bright with the dots of light Lon couldn't always see at home, but there were many, lots, and oh my goodness of them here.

They made it easy to see the wolves. Even the dark one stood out against the ground and had a shadow to blend with. The white wolf pawed at his neck, and every time he did, the dark wolf growled.

Lon was so hungry his tummy hurt. The wolves would be hungry too. The babies were satisfied. They'd stuck their fuzzy muzzles against Mama Lu for milk. She hadn't eaten either. Everyone was hungry here, and there were fish in the stream. Only the wolves kept Lon from hunting.

The two-leg wolves outside the pen had a fire and food over the fire. The scents carried and made Lon's tummy hurt more. Someone Lon liked ate that kind of food. So did Lon, sometimes, and he'd like some now. But the two-leg wolves weren't sharing, not even with the fighters.

Their voices carried in the night. Sometimes they called out to the wolves. "Hey, Whit, just finish him!" or "Melvin, just fucking give up already!" but mostly they talked among themselves and two of them went into a little house on the back of a truck.

There were fish in the stream. There was a reason Lon wasn't supposed to eat these fish, but it was getting harder to remember and his tummy growled almost as loud as the wolves. He didn't have to keep watch all night. He slipped down to the den where he could be near his kind. He'd sleep a while.

He should take his fur off. But it was so comfy. If he took his fur off he'd be hungry and cold. But he'd had his fur on a long time. Fur was nice. He could wear his fur forever and play with the water and Lu. The babies would grow up and he could play with them too. And there'd be more squeaky little babies. Have to teach them to swim.

Stay forever in the stream. Not this stream, this had a nasty fence, but they'd find a place to dig under and escape. Lots of fish upstream from here. Lon had found them. He wanted one. Maybe those fish were okay to eat.

Lu stuck her nose out and woke Lon. She nuzzled Lon's cheek. He nuzzled back. The wolves weren't paying attention. Good.

She slipped into the stream. Her flat head made a V in the water for an instant and then she dived. She stayed under a long time. Lon's tummy grumbled again. He'd join her in the water.

The world looked different underwater at night. Lon wasn't used to it. He liked to swim in the day with… with… Somebody liked him to swim in the day. But he was an otter, and he was nocturnal. Lu flashed by underwater, a fish in her mouth. A little one. One of the "don't eat this fish" kind. But she was hungry and so was Lon, and there was another one! He chased.

Terrible thrashing and flailing in the water behind him! Lu! Lon popped to the surface. The wolves were fighting, right there, and Lu was in the middle. She screeched. The dark wolf grabbed her. The white wolf crashed into him. Lon swam as fast as he could. Dark paws in the water! Hard to catch, all bounding around, but Lon could catch fast fish. Legs were easier, legs didn't swim away. He bit one, hard as he could. His sharp fangs went through skin and down into crunchy parts.

The wolf tried to run away, but Lon hung on. Bite that bad wolf! Wolf dragged him through the water, howling, thrashing. All the way across the stream. Lon went bump bump on the bottom of the stream when the wolf ran. Dragged him up onto the bank. Lon didn't let go, even when the white wolf nearly stepped on him. The dark wolf growled and snapped everywhere, biting back. Ow! Lon let go and slid back into the water. The white wolf chased the dark one away.

Lon popped up for a breath. The wolves ran and snarled, on the other side of the water from the gate. The two-foot wolves yelled, "What's going on?"

Where was Lu?

Lon climbed out onto the rocks. Lu lay panting, her fur dark with water and even darker on her shoulder. He smelled blood. She whimpered when he sniffed her, and cried out when he licked. Blood seeped through her fur. Bad wolf!

The bad wolf might come back. He nosed her toward the den. All this for a fish. But she was hungry. She slid down to the den, crying with each step. She should stay there, rest. She'd caught a fish. Was the fish lost? Lon sniffed around, but he didn't find it, so he slid into the water. Maybe catch another one. But there was Lu's fish, not swimming, still tasty. He snatched it out of the shallows.

He dropped the fish into the den. She chittered and squeaked and the fish disappeared. Maybe she'd be okay.

The white wolf returned, streaked dark across snout and chest. He smelled of blood. Lon looked at the wolf and the wolf looked at him. Then the wolf turned three times and lay down, watching the woods. He scratched at his neck with a hind foot. The ridge of fur still stuck up. Maybe it itched.

Lon didn't like the wolf being so close to the den, but he wasn't attacking. Maybe the dark wolf wouldn't come near if the white wolf stayed. The wolf's head bobbed, but he jerked it up. The third time, the white wolf's head drooped to his paws.

A shadow came limping between the trees. If it made a sound it was lost in the water's laughter. It dipped a paw into the stream, trying to find footing. The water was fast there. It came closer. The water didn't run so fast here. The dark wolf stepped into the stream and began to pick his way across.

Lon screeched. The white wolf jerked to its feet and leaped at the dark wolf. He knocked the dark wolf under the water. It thrashed and struggled, and when it got up, it didn't fight. It scrambled to its feet and ran, back where it came. Away from the gate.

The white wolf didn't follow. Instead it padded slowly to Lon's rock. Silently, with covered teeth and ears forward, the wolf offered its muzzle to Lon. He sniffed the wolf and the wolf sniffed him.

The white wolf was tired, so tired it trembled while it offered peace. Lon had a nap but he was still hungry. He hadn't eaten even a nibble of Lu's fish, only had a lick while carrying it. The wolf hadn't had even that much. The wolf snuffled into Lon's fur and retreated to flat ground to lie down. Lon slipped into the stream. The fish were too quick on this end of the creek. All that thrashing scared them. Lon swam downstream, where the fish were dozy and slow.

Also the fish were bigger here. Lon sneaked up on a torpedo shape, which didn't begin to flash away until it was too late. He pulled the trout upstream, a long hard paddle with a fish a quarter of his length.

The wolf remained on guard, but its head was bobbing. He came to full alert when Lon dragged his prize on the bank. His ears pricked forward. He didn't get up to steal the

175

fish, but his nose wiggled and twitched, and he licked his chops with his long tongue. Lon pulled the trout nearly to the white wolf's paws. He'd defended Lu. Lon would share.

The wolf wouldn't. Or maybe it was just better not to try for a bite when the wolf held the fish between his paws and gnawed with his back teeth. Lon slipped back into the water and found the closer fish had calmed down. He caught breakfast and joined the wolf on the bank. He ate his small fish and thought about finding another, but the wolf's head was bobbing again. Someone needed to keep watch.

Lon stayed with the sleeping wolf, just in case the bad wolf came to bite him. Maybe the bad wolf only wanted to sneak out. He'd tried that, and the white wolf wouldn't let him. Bit him hard. Lon bounded along the creek, just in case. Letting the bad wolf run away seemed like a good idea, but the white wolf didn't want him to run away outside the cage. Lon didn't know why.

The dark shadow limped to the creek. Lon watched from under a willow, all whippy branches and only the tiniest leaves to hide him. The willow might not hide him enough. If the wolf only wanted to drink, Lon would stay hidden. They were both nocturnal hunters, but the wolf might be better at it than Lon was.

Bet his paw hurt! Lon could still taste wolf. *Pfeh*. But Lon would bite him again if he had to. His own stepped-on paw felt much better now.

The wolf lapped from the burbling waters until it was satisfied. It stood still, head down but his tongue not moving, for long minutes. Lon watched. Would it go back into the shadows?

No. The wolf took one shaky step into the water, and then another. Two feet in the wet was enough for Lon. He screeched louder than he'd ever screeched before, even when his paw got smushed.

The white wolf staggered to his feet, rushing slowly. The dark wolf kept coming. Maybe he would get all the way

176

across the creek before the white wolf could stop him. He hurried and stumbled, dunking his face into the water.

The white wolf snarled from the bank, daring him to keep coming. The dark wolf stood in the water, his head down. Slowly he turned and once on the far bank, he limped back into the shadows.

Lon rustled out from under the willow to touch noses with the white wolf. Maybe not all wolves were bad. The wolf poked at Lon with his snout, shoving him around the other way, and then nudged Lon's butt. Hey! He started to hiss, but the wolf trudged along the creek, looking over his shoulder. The wolf took two more steps.

Okay, Lon would see what the wolf was doing. He bounded behind the wolf, who started to trot when he saw Lon was coming. He came to the end of the pen and snuffled at the fence.

Lon knew those smells! Some were him when... when... When he was different, but how was he different then? His own smell mingled with the pretend fur stuff two-foots used. Lon remembered using pretend fur. Why did he need pretend fur? He had good fur! That stuff wasn't even furry and was nasty when it got wet. Bad for swimming. But... Another smell, a smell he knew. A person, with a woodsy kind of scent. Plants, but not really plants, and Lon remembered the smelly stuff was bad to lick. He must have tried it once, because that smell was with the two-foot scent Lon liked a lot. Who did he like that was a two-foot?

Someone tall, who went *hurr, hurr, hurr* with Lon. Someone who let Lon climb up and sit by his head to be carried. Someone who challenged wolves for Lon. Someone... who loved him with his fur on. And...when he didn't. If he didn't always have his fur on, what was he? Lon tried to remember not having fur.

Not...having...fur... Lon could barely remember what that was like. He sniffed and sniffed, trying to remember.

Something glittery lay on the ground, something that smelled of the human. He knew what that was. Once. Lon strained to remember. It was something important. Something the human wouldn't want to leave. Something....

He could remember better if he was... If he was... Thoughts that needed words danced at the edges of Lon's mind, and he wanted to pursue them. They scattered like a school of fish and he had to find them, he had to capture them. It would be easy if....if...

He pushed, trying to catch the thoughts. He needed to be bigger to catch the thoughts. Lon made himself be bigger, and his tail went away. His fur went away. Most of the smells went away. Only the strongest scents stayed. Pine duff and wolf and water. Corey's scent disappeared but his truck keys shone in the starlight. His keys! Where was Corey?

Lon sat up, shivering in the mountain night. How long had he been in fur? Time didn't mean much right now, but darkness swept with a million stars meant too long. Corey'd watched him jump into the creek in the late afternoon.

He leaned his forehead to his knees, hugging his legs for warmth and to collect the scattered bits of his humanity. Words came back in chunks. Cold brought clothes, houses, fire, furnace, cuddle, blanket, bed. Ideas followed in great streams, filling his mind with home, love, happy, close, and then chased them with negatives: stranger, fighting, far away. Long moments passed while ideas formed into thoughts and shaped memories, filling the vast spaces of Lon's mind. He came back to himself, concept by concept, memory by memory.

His companion waited silently at his side. The wolf Lon feared so much leaned into him. Sharing his warmth. He had a name—Melvin Vadas. He was Corey's colleague. He made decisions for the werewolves. And he was fighting for his position, if not his life. All the while, he'd looked out for Lon. Fought for him. Taken wounds for him.

Words had been far away: Lon's voice came out rusty. "Thanks. I think I was in fur a little too long."

The wolf nosed Lon's face for a moment and padded to the fence. He put both paws up on the chain link and looked over his shoulder at Lon.

"Good idea." The fence hadn't been the problem before: what lurked outside the fence had been the issue. "I'll tell Corey what's going on, okay? I don't know what he can do about wolf business, but…" Lon knelt to hug the great shaggy form, on four feet again now that Lon understood. "Thanks for defending Lu."

The fence was made of handholds, and the overhang was nothing when he had hands. Up, over, away… Over that fence, scoop up clothes and keys, and he'd make a mad dash back to the truck before his nads froze off in the chilly mountain night.

The metal clanged with the impact. Hot breath scorched his foot—Lon jerked back, fighting not to fall on the side with the teeth. "Not again."

Yes, again. Two wolves crouched at the base of the fence. Three, but one was on his side, and Melvin's snarl meant nothing to them. Because of stupid wolf rules? Lon perched on the overhang.

Enough starlight to read by filtered through the wide-set trees, more than enough to see white fangs and lightly marked coats. One crouched for a jump. To scare him? Or for more?

The wolf sprang. The clash of teeth in front of Lon's face made the point. He toppled back, landing hard on his back. With the breath knocked out of him, he could barely summon fear for his spine.

Melvin threw himself against the fence, snarling wolf threats but not going over. When Lon could move again, the two wolves had backed up. One sat down, stretching his paws out before him, apparently there for the duration. The other licked his ear and dashed off around the fence. To warn Whit? Lon sat slowly, every vertebra and joint rattled completely loose. Melvin left off his imprecations to come sniff.

"Looks like they aren't going to let me out of here." He wrapped his arm around the great hairy shoulders, for warmth as well as appreciation. "Do you need to sleep? I can watch over you." He might be able to yell fast enough if their silent observer decided to come over the fence.

Melvin lay down, his head on his paws. A great whuff came out, blowing the fallen pine needles away from his muzzle.

The afternoon was jacket weather for Corey, and the temperature fell with sundown. Frost was possible tonight, and Lon was quite sure a coat of rime was forming on his bare skin. A heat source lay next to him. He cuddled up to the wolf, pressing every possible inch of hide against him. He dared not fall asleep. The cold couldn't seduce him yet.

Lon had to switch sides, warming his back against the shaggy form of the sleeping werewolf. The guy was old, well, older than Lon and Corey, and he must be exhausted. Because why else would he opt for rest when he could be making Lon open that gate? He could see the gate from here, and would yell if the dark wolf went anywhere near it.

Staying vigilant for movement and sound took part of Lon's thoughts, but puzzling out Melvin's reasoning kept him awake. "Shift and walk out of there" tumbled through his memories, words that didn't mean enough when he had his fur on. Lon didn't know the wolves' rules, but everything that happened today pointed toward the winner walking away from the fight on two legs. "Then we'll shoot Vadas" sounded like the victor didn't have to kill his opponent, only leave him. Whit had tried opening the gate as a two-foot, and Melvin pounced on him and made him shift back.

No wonder Whit had tried to cross the stream while Melvin slept. Lon strained to see movement between the stream and the gate, but only the pines rustled and creaked in the night air.

Whit seemed cowed into staying on the far side of the creek. So why the hell wasn't Vadas on his feet, marching out that gate? Because of the five wolves on the far side who wouldn't welcome him?

Vadas sighed and rolled, curling up into a large furry ball. He'd better be able to wake in a hurry. Lon swapped sides, warming his now chilled front on the sleeping wolf. Where was Corey sleeping tonight, and was he okay?

Corey'd done everything he could to get them both out of this mess, and he wouldn't just give up. But what would he try next? And when? Corey couldn't be a pile of bloody, cooling meat. He just couldn't.... Lon's heart crushed into a tight ball and refused to unclench, no matter how many times he repeated Jack Schwimmer's instructions to Barbara. Melvin was still alive and keeping at least part of Lon from freezing, and every breath he took meant his protection over Corey still held.

Lon squeezed his slumbering protector, not that muddy, exhausted wolf was a good balm for his tattered composure. Twice now he'd spent more time in fur than he should. The water called him, suggesting how much fun it would be to slide down the bank and into its embrace. The water loved him, the water wanted him, and he couldn't block out the call of his first lover, which would babble enticements to him until the earth dried to a desert. Holding on to Melvin kept him from following that invitation. The cold night nipped his unprotected back. He wouldn't even notice the chill if he wore his fur....

No. Lon clenched fingers woven through Melvin's coarse outer coat and into his fluffy undercoat. The tug woke his companion, who got up to stretch with rump up and forequarters down. He yawned, showing every sharp tooth, and sat to lick his chops.

Another fish wasn't an option. Lon had his urge to put on fur under control—for now—and wouldn't hunt again. But a drink, for both of them, even if it meant dipping his hand into the snowmelt waters, was within reach. Melvin lapped from the stream.

Thirst slaked as much as he could without giving his cupped hand or his stomach frostbite, Lon sat back on his haunches. "So why don't you march right out that gate? That seems to be the goal, leaving on two feet."

Melvin lifted one side of his lip and flattened his ears. With one hind foot he started scratching his neck, aiming at the odd ridge in his fur. No itch ever got that deliberate a treatment.

"Need some help there from the fingers and thumb brigade?" Lon reached out with a certain amount of trepidation. His companion had permitted the familiarity of sharing warmth, but premeditated touching still seemed dicey.

Melvin all but dove into his hand, snout first and creating a stroke.

Okay. Lon didn't figure this was about affection. He worked his fingers through Melvin's heavy fur to the ridge. "Oh fuck, they didn't!" He had to fix this right now! No wonder the fight had lasted all these hours. No wonder Melvin hadn't already kicked furry butt and taken names with the group camped out by the gate. "Those sons of bitches."

His drinking hand was still nearly numb, and his fingers didn't respond well. But he could twist—Wham.

A fury slammed into Lon, putting him on the ground. Coarse hair and fetid breath, too many legs, snarling and snapping. Lon rolled away from his attacker. Whit went down, slammed by Vadas, but scrabbled past his opponent to come after Lon. He threw up an arm to take the attack. The wolf bore him backward, pushing him into the creek.

God, it was cold. The water wanted to kill him as badly as the wolf did. Whit thrashed and snapped. Lon's head went under the water, the weight of his assailant on top of him, and he…might…not…get…

Lon threw his fur out. With a slash of sharp canines at the wolf, he fled downstream.

Lu's den would be warm.

182

CHAPTER SIXTEEN

Five o'clock came after only a few hours of sleep. The couch was comfortable enough, even long enough for a man of his height, but the lumps of guilt kept Corey awake into the wee hours. How the hell had his pride gotten them into this? Why hadn't he listened to Lon? Now he had to depend on an unknown team to get his lover back, and only one of them knew what Lon was or what the others were.

Not to mention, the handcuffs were a hindrance.

He could have sworn he'd noted exactly where Ray hung the truck keys. They'd eaten and come back to Ray's gingerbread Victorian cottage to get some rest before their dawn raid. Guess Ray wasn't all that trusting, because when Corey sneaked into the kitchen intent on boosting the pickup, he'd tripped over a stack of pots and pans in the doorway. He'd spent the rest of the night handcuffed to an antique maple breakfront that had to weigh more than the pickup, with instructions not to mar the finish.

Guess he'd telegraphed his intentions a little too clearly at dinner, trying to convince Ray not to wait for the others, dawn, or even the check.

Corey dreamed of snapping teeth and bloody scraps of fur, when he'd slept at all. The long wakeful hours he spent convincing himself that Lon could get back to human in the night. That he'd scamper up some sturdy pine and shift back where the wolves couldn't reach him. Ray interrupted snarls, snaps and screams when he shuffled in before dawn with the key.

Advice and coffee came with Corey's freedom. Ray DeLuty wasn't fool enough to try to sell the rest of the team on werewolves. "If they look like humans, we have to assume they're humans, and if they look like wolves, we have tranquilizer darts and shotguns. If they switch back and forth in front of us, we don't have to convince the rest. And I don't have any silver ammo."

"I have it on good authority you shouldn't use movies for data." He'd trust what Lon had told him and what he'd seen. Corey raided the fridge while explaining. Ray could cough up a roast beef sandwich for the cause.

Ray wasn't relieved enough by the answer to let him carry a Remington 870 of his own. "You're still a civilian and a nuisance, and your only function is as a guide." He did let Corey sit in the front of his pickup truck, with the other officers following behind.

Corey steadfastly refused to look at the map, but called the few turns that surprised Ray not at all. "Full Moon Conservancy, huh." He pulled up beside the crude sign at the turnoff. "Could have found this place without your 'help'. Damn but you are a know-it-all pain in the butt. Stay in the truck."

Ray shut the door quietly. Had to be for the wolves' benefit, because he was royally pissed with Corey. They'd planned to go in friendly rather than combative, even knowing some regulations were being violated. The white Sheriff's Department Suburban and the olive green Forest Service pickup carried six men with a sizable armory, which amounted to a small army. Corey hoped it would be enough.

He didn't know how far that track went to get to the water, but Ray'd left a map behind. Corey found Whiskey Creek and the thin line of the tertiary road, and he'd hiked a lot farther than that yesterday. He measured the

184

map against his memory of the gate's location and the few vehicles the wolves had there, and came up with a couple of hundred yards to the entry of the creek. If nothing else, he'd retrieve his keys and Lon's clothing. Poor guy probably spent a cold night under a bush.

Or a warm night in fur.

He eased out of the pickup truck into the nippy dawn air. This side of the mountain got the sun first, but the sun would have to rise a lot farther to reach this face of the range. He could see enough not to stumble into trees.

Corey cut right, away from the road, listening intently for voices and for the rushing of the water. That would be enough to guide him to the upstream edge of the pen. The stream ran unenclosed here—he'd gone too far north. Corey followed the creek downhill to the pen.

Well, hell, there were his keys, right where he'd dropped them in his rush to play Lone Ranger. At least the Masked Man would have had a silver bullet for his revolver, unlike the *tonto* here. Corey pocketed his keys, hunted a little farther, and found Lon's clothing. One of his athletic shoes was five feet away from the pile with teeth marks in the leather toe and half a lace missing. Please let that be the worst damage from last night!

From his vantage point at the fence, Corey could see the gate, where the game wardens and other law enforcement officers stood, chatting with the group that had stayed the night. A much smaller group than had been here yesterday. The good guys weren't outnumbered after all. But he didn't see Lon or any otter sign, and he didn't see any wolves. Had the fight ended? Had Vadas prevailed and taken Lon away with him? Or was Vadas so much carrion among the trees, and Lon still trapped? Not knowing twisted Corey's guts.

He could hear discussions, some distant, some growing louder. "This pen is closing off water access for the wildlife. You've blocked off a lot more of the stream than you're allowed" wasn't going over so well, from the sounds of it.

185

Neither was "What do you keep penned in here? There's been reports of wolves."

Since Corey was certain he was the only one who could have reported wolf sightings, he'd better brace for the ass kicking sure to follow. The only wolf who knew him well was on his side. Where the hell were Vadas and Lon?

A flash of white through the trees caught his eye. "Psst! Melvin!" brought a wolf staring directly at him. The icy blue eyes could belong to no other. "Melvin!"

Why he was calling the wolf, Corey wasn't sure. Communication would be awfully limited. Was Melvin trapped in this form for some set period? Lon—*don't think about Lon as trapped.* Yes or no questions, they could manage. The wolf trotted to the fence, meeting Corey's eyes through the mesh.

"Is Lon okay?" Corey whispered. The wolf flicked an ear: that could mean anything. "Can you shift back so we can talk?"

Melvin sat down to scratch at his neck. Some kind of thin collar ruffled his fur.

"Should I take that off?"

In a flash the wolf pressed up against the mesh, presenting his neck.

"Okay, got it." Corey wiggled his hands through the wire, searching out the buckle. Not a collar, too thin, more like jewelry. A chain. Corey worked the chain around, searching for the clasp. Melvin whined softly. "I'm hurrying, I'm hurrying."

Finally he found the lobster clasp and worked his thumbnail against the lever. "Silver, huh. Your friends play dirty."

The necklace, a sturdy silver box chain, fell away from the wolf's neck. Tension seemed to flow from the animal, who stretched front up, rump up, and then wasn't an animal any longer.

"I need to eat. Something. Anything." Melvin wasn't getting up from the pine duff, but sat, hunched and gray.

Corey'd packed his pocket for Lon. But—"Here." He knelt to poke half the roast beef sandwich he'd brought as otter recovery chow through the chain link fence.

Vadas wolfed the bread and meat down in two bites. "More." He clung to the fence, color returning to his face.

"That's for Lon." Corey jammed the rest of the sandwich back into his pocket.

Vadas shoved his hand through the links to drag Corey against the fence. While the clang of impact still reverberated, Vadas raided his pocket. "If you want Lon back, feed me."

With his cheekbone crushed into chain link, Corey couldn't see past the bright pain. He fell back on his ass when Melvin thrust him away. Clawing at the disappearing food didn't keep Melvin from devouring it, in four bites this time, and with a bit of chewing. Damn it!

"If you've messed with Lon because of that..." Corey would find a way to exact payment.

"Lon will be fine, if and only if I get down there before your army finds him." Vadas snarfed up the last crust. "Now, where were we?" Dr. Melvin Vadas dusted crumbs from his fingers. "Ah, yes. I don't believe they are my friends."

Food was a shifter miracle. Vadas pulled himself up the fence to stand as assured while stark naked, muddy, and bloody as he ever was in a suit in a lecture hall. "They are, however, still subject to my will." He said nothing about his appearance or his condition. "And they will stay that way. Hand me those jeans, please." He pointed behind Corey.

First Lon's sandwich, then his clothes. No. Corey clutched the heap of clothing. "How's Lon? Is he okay? Where is he?"

"He was fine when last seen or heard from, and I believe he's still in the den by the creek." Vadas snapped his fingers. "I need to be dressed to get him out of here. Now."

Damn Vadas for being right. He'd have to do the talking; the Fish and Game team wouldn't listen to Corey. He threw

187

the clothing over the fence. Vadas dressed, mashing his feet into the sneakers that looked far too small. "The chain, please." He snagged the strand of silver through the fence and strode away, heading to the gate like he was taking the podium for a Nobel Prize.

One of Ray's law enforcement officers came along the fence line on the far side of the creek. "You. You just can't follow directions, can you?"

"I needed to find my keys," Corey shot back, knowing that didn't explain chain link marks across the bridge of his nose. "I'm not messing with your operation." Much. "Find the otters?"

"No," the LEO admitted. "Did you see any wolves?"

"Last night I saw one that was brown on top and buff underneath." Corey could say that with perfect, if incomplete truth. "I think it would blend in pretty well." He gestured to the ground, gray and buff with fallen evergreen needles and sprouted with flexible, mostly leafless deciduous stems.

"Yeah, it would." The LEO carried his rifle at the ready. "This enclosure's big enough to hide a couple of them, damn it. There'll be some arrests for sure if we can find the animal."

Vadas was drawing near the gate. "Ho, gentlemen! How good to see you."

The feeling was not mutual—the glares and stares of the three werewolves standing with the sheriff could have cut Vadas in two. The Forest Service LEO interviewing them dropped his clipboard and stared.

"You know anything about wolves in here, mister?" One of the LEOs stopped Vadas some thirty feet from the gate.

"There's one. I spent a rather uncomfortable night in here with it. Alone and unarmed." Vadas adjusted the cuff of Lon's jacket. "Violent beast."

"Lucky you, then, walking out of here," commented the LEO.

"You have no idea." Vadas headed for the gate. The three adults outside the pen started, as if they'd push him

188

back, but didn't take more than a step forward. The LEO shrugged and headed toward the stream.

"Hey!"

Corey whipped around to the source of the shout.

"You can't just—" Jack Schwimmer, clothed now, dashed to the gate. "You can't!"

"Can't what?" Vadas sneered. He marched on. "Leave this pen? I believe I can, and no one to stop me."

"No!"

A brown streak pelted from under a spruce tree. Corey stopped breathing. No! That wolf attacked in full view of the officers. The wolf covered the distance in two huge bounds, headed directly for the gate. Or Vadas. After everything, was he going to be slain?

Schwimmer crouched into a two handed stance, a pistol raised. The wolf leaped. Schwimmer fired twice. Vadas went down, knocked off his feet by a wolf as large as himself. Oh fuck—Corey's department head would get mauled to death while bleeding from a bullet wound.

Man and wolf fell. Both lay still. Corey gripped the fence tightly enough to cut. *Melvin, no, no...*

Every officer in the pen came running. They rolled the wolf away from the man, splitting their efforts to save both.

Schwimmer dropped his hands, the pistol dangling loosely from one finger. "Oh fuck, I didn't, oh fuck, no, oh fuck.... Whit, I'm so sorry." He folded in on himself, and didn't offer resistance when another officer came running to confiscate the gun.

"Heart shot," said Ray, his hands smeared with great gouts of blood. "Total goner." He put his hand to the wolf's throat in search of a pulse, but no matter how he groped, he didn't declare a heartbeat.

Vadas sat up. "Winded but unharmed, gentlemen. I do believe we need to congratulate our marksman." He let a LEO give him a hand up from the ground, in keeping with his "elder statesman squashed by the beast" demeanor.

Schwimmer watched Vadas approach, his eyes wide and his fists clenched. Vadas clapped him on the shoulder. "Good shooting, Jack. The skill will serve you well in Wyoming." One more pat, hard enough to buckle Schwimmer's knees, and then Vadas passed through the gate. He came to stand in front of the man, woman, and a boy of perhaps twelve. He stared into the adults' eyes, passing from one to the other. "Thank you so much for your concern. Barbara, you and your family are going to enjoy life in Wyoming so very, very much."

Corey let go of the wire, not caring about the blood dripping down his palms. Running down the hill, he couldn't reach the gate fast enough. The wolf-shaped wolf was dead, the rest couldn't give themselves away, and there was no reason now why he couldn't barge in on this operation. He had to find Lon. Ray would understand.

The pines rustled and creaked in the breeze, and sometimes kept him away from the fence, like they knew he couldn't stop to really look. The glimpses he could spare from his footing didn't show him Lon in any form, but that might have been the tears trying to blind him.

He burst through the gate, panting hard and looking around wildly. "Did anyone see the otters?"

"You probably scared them into the next county, jerkoff." Ray looked up from the carcass. "Besides, you were told to stay in the truck."

"I had to know." Corey headed to the stream, to be stopped by a Fish and Game officer.

"Why do you need to know so bad?" he asked.

Think, think, think. "Part of my research involves otter habitat. This wolf may have interfered with my data." That was so half-assed, but the officer seemed to be considering it. Corey begged Melvin silently for some sort of backup.

Vadas rose from the wolf's side, where he'd been doing something to a front leg. "Absolutely. Dr. Levigne's data is essential." He came to join Corey.

"You two know each other?" demanded the officer.

"Certainly. Dr. Levigne is one of my department's up and coming stars." Melvin stuck his hand out. "I'm Melvin Vadas, head of Economics at the University of Colorado." The officer took it, and from the twist of pain on his face and the roiling in his forearm, was probably sorry for it.

"Doesn't explain why you're both knee deep in this operation," Officer Suspicious grumbled, once he got his hand back.

"Dr. Vadas is here to check on my fieldwork in endangered species impacts," Corey improvised an explanation that worked for both two and four-legged versions of his department head.

"Absolutely. We need to check on the otters." Melvin strode forward with the unstopability of a frigate under sail. Corey trailed along in his wake.

"Hey!" The Fish and Game officer tried to stop them by grabbing Corey's arm. "You said 'economists,' not 'biologists.' This is bullshit! Stop!"

"We said 'economic impact of endangered species'," Corey bluffed. "We're still interested in the species." He pulled out of the officer's grip. Even if he'd been identified as "not the alpha", Corey wouldn't suffer manhandling. He followed Vadas to a very tracked-up section of bank, damp enough to form good prints and dry enough to hold them. Corey helped stomp them flat. No sense giving away the number of tracks vs. the number of carcasses.

Vadas knelt. "Otters. Oh, otters."

"Lon," Corey called. "Lu. Come on, guys, we're here. It's safe. Lon!" He stayed farther back on the bank. "Psst, Melvin, give the otters some room before they drag us back." He inched sideways, disturbing more evidence.

"Oh, right." Melvin scooted backward, obliterating paw prints with his knees. "Otters!"

Corey called again, adding "It's safe" to every blandishment. Surely Lon would remember those words?

191

Surely Lon knew the sound of his voice? Surely Lon was okay, and not chomped to hamburger somewhere in the woods?

How long had it been? Lon had restarted his fur clock during daylight yesterday. But still, even in the misty morning not long past dawn, he'd been in fur for more than twelve hours. Ten was his practical limit, he'd said. Would Lon remember why he should care enough to come out of the den?

Please, please, please, let Lon still be in that furry body. Let an intelligence far beyond mustelid normal still lurk in his little flat head. Let Lon remember that life without fur was possible. "Lon, buddy, come out." He knelt by Melvin and held out both hands. "Lon!"

Corey held his breath and shushed Melvin—was that Lon's soft chitter?

"Yeah, baby, it's me. You can come out now." Maybe he should have called Lon "Fuzzface" instead, but he was done catering to other people's sensibilities. He wanted his lover, and he wanted him now. How much coaxing would it take? "Please come out now."

Besides, Melvin was the only one who knew how much he meant that endearment. "Lon, it's okay."

A tail emerged, broad and strong, attached to a flexible spine and short leg. At last the front end of otter appeared. Lon, with a fuzzy, wiggly bundle in his mouth. He lifted his head, looking at them as if to say, "Isn't this the silliest thing you've ever seen?" The baby otter paddled the air and squeaked in the weak sunlight.

"Oh, my goodness," Corey mumbled, and then his breath caught, for knowing Lon would correct him: "No, just one." "Who's your little friend?"

"Nothing should be that cute." Ray startled Corey for speaking from behind. "That much cute is flat unfair to the world."

"I can live with it." Corey smiled.

Lon clambered over the stones to deposit the baby gently in front of Corey. "Aw."

192

"Aw is right. And so is fuck, except I'm not supposed to cuss in front of the kids," Ray groused. "Hey, George!" he called over his shoulder. "Go get the carrier out of your truck! We got otters!"

Lon nosed the baby and disappeared between the rocks. More squeaking, and he returned with a second baby, who wobbled on unsteady feet to his brother. Or sister. Corey would only swear that the second pup fell on the first one. A chorus of squeaking ensued. The little fuzzballs toppled on each other, sounding like dog toys gone wild. If he wasn't about to explode of worry, Corey'd die of the cuteness.

"Yes, you are a clever fellow," Corey told him. Where was their mama? And had he and Lon just been tapped as foster parents? Lon bounded back to his bolt hole and disappeared into the rocks again. Corey cast a quick sideways look at Vadas. "How many, do you think?"

Vadas shrugged. "There were two adults last night. One of them had an incident with the wolf. I hope she's not hurt too badly."

Melvin creaked to his feet like he'd petrified. Corey felt more than heard a hip joint snapping on the journey to upright. Must have been a hell of a night, but not a peep of complaint did Melvin utter. He did lean on Corey's shoulder for those last few inches. "Adorable," he pronounced, as if baby otters couldn't be darling without his imprimatur. "And an excellent sign of the health of the creek."

Chittering from the rocks kept all the humans rooted to their spots. The babies wiggled and squeaked, finding Corey's knee with their little fuzzy muzzles, and proceeded to suck wet spots into the fabric. Charmed in spite of his worry, Corey was annoyed with George for showing up with a wire mesh cage. He scooped the infant otters into a towel, bringing a chorus of high pitched squeals, and that, more than Lon's soft encouragements got Lu out of the den.

She moved stiffly, unwilling to put weight on one foreleg, hopping to the bank. Lon stayed by her side, nuzzling her neck and chittering. Step by step, he stayed with her to the humans. She stalled at the cage, torn between her babies and her need to run. She trembled.

"It will be okay, Lu," Corey tried to reinforce Lon's message, even though she didn't speak human. His soothing tone had to mean something to her.

Lon pushed her near the cage. He stuck his nose in to sniff the babies, who squeaked all the more. He backed out and licked Lu's cheek.

"You know her name?" Melvin asked.

"I've seen her along the creek. I couldn't keep calling her Otter A." Was that enough of an explanation?

Apparently not. "And what do you call this remarkably helpful fellow? Surely not Otter B?" A guy who was stuck in a wolf body until about ten minutes ago shouldn't be razzing.

"That's Lon. He's a great guy." Corey cut off the questions by offering more encouragement to the wounded female otter. "Yeah, Lon's pointing you toward help. It's okay, go on in with the babies. "

The female otter touched noses with Lon, nuzzling and finally licking his vibrissae down along his cheek. Then she stepped into the cage and didn't protest when George closed the door. Corey heaved a sigh of relief. Get all thoughts of otter catching out of people's minds, just so no one was tempted to pop a towel over Lon. Not that he couldn't shred terrycloth at will. Maybe if they tried a Kevlar cloth...

"We'll get her to the vet and all patched up. Any idea where her den is?" Ray asked.

Corey stood up, his eyes never leaving Lon, who'd backed up a couple of steps and was eyeing him thoughtfully. "When I first saw her, she was downstream from here. I don't know how she got caught, but she might have been dug out. You'll need to check."

"I certainly will." Whoever Ray checked on wasn't going to enjoy it, not from that tone of voice. "Now, about Mr. *Lontra canadensis* here. Where does he go?"

194

"Upstream, about a mile." Upstream, toward Corey's RAV4. Because explaining a trained otter, though for some reason Ray wasn't asking, imagine that, was slightly easier than getting a nude man through the woods. "I think if we let him out, he'll head back to his proper territory." And if not, Corey would coax him into the truck and hope he didn't stick his head up when a cop was patrolling I-70. If Corey couldn't get him to take his fur off. A chill ran through Corey. Had Lon restarted the clock on fur time?

"You want to follow him?" Ray inquired. "See where he goes?"

"Yeah, absolutely." Thank God for a man who'd dated a shifter—he was feeding Corey all the right lines. "Hey, Lon, ready to blow this joint?" He put on a happy face, which might not have fooled a guy who smelled emotions, and started toward the gate. "Come on, let's go!"

Lon bounded past Corey, looking every bit as happy as a man unjustly imprisoned would look for being released, which was about as happy as he usually looked with his fur on. He humped up and stretched out through the gate, and turned to look at the three wolves in human form huddled against the side of the Forest Service pickup.

For any other otter, sticking his tongue out would be anthropomorphizing a little too much, but Corey knew damned well what *hurr, hurr, hurr* meant.

"This way back to the stream, Lon." How the hell was Corey going to get rid of Ray?

They followed Lon until they reached the end of the fence, and then Corey started to direct their path. "No, Lon, not to the water yet. Come on, this way!" He kept up a steady patter, punctuated with pats on his thigh. He had to keep Lon away from the creek. How long had he been in fur? How loud was the water calling? Terrified that the water's voice could drown out his own, Corey kept talking to Lon, who occasionally bumped his leg, sometimes stopped to groom, and in general seemed happy enough to amble along with the humans.

"Where ya going, Corey?" Ray inquired. "I gotta get back."

"Oh, don't let me stop you." Perfect! Corey leaned down to stroke Lon's head, mentally promising caresses of a wholly human sort, once Lon stood five foot nine again.

"You can't." Ray didn't leave. "See, this whole endangered species thing means I can't risk you absconding with a wild specimen, no matter how habituated to humans he seems. But if you were to get into your truck with a human who needs a pair of pants, that's a whole 'nother issue."

"You already know the score. You don't have to watch to keep me from taking a wild otter, who's about as wild as your Aunt Matilda's pet Pekingese," Corey grumbled. "You just want to see him shift."

"Something wrong with that?" Ray drawled.

Yes, actually. The whole habit of secrecy. "We're almost there, Ray. You can see the truck ahead." Corey nodded to the blue RAV4, which made a strange cool note between the evergreens at the picnic ground. "You don't need to watch."

Ray took a good long look at the truck, and then at Corey. "Either you got that purty SUV at a bargain price, or you don't want company after your pal stands up."

Wasn't the first time someone had drawn conclusions from the baby blue shading to lavender of the truck. Since it was the right conclusion, he didn't argue.

"Don't want company," he said, and made himself smile brightly at the Fish and Game officer. Absolutely not. Not for Lon's successful de-furring, and, not… Corey didn't want to think it could happen but… what if Lon couldn't take his fur off?

"Gotcha." Ray chuckled. "Well, dude, you two have fun. Glad we got him back. You'll be hearing from me, since there's probably going to be a prosecution about the animals, and we could make it stick about hunting without a

196

permit, since Jack Schwimmer shot that wolf. But you know what? I don't think he wanted to shoot the wolf at all."

"He didn't." Corey knew with absolute certainty.

"Now, how'd you know that?" Ray gave him a sharp look.

The remaining distance to the truck had looked too long a minute ago and looked way too short now. Corey'd have to answer. "That gun has a couple of quirks. It was my grandfather's."

Ray let out a long whistle. "Don't know how long it'll take to get it back, but I'll make sure you're listed as owner of record. Seeing as so many pistols of that vintage don't have proper registrations."

"Thanks." Corey shook the officer's hand. "Thanks for everything, and sorry about last night, but..."

"But you were worried. I get it." Ray ground Corey's knuckles just a little, probably paybacks for the fright of all those clattering pans after lights out. Corey'd waited quite a while to commit his burglary. "You guys give me a call sometime. We'll all go have a beer." Ray knelt to stroke Lon's fluffy sides. "And then you both have to tell me the rest of the story."

"Thanks. What you don't know you can't tell. So after the case is wrapped...?" Corey wanted this man out of sight right now. "We'll keep in touch. Bye."

Lon slid out from under Ray's hand back to Corey.

"Got it. Have a good one." He turned back, and if he kept peeking over his shoulder, Corey couldn't call it unreasonable. But still...

"Okay, Lon." Corey knelt to hold Lon's face close to his, silently cursing his lack of roast beef sandwiches. "He's a friend. Now please take your fur off."

Lon whuffed into his face.

"Come on, Lon, I know you can. It's been a while since the cavalry came over the hill, you have to be ready. Aren't you?" Corey showed Lon his watch, which they used as a "is it time yet?" signal, but Lon didn't seem interested in it. "Come on, Lon, take your fur off, let's go home. Please? You said I should keep talking to you, and I will, so please take your fur off. Please? You have to tell me all about last night, and what happened to Lu, and…"

Lon pulled away from Corey's hands but instead of stretching out and making his fur go away, he groomed a hind foot.

"Very flexible, Lon, and you know I love it when you get your leg that high in bed, but you're wearing fur. You don't come to bed wearing fur. Please take it off, please."

With increasing desperation, Corey started basic explanations. "You aren't really an otter. Well, you are, but only part of the time. You've been in your fur a long time these last couple days, and it's time to take it off. We'll get your clothes back from Melvin, he needed them right then. You have more clothes at home. You wear clothes like I do, like this"—Corey held out the hem of his shirt, which Lon sniffed curiously and nibbled. "It's clothes, babe, you wear T-shirts and sweatpants around the house, and you wear dress pants and button-down shirts to the bank, and you're supposed to be there tomorrow morning. You have a job; you go there to earn money…"

Oh shit, he was boring Lon with human details. Every sharp tooth in his head showed with that huge yawn. "Yeah, the job's a job, but it got us into this adventure. Please, babe, put your fur away. Let's go home. We need to feed the koi."

Oh, yeah, that got Lon's attention. He stretched out and trembled. That usually presaged a shift, but the trembling went on and on. Lon relaxed and looked quizzically up at Corey. The cuteness of his whiskers standing out around his muzzle didn't make up for him still having vibrissae. "Come on, Lon, you need to put your fur away. Try again."

Lon licked his front foot.

"Babe, otter life might be a lot simpler than human life, but I can't share it with you. We have a life together, Lon, remember? And I gave you a ring, and I'm sorry it was silver, but at least I knew what was wrong with Melvin, and please, Lon, please, put your fur away."

Lon circled around Corey's feet and whuffled at his now-empty pocket. "I know you remember what it's like to walk on two feet. I know you remember what it was like to hug me and kiss me and take my clothes off and roll in bed with me." If Ray had hung around to listen, too bad for him. "I know you remember that, I know you like doing it, I know you want to do the things we have to both be human to do. Come on, Lon, please?"

Lon twisted under Corey's hands again, and tensed for his shift. He trembled, and trembled, and... Oh fuck, usually he had his fur off in about a tenth of this time, but Lon was still trembling.

"Please, don't give up, please, Lon, keep trying, please come back to me the way you were, please," Corey begged. Lon had been in fur so long, but he remembered what Corey was asking him to do. And he was trying. "Please, Lon, take your fur off. I love you, I need you, please."

Corey put his arms around Lon, trying to push hope and effort and desire for his old life back into him. "Keep trying, please, don't give up, please don't stop trying, please..."

Lon collapsed on the ground, still an otter. He closed his eyes.

No, no! "Lon, love, please, don't give up, not now. You're so close." Corey scooped Lon into his arms, burying his face in the fur he wanted so badly to be gone. "Don't give up, Lon, please..." He rocked Lon gently, imploring with all his heart, longing for the sweet, playful man who shared his home and his life to come back. "Your name is Lon Ewing and you cook sweet potatoes and kale to make me happy, and then I kiss you until your clothes fall off. I can't kiss you with fur on, and you like kisses and you like making love with me."

Lon trembled and went limp. "You can do it, Lon, I know you can do it, please, please." Corey's tears dampened the fluffy brown fur, the hateful, hateful fur that wouldn't go away. "Keep trying, babe, Lon, I love you so much. Don't leave me, please."

The otter in his arms might be an otter forever. Corey wept, begging though his tears. "Lon, please, try again, please…"

The otter shook, terrible spasms shaking him from head to tail. His limbs went stiff and his entire being vibrated. "Yes, babe, yes, you can do this, you can!" Corey urged into the furry shoulder where his face rested. "I love you, I love you so much, you love me, I know you do, keep trying…"

Corey's armful went limp and nearly pulled out of his grip for being more than a hundred pounds heavier. In an instant Corey's face rested on smooth skin; his hands touched arms and not paws. Lon's sweet bottom was two rounded mounds, and had no tail. Corey wept harder for the success. "Lon, babe, you did it. You're you again! You were you, but, you're all of you again. Oh, Lon." Carefully he turned his lover to sitting, holding him and maybe squashing him out of relief for holding a human form once more. "You put your fur away."

Corey pulled back to look into his lover's face, to share the triumph when he didn't think he would ever see those deep brown eyes shaded by lashes and brows, and a mouth of human teeth, with a tongue and lips made for kissing.

Lon lifted one hand, gazing at it with his lips parted and confusion in his eyes. He offered his hand to Corey as if he needed it identified.

"Yeah, you've got hands again." Corey sniffled and grinned. "Isn't it great?"

Lon made a squeaky noise. In only the most distorted of sounds, he might, might, if Corey really squinted, have said, "Hands."

CHAPTER SEVENTEEN

Lon opened his mouth again, and more not-words squeaked out.

"Come on, Lon, let's get you home, and fed, and cuddled." Feeding him had helped before. It had to help now. Not fish, though. Nothing to remind Lon of his other life.

Lon had struggled so long and so hard to get back to his two-foot status that Corey had almost despaired. He wouldn't have to release Lon into the wild, but this human-shaped person that looked like his boyfriend wasn't Lon in any meaningful way. Had Corey fucked him up beyond repair?

"Come on, yeah, there we go." Corey helped Lon up off the ground. He wobbled, like standing upright was a novel thing. "Yeah, that's how us two-foots do it, we stand up. And we walk…" Corey wouldn't try Lon with walking just yet. Too unsteady, and if Corey hadn't grabbed on tight, Lon might have hit the ground after one second on his own. "Balance, balance."

Lon leaned against Corey, like he enjoyed it, but this not-hug shit scared Corey. Lon didn't seem to know how to use his arms. Not even his hands, his arms. Retraining—yeah, he'd coach Lon through. Struggling to recall how the evening after the aquarium went, all Corey could remember through his alarm was that Lon's skills came back. Eventually.

"Walk, let's try walking." Trying to sound chipper so Lon wouldn't panic, Corey sounded false in his own ears. If his words didn't have any meaning, they were really screwed. "We're going to get in the truck, and we'll go home, and you'll be in nice, familiar surroundings." All Corey had to offer were words, and Lon hadn't had a lot of words since yesterday morning. Ten hours was his outside practical limit, he'd said. Twelve was pushing it.

Lon put his fur on yesterday afternoon. Sixteen hours ago.

They had only a few feet to go to get to the truck. Arms around shoulders and waists, Corey half carried, half led Lon. With baby steps they covered the distance. Lon seemed to have no idea what to do once Corey opened the door. "Get in, sit down," didn't have enough meaning: Corey ended up lifting Lon into the truck and swinging his legs around, narrating every step.

Covering Lon's lap with his jacket and strapping him in solved the worst of the public nudity issue, and parceling out his layers dressed Lon's upper body enough to not attract attention. It would have helped a lot if he could follow instructions or had any idea that a waffle weave Henley went on over one's head. Was this what dressing a baby was like?

Food, food… Lon needed something. A chewy granola bar lurked in the console, emergency rations. If this wasn't an emergency, Corey didn't know what was. He unwrapped the bar and handed it to Lon, who held it between his hands to sniff.

"Eat up, Lon!" Corey threw the little SUV into gear. "Eat the chewy bar. It has cranberries, your favorite."

Lon licked the bar, considered it carefully, and flipped it out the window.

Damn it all! Granola wouldn't look like food to an otter.

Corey fought not to spin up to NASCAR speeds on the dirt road. Getting airborne might get them to food faster only if they could stay in the air for more than ten feet. Twenty over the speed limit once they hit pavement wasn't half fast enough to get to food. Idaho Springs was way over on the rustic side, but there was a chain burger joint by the highway. This damned road got longer and longer, or maybe what he needed at the other end just kept getting more important.

They sat in the parking lot with a bag of precious food. Corey wouldn't risk Lon feeding himself a second time: he held an English muffin sandwich to Lon's lips. "Egg and bacon, babe. Open your mouth." Oh man, if they couldn't manage anything as basic as eating… Corey nearly crammed the sandwich into Lon's mouth. "Take a bite, damn it!"

Lon pulled away, shrinking into the corner of the seat. He batted at Corey's hand with an arm that at least he was using, even if he seemed to be using it as a club.

"Sorry, Lon, sorry." Corey forced himself to calmness, a surface phenomenon if ever there was one. "Let me show you. Mmmm…" He nibbled a bite of sandwich and chewed his mouthful of ashes with exaggerated jaw movements. "Mmm…" he repeated, when Lon's eyes grew a little brighter. The first spark of interest since he'd shifted. Corey'd take it.

He pulled off a bite of the breakfast and offered it. "You eat this bite, Lon. This is for you." Would Corey be coaxing Lon to do everything for the rest of his life? Could he even get results with coaxing? He didn't try to force the morsel in this time.

If Lon had vibrissae on, they'd be pointing forward with his interest. His brown goatee had an entirely otterlike mien right now, but at least he was approaching the food with the sort of intent that spoke of eating. He leaned in and nipped the egg and bread from Corey's fingers. He chewed and swallowed, and opened his mouth again.

"More?" Oh thank you, God, that was progress! Not enough progress to let Lon feed himself, but he ate every scrap of the breakfast sandwich and licked grease off his lips after the potato cake.

"Drink?" Corey demonstrated with the orange juice, sucking through the straw. Lon tried twice before he got the hang of steady swallows, and glory be, he held the cup for the last third of the liquid! Maybe Melvin's sandwich theft was only a setback, not a calamity.

"See, it's coming back," Corey crooned. "You'll get your skills back, the big ones and the little ones, and you'll be fine. Words and tools and good times for both of us."

Prattling on about anything and everything while he pointed them back to Boulder, Corey watched from the corner of his eye when Lon started touching things in the truck. He was using his fingers! Clumsily, like they were barely more than floppy sausages on the ends of his arms, but he was using them! Running his fingers over his shirt, his seat belt, the jacket, the armrest, he explored the tiny bit of universe inside the truck. Corey hit the lock button, praying the sound wouldn't excite Lon's curiosity to trying to open the door. "Careful, babe," he had to say, when Lon turned his attention to Corey, stroking his arm and tugging at his sleeve.

Maybe fine motor skills weren't the best thing for right now, not when Lon discovered his fingers worked together and pinched the underside of Corey's arm. When Corey got the truck under control again and determined that the damage was all honking, frayed nerves, and possibly soiled trousers in the big rig they'd swerved in front of, he twined his fingers through Lon's. "I like holding hands with you, and this way you won't cause any accidents," he suggested, not entirely sure he didn't need new britches.

Damn every time he'd respected Lon's need not to be poked and prodded with a thousand questions. He should know more about Lon's otterness! Or he should be able to ask someone! Lon's mom? His dad? Corey'd spoken to them both: they'd know him. They'd know he was asking for a reason. Except Lon's parents were voices through a cell phone. Lon's cell phone, password protected. And Lon had no concept of password or cell phone right now. He'd probably bite the case.

Just as soon as Lon was back in his right mind, they were making emergency contact lists. Moms, dads, bosses.... Might need that one real soon.

They held hands all the way back to Boulder. Lon played with Corey's fingers while Corey kept up his chatter, naming objects and telling stories, suggesting things they'd do. Asking questions, not so much. Corey could ask, but Lon would only give rusty squeak answers, and nothing that seemed like a word.

But damn, it was better than it had been forty-five minutes before. Corey pulled into the garage and unclicked Lon's seatbelt.

He still had to come around the truck to open the door, but Lon put his bare feet down and hopped out without prompting. Corey nearly hit the ground with relief. Progress!

But Lon seemed perplexed by the door knob and had to twist it over and over, watching the latch appear and disappear. When he finally tried shutting the door and opening it, his face brightened with the discovery. Then he had to try it again.

This could be a really long rehab.

"This is our home, Lon. We live here." Feeling stupid with the simplicity of the explanations, Corey still kept up a waterfall of words. If Lon heard enough words, if he was deluged with enough ideas, perhaps they'd wear back into the familiar channels in his mind. "This is our kitchen. We make food here. Are you hungry again?" Feeding Lon helped bring him back before, and that breakfast sandwich might have been all Lon had since the wolves accosted them yesterday. What could he make that was fast?

Cereal, no, absolutely not. A food that required tools to eat neatly, and had too much possibility for not being eaten neatly, worst possible choice while riding the thin edge of panic. "Let's give you a sandwich. We have turkey and cheese. See, the cold food stays in the refrigerator..." Lon explored while Corey built sandwiches, alert to his whereabouts and glad Lon didn't try to go near the butcher block full of knives. Mishing in the drawers of dishtowels and plastic containers was safe enough, and Corey parked his hip casually in front of the tool drawer, lest Lon try to play with pointy, sharp, pinchy things. Good Lord, trying to think like a recovering otter was making his own mind go to mush.

Lon stuck his head into the fridge, sniffing and touching, picking up a tub of cottage cheese to bite at the rim. Corey took it away from him. "Come eat your sandwich, Lon. We'll eat cottage cheese once you've remembered about bowls and spoons." He offered the plate with a smile, luring Lon to the table. "Come sit, this is a chair, we sit on the chairs when we eat our food."

Lon abandoned the fridge and the cottage cheese, which yay, Corey wouldn't have to wipe off the floor today, but left the door hanging open. Corey patted the seat of the chair, which got Lon to park his butt, and scooted him close to the table. "Can you feed yourself?" His stomach dropped even further, contemplating a "no" communicated by inaction.

Picking up the top slice of bread, Lon studied it for a moment. He sniffed the bread and licked at the mayonnaise. Good, he was using his fingers... Corey willed himself to find any speck of hope.

"It's all good to eat, Lon." Corey smiled and *nom nom nommed*.

Lon ate the sandwich, one layer at a time.

Pumpkin materialized between Corey's feet, meeping furiously. Lon cocked his head at her. "This is our kitty cat. She's hungry. She missed us..." Corey put some wet glop and kibbles into her dish and wondered if he was reteaching Lon language all wrong. "Missed" was now redefined as "swat with claws that doesn't connect." Lon yanked his hand back much faster than he put it out and returned her growl about two octaves deeper.

"Well, she missed me more than you, I'm afraid." Corey took Lon's hand to lead him farther into the house. How much otter still clung to him after spending too long in fur? "One day she'll get used to you."

Lon surveyed the hall and the bedroom with curious eyes, following where Corey led.

"This is our bedroom, Lon. We sleep here. Both of us sleep in this big bed…" Was that ever going to work again? Trying not to think about a Lon stuck in nonverbal, no-tools, otterlike mode, Corey chattered on and on. "Here's the bathroom. Do you remember what we do in the bathroom?" At least he didn't have to get Lon's britches down—he still wasn't wearing any. "This is the toilet, we pee into the toilet."

Corey's heart dropped somewhere into the vicinity of the Earth's core: would he have to toilet train Lon? Could Lon be toilet trained? Or would he remember? What the fuck had Corey done to his lover by not rescuing him sooner? He should have just shot the wolves, they were dangerous animals… That walked and talked and ate with forks most of the time. Hating himself for everything he'd done and not done, Corey tackled the practical matter before him the only way he knew how. He stepped out of his own jeans. "See, when you need to pee you aim at the toilet…"

Lon did nothing. Corey's only relief was in his bladder, draining of hope and urine.

"Pee."

Lon's voice was breathy and rusty, but that was a word! A Word! Corey would have happy danced to hear it, risking hosing down the bathroom. "Yes, pee. Do you need to pee? Come stand here with me." The first genuine smile he'd been able to give his otter lover stretched across his face.

207

And Lon peed. And shook. And turned to the sink, though he seemed confused by what to do next. Corey turned the water on for him. "Yes, great! We wash our hands after!" Lon reached for the towel unprompted. Corey undied a fraction.

Toothpaste, oh heaven. Corey squeezed a dab onto his brush. Lon reached for his own toothbrush. Was that a clever mimic or did he recall what to do? Corey squished pale blue goop out for Lon. And oh! Even better than removing twenty-four hours of crud from his mouth was watching Lon scrub his teeth without seeming to think about it, just up and down and all around and spit the foam away when he was satisfied.

What else had come back? Corey peeled out of the T-shirt he'd slept in, revolted by his own scent. Lon struggled to lift the Henley over his head, but got it off without assistance, even if it was inside out now. He tossed the shirt at the hamper, and who cared if he only got it part way in? Corey turned on the water in the shower, mindful of how he'd first seen Lon's otter form in the tub. "Let's take a shower. We're scruffy and gross."

Was this safe? Would the water call Lon's fur back? Too late now—Lon hopped into the tub to push his face into the spray. He batted at the streams with both hands. Playing, okay... Corey jumped in after and pulled the curtain to keep playtime off the tile floor. "Get your head wet, Lon, and I'll wash your hair." Corey stuck his scalp into the water and reached for the shampoo.

Lon luxuriated under his hands, so much like other days when a lazy shower was foreplay. Don't even think about sex now, not when his partner was not in his full right mind. Not when he was stuck in some weird twilight state between his animal self and his human self. With both hands hooked over Corey's shoulders, he seemed far too otterlike, rubbing and wriggling against bare flesh. "Calm down there, Lon." Corey willed his cock not to notice the goings-on.

208

Thinking about the bandages on his leg getting wet turned his little head's attention. Being under Melvin's permanent protection might be more than a formality now. Problem for later—not a damned thing he could do about it. He wasn't craving red meat. Yet.

He got them shampooed and Lon recovered the idea of soap pretty fast, swirling his foamy hands over all parts of both of them that he could reach. "I think we're clean now." Corey redirected him once they'd both been scrubbed down for the third time. "Really clean. Let's go get dressed." Damn but Corey needed some clothing—his body was screaming *Safe! Relieved! Lon! Home! Sex!* But his head was having none of it. Even when Lon discovered Corey's erection and had to get it clean. "Later, babe. You have to be able to tell me in words what you want." He caught Lon's hands to rinse them. "Do you remember towels? Nice soft towels that get your skin and hair dry?"

He did! Lon rubbed himself all over with the green terrycloth and scrubbed at his hair. He stopped, grabbing Corey's attention with half his face peeking through folds of towel. He'd played peekies that first time, too, only then he'd been four-footed and fuzzy. The look was the same.

"Clothes, Lon."

But Lon stopped to comb his hair, even running the tines through his goatee and smoothing down the whiskers.

Yes! Yes!

The drawers of clothing fascinated him. Corey opened Lon's underwear drawer, only to be pushed aside. Lon picked up the skivvies one pair at a time, examining them and then tossing them over his shoulder.

"Just pick one pair and put them on. Underwear keeps your junk from swinging." Corey wanted Lon's junk out of sight and not taunting him with promises of a homecoming celebration that would be totally skeevy if Lon wasn't tracking. Even running on instinct, it would be taking advantage.

"Put some underwear on, okay?" Corey collected a pair to demonstrate with.

Lon didn't care. A pair of blue bikinis turned into a hat. Staring out at Corey through one leg hole, Lon grinned and stuck his tongue out. He went back to mishing in the drawer.

Should he laugh or cry? "Lon, babe, I don't know if you're teasing me or if you really don't remember. Underwear goes on your butt when you aren't being silly." He plucked the unconventional headgear off Lon's head and knelt at his feet. "This is your foot. Put it through the leg hole." Lon cooperated, sort of, letting Corey maneuver him into the underwear and pull them up over his hips. "See, you're getting dressed. Two-foots wear clothes. You're a two-foot right now, so you wear clothes too."

Lon snapped the waistband against his skin a couple of times. He looked in the mirror. Corey held his breath—thoughts seemed to be chasing through a mind that worked in who knew what sort of fashion. Then he opened another drawer. He had to examine the jeans he pulled out, but he slid his legs into the denim and worked the zipper with only a minor bobble. The shirt gave him no trouble at all.

"Shoes and socks too. We need to go outside." Or maybe Corey needed to go outside alone. Was it safe to take Lon? Or was it less dangerous to leave him in the house alone? Keeping an eye on him won out.

And Lon put socks on without coaching.

Every little bit of progress made Corey hope that more would come. He'd wait until Lon was asleep for this next task, but the fish had missed meals as it was. He couldn't make them wait as long as it would take for Lon to fall asleep. With his joyous explorations of all the familiar things in the household, it might take him until midnight. Corey got his head through his shirt in time to see Lon rolling himself in the blankets. "Maybe I should leave you there while I run outside?"

But what if Lon drank something poisonous before he got back? Otter curiosity, human hands, no supervision? Oh, recipe for disaster.

The lump in the blankets sat up, the covers falling away from his head and his eyes frightened-wide.

"I won't leave you, Lon." Corey held out his hands.

His arms were suddenly full of Lon, who clung tightly. He burrowed his face into Corey's neck, clutching handfuls of shirt and vibrating with his tension.

"I promise, I won't leave you." Corey held his trembling lover and stroked one hand up and down Lon's back. "You'll come outside with me for a while." He offered reassurances with voice and body until Lon relaxed into something approximating a hug. "I'll hold your hand, okay?"

This had to be progress, right? Lon responded to ideas, not just show and tell. He'd understood, that had to be good. Corey clutched him a little tighter. Everyone needed something right now, but the hundred and fifty mouths that needed breakfast weren't nearly as important as the man in his arms.

Not a word did Lon utter, all through getting shoes and jackets. Corey led him outside, trying to leave some breaks in the running commentary so Lon could get a word in edgewise if he wanted to, but he didn't try. "One scoop of fish food for the koi should be enough for now." Corey filled his measure to the top. "We'll feed them again this afternoon. We'll throw some food on the water but we won't get wet."

Shedding the top layer of fish food into the greening grass as Lon tugged him toward the pond, Corey hoped there'd be some fish left if they'd been visited again. A black feather floated on the surface. Cormorant. The netting looked intact. "Slow down, Lon." Oh shit. If he hadn't been feeling his responsibilities to the creatures he'd brought home, he'd say "Fuck it" and pull Lon back inside. "We'll feed them, that's all."

211

P.D. SINGER

Orange, black, and white shapes writhed below the surface, attracted to the patter of morsels Corey threw in. Fishy mouths hoovered up the pellets, which Lon scattered with wild abandon. "Fiss!" he breathed, and it was almost a word.

"Yes, fish," Corey agreed. "Koi. We brought them home for the pond. You dug most of this pond. You know how to use a shovel and other tools." He offered the scoop to Lon.

"Fiss…" The hand reaching into the scoop was brown and webby.

"Lon, no!" Corey dropped the scoop and grabbed that hand, willing it with all his might to be a human hand again. "You have to stay human. No fur! Not now, no fur!" He pulled Lon away from the edge of the water. "Please no fur, you have to remember how to talk and use tools again. Inside, we have to go inside." He hauled Lon across the lawn, begging with every fiber of his being for Lon's hand to be a hand.

Lon fought him, trying to turn back to the pond, and his hand wavered pale and brown.

"No fur, we're staying dry, we're staying inside," Corey babbled, tugging Lon toward the house. "You're human now, you have to remember about being a human." He pushed Lon through the door and threw the deadbolt, hoping the knowledge of how to defeat such a simple barrier from the inside would elude his captive until he recalled why Corey had to latch it.

"Human, Lon, you're on two feet and have to stay like that." Corey pulled Lon into a hug once they were safely in the kitchen. Maybe not so safely—Lon craned to see over Corey's shoulder, and the only thing that would interest him that much was the pond, visible through the window. Corey turned them so he faced the window. Lon's head swiveled, though he didn't let go.

"Lon, babe, look at me, Corey cajoled. "I'm right here, you have to look at me. See? Human, we're walking on two feet for a while." He used both hands to redirect Lon's gaze. He stared deeply into Lon's dark eyes, which only slowly lost their wildness and focused on Corey's face.

Oh, okay. Crisis averted. For a moment. Corey brushed his lips across Lon's. "You have to be human for me to do this, babe, and you like it. You like it a lot." He swept across Lon's lips again.

Lon reached back, and Corey stayed lip to lips with him. Lon didn't seem to know what else to do, and Corey wasn't going to take advantage, making him grateful when Lon sighed into a warm pressure against his torso, his head on Corey's shoulder.

They stayed like that a long time.

The fish still needed to be fed. Lon went to explore the laundry room. Corey followed, ready to snatch the bleach away if Lon tried to taste it, punching up a number on his phone.

"Steven, hi, it's Corey. Can I ask a favor?" Their musician neighbor and his Irish lover Hugh were his best bets for a helping hand. "Do you mind coming down and feeding the fish? I dropped the measure by the pond. They just need the rest. Um, Lon's… he's…not well." He should have thought up a good reason before he picked up the phone. "I can't leave him, not even to go out back. Okay, thanks." Corey drew the blinds over the kitchen window, lest the motion of their neighbor's visit attract Lon's attention again.

Lon had all the clothing out of the basket and on the floor. Corey opened the washer. "Now you can throw all the white things in here, Lon! See, these are white…"

Corey called again that evening, while Lon built towers out of canned corn and condensed soup. "Thanks, and um, yeah, if you or Hugh could feed them in the morning? Um, no, I don't think Lon needs to go to the hospital, this will pass…"

He hoped. Lon seemed to be recovering human things, slowly, and he hadn't said much yet. Corey grew hoarse with his commentary, hours and hours of it that ran late into the evening. "Lon, time for bed, okay? You probably had a bad night. I sure did. Come cuddle with me. We'll sleep, and you'll wake up with more words. Lots of words. You'll be fine."

Corey woke in the night, his drowse lost in the freakout of being alone. "Lon?" He followed the hollow thud of a hand against wood. He found Lon on the floor in the light from the front window, his guitar in his lap, the neck pointing the wrong way.

"You'll remember how to play this." Corey turned the instrument the right way to, and placed Lon's left hand on its neck. Lon would have to recover this knowledge without Corey's active coaching—he didn't know how to play. "Want to try?"

Lon plucked an open string. The tone sounded louder than it was in the silent dark. He tried again. They sat until the moon moved past the big window, listening to the open stringed notes, sounding one at a time.

What was Corey going to tell Lon's boss? Monday morning rolled around too fast. Corey was on the phone half an hour before the bank opened. "Sorry, Petra, but Lon can't come in today. No, he's not well…" Thank goodness for her sympathy. "In fact, he can't even talk right now." That was the absolute truth. Corey'd tried to coax speech from his boyfriend and gotten a few half words.

Unfortunately, his own responsibilities couldn't be solved with a phone call. Two hundred and fifty-some undergraduates expected him to enlighten them on the effects of governmental policies on the stability of the economy, starting at eleven a.m. sharp. "Shoes and socks, Lon. We're going for a ride." There were usually a few front row seats not occupied by future bankers, lawyers, and politicians. Corey could keep an eye on Lon, and if the universe smiled, Lon wouldn't be disruptive. Corey stuck a ball of rubber bands in his pocket, which might amuse the universe and Lon for an hour.

"Ride." He opened his own truck door this time, and fumbled with the seat belt. Corey held his breath. It took him four tries, but Lon got himself buckled in. Win for sure.

He wouldn't get anything else done on campus today, but they made it to the classroom with about thirty seconds to spare. Lon sniffed the air and patted trees and rocks between the parking lot and the building. Since he didn't act much different than a particularly giddy version of a student with spring fever, Corey let him ramble.

At the top of the stadium-style lecture hall, Corey paused. Perhaps he wouldn't have to cajole Lon into an hour of immobility. Melvin Vadas, in a suit and dress shoes, his only concession to the informality of CU in the form of a regimental stripe tie pulled away from his undone collar, flicked some PowerPoint slides across the screen. Maybe there was an upside to a department head with access to his office.

Melvin turned to face the steeply raked lecture hall. "Thank you all for joining us today," he boomed, disdaining to turn on the sound system. He caught Corey's eye briefly in the middle of a piercing scan of the students. "Dr. Levigne is indisposed this morning, so I'll discuss the Federal Reserve System in his stead...."

There was absolutely nothing Melvin couldn't expound on at length for an undergraduate class, so Corey pulled Lon out of the way of the latecomers. "Let's go for a walk," he suggested. "You went to college here, so let's go see the campus." Maybe it would jog something loose in Lon's head. "Did you have classes in there?" Out in the sunshine again, Corey asked questions and pointed out landmarks, and only a few students eyed him like he'd grown a second head.

A Frisbee sailed past their noses on the quadrangle next to the library. Lon plucked it out of the air and sent it wafting back.

They ambled around campus; Corey steered them away from the student union. He would have liked a cup of coffee, but that big fountain in the courtyard might be a problem. No koi in it, but no sense tempting Lon with water deep enough for him to swim in. If he was wearing fur. Had Lon ever taken a midnight dip in the fountain, or played in the turtle pond on the north edge of campus? Had he rustled through the reeds in the small creek that ran beside the Anthropology building and Old Main?

How long until it would be safe for Lon to shift again? If he didn't wear his fur again by Sunday, what would happen? And what would happen if he did wear it?

Corey had to stop borrowing trouble—focus on getting Lon to talk again. "Do you remember where my office is?" He was running out of simple things to talk about.

"Yes." Lon grinned at him and pointed the right direction.

Corey stopped and stared. A word! A whole word, unslurred, unhissed, a whole word! An answer to a question! Correct, even! The implications weakened his knees. "Well, then, lead on!"

Melvin Vadas met them halfway down the corridor.

"Thanks for taking my lecture this morning," Corey said. For the first time since he'd met Lon, he wasn't afraid of his department head. Lon skittered to Corey's other side, but didn't flinch away more.

"Considering how this weekend went, it was the least I could do. In fact…" Melvin paused until Corey opened his office door and all three of them were inside. He shut the door behind them. "It doesn't begin to cancel the debt. Your friend, my possibly ex loan officer, and you got me through this weekend. Our endangered species problem is resolved, therefore our building plans can go ahead. I removed the biggest threats to my leadership of the pack. Although—" Melvin stopped to scowl. "The threats either weren't as united as they led me to believe, or something else entirely was at play."

216

"Something else," Corey muttered, unwilling to stop Vadas' train of thought.

"Oh?" That raised eyebrow demanded explanation. "I stared down the barrel of a pistol at close range and thought I was dead."

"Jack meant that bullet for you." Corey drew the only possible conclusion. "My grandfather's Luger throws low and to the right. I'm the only one who can hit the broad side of a barn with it."

"Indeed." Melvin regarded Corey thoughtfully. "Jack will have a great deal to contemplate from his new territory somewhere south of Worland."

"Where's Worland?" Corey'd never heard of such a place.

Melvin grinned with every tooth suddenly as sharp as before Corey'd removed the silver necklace. "Few know. Roughly the middle of Wyoming. Wish him and his little pack luck. Barbara won't forgive the loss of her brother."

"Ouch." Corey'd done all he could to thwart the werewolves with sub-lethal means, and they'd brought death to each other. "Better him than you, but... I'm sorry anyone died."

Vadas went solemn. "As am I. We are predators, and quick to assert dominance, but I wouldn't have sentenced him to death." He stopped to consider. "Though he did put silver on me. That's cheating."

"He or someone else?" Corey'd seen the mêlée but couldn't say who had done what or with what degree of furriness.

"Perhaps the rest should be grateful that I don't precisely recall, though it seemed to be a group effort." Melvin's smile was all wolf again. "As may be, the challenger didn't walk out of that pen on two feet, thanks to your grandfather's inaccurate pistol and our curious friend here." He turned to gaze fondly on Lon, who'd clearly decided that listening to Melvin wasn't as much fun as spinning around and around in Corey's office chair. "Lon called alarms several times for me, and would have removed the silver had Whit not nearly drowned him."

217

"Removed…" Corey choked. Drowning hadn't happened and couldn't be worried about now. "With hands?" And that all probably explained itself….

"Indeed. I couldn't have prevailed without him." Melvin patted Lon's shoulder as it whizzed by. "Consider him, no, consider you both under my permanent protection."

"Thank you." Corey hoped never to invoke that protection, although come tenure time he might need to, should someone in the department prove hostile. Except… Corey'd removed the bandages the game warden had patched him with, and the wounds seemed to be healing cleanly. He'd had too many things to be frightened of in the last few days. Corey's fear for himself surged up to choke him. "I got chewed on by one of your buddies. What should I be planning for the next full moon night?"

"Dinner and a movie with Lon." Vadas didn't miss a beat or ask to see the bites. "Or a concert. Full moon falls on a Friday this month."

"Are you sure?" How could he sound so nonchalant?

"Certainly." The corners of Melvin's mouth turned up. "There's a new werewolf movie coming out. Take Lon and rejoice in the knowledge they got most everything wrong. They always do. He'll still be the only shifter in this couple."

"The only…" His knees threatened to drop him.

"Unless you wanted to join the pack?" Vadas lifted one eyebrow. "It could be arranged. Our numbers are a bit low lately."

Lon stopped twirling. Clutching Corey's hand hard enough to hurt, he stared up with huge eyes.

Corey didn't need his lover's fear to make his decision. "Thanks, but no thanks. Your protection is more than enough." Corey squeezed back. Lon rubbed his face once against Corey's forearm and resumed twirling.

One less thing to worry about—back to more immediate concerns. "Lon spent a lot of time in fur, and he's… having a rough time coming back from it." Corey had to stop Lon's

218

whirling before he threw up from watching. "He gets bits and pieces back, sometimes chunks."

Lon must have gotten a lot of ideas from "twirly office chair" because he picked up a pen and started scribbling across a blank sheet of paper, and two that weren't blank. Nothing there Corey couldn't salvage; he let Lon scribble. He held the pen correctly for writing, so maybe....

"But he's not talking, except for one real word a little bit ago. And he's a long way from his old self."

Melvin stopped Lon's attack on the papers to cup his chin and look deeply into his eyes. Lon didn't need words to say how much he hated the direct examination—he twisted this way and that to escape what proved to be an iron grip. He calmed, and went meek, dropping his eyes away from Vadas' gaze. Once Vadas released him, he scooted the chair backward into the corner and stayed hunched over. Corey wanted to smash Vadas' face for scaring him.

"He's still in there, Corey," Melvin told him. "I don't know how much he can come back out, or how long it will take." Vadas spoke with sympathy Corey hated for needing.

"Sounds like you were in fur longer than he was, but you're bossing law enforcement around and teaching classes." Corey pulled Lon against him—his lover responded by wrapping his arms around Corey's hips and hiding his face in Corey's waist. "Is one sandwich at the moment of shifting that big of a deal? Or...?"

"He's an otter, born to the otter clan." Melvin took a step back, which let Lon relax a fraction. "We wolves... operate a little differently. And I'm the strongest among us. Even so, I'm glad you and your hands came along when you did. Things were getting... a little black and white."

"So what do I do?" Corey stroked Lon's hair, too reminiscent now of the pelt that had covered his whole body. "How do I help him?"

Vadas shrugged. "Talk to him, do things with him. Help him find the familiar pathways of his life."

219

"I'm trying." And apparently succeeding—Corey had to confiscate the stapler before everything on his desk ended up in one well-attached mass. Lon pulled a length of tape out of the dispenser. Corey ripped the tape off the cutter edge and let Lon fight with the strip that clung to his fingers.

"And don't let him shift until he absolutely has to," Melvin concluded.

Nothing new there, Corey'd been doing all that, but the confirmation of his methods made him feel a little better. "We had a moment yesterday, but he stayed two-foot."

"Good. There is hope." Melvin's words were small comfort.

"I called him in sick to work today. Guess I better ask for the whole week." Not having firmer directives from his only shifter expert worried him.

"A pity." Melvin smiled, and it was the small, human smile that went with the search for silver linings. "I could have gotten that construction loan."

"You might still," Corey offered. Surely not all the wolves were like the ones he'd met. "Once he's himself again. Maybe it won't take long." *Please let Lon be himself again, soon.*

CHAPTER EIGHTEEN

Some of the bounce had gone out of Lon—he marched by Corey's side to the sub shop on the far side of Broadway. Not wanting to jinx what might be progress, Corey asked yes or no questions, and observed what looked like normal human alertness from the corner of his eye. Feeling greatly daring but determined to shake a little more out of Lon, Corey followed him through the shop door and asked, "Roast beef or tuna salad?"

"Roas' beef." Lon grinned at him, and Corey grinned back, as much for the words as for not finding out if "cooked fishy from a can," as Lon had dubbed it once, would prove a setback. Lon directed the sandwich maker to add mustard, lettuce, and tomatoes, with a yes here and a half a word there, but he not only managed to get his sandwich built to his specs, he unwrapped one end, ate roll, meat, and veggies in the usual fashion, and wiped his mouth with a napkin. The soda with a straw presented no problem. Corey tried not to pump his fist with a yes! with every familiar, uncoached action that would have been impossible twenty-four hours earlier. And Lon looked both ways before crossing the busy four-lane street between College Hill and the campus, when on the way to the Hill he'd watched Corey for cues.

Progress! And more progress! "Let's go home," Corey said, and nearly buckled when Lon responded.

"Feed kitty."

"Yes, and feed Pumpkin." A whole thought! With multiple words! And he did it again!

"Feed fishies."

"Yes, we'll feed the fishies too." Driving became a bit hazardous—Corey tried not to let the film of tears lead him into any crashes. Lon had more to say on the way home, two and three words strung together, and Corey'd never been so happy to hear about red pickups and roads going up to the mountains.

"Yes, we can ride our bikes up the canyon," Corey agreed. Lon—wasn't back, exactly, but he was more of his human self than he'd been since he put his fur on to hunt for silverscale dace. Best conversation in days!

"I like Melvin," Lon commented. "He's warm." Now that nearly got a spit take, but Lon amplified, "All furry. Hugged him."

At last, Corey could find out what happened while he was cuffed to an antique. "So you changed back to two-foot in the night?"

"Yesss." Lon shivered theatrically. "Cold! Climb fence. Run away. Bad wolf!"

"Ohh... So another wolf kept you from getting away in the night?" Shit, Lon could have scooped up keys and clothes, and high-tailed it to the truck. He could have been out of there. If he'd gotten away when his mind still worked like a human's.

Lon nodded hard enough to rattle his brains. "Bad wolf! Two bad wolfs! Stupid Whit"—Lon lost a word and demonstrated with both hands—"me in the water!" He peeked sideways at Corey, who wanted to hear the rest of this story without the hazards of moving vehicles.

"He pushed you into the water? So you had to put your fur back on?" Corey supplied the missing verb and tried not to count the words in the growing sentences.

"Yesss! Stupid dumb Whit! Bit him!" Lon crossed his

arms with a *humph!* that would do a grandmother proud. "Wanted to hurt Melvin. And me."

"I guess Melvin is our friend now." Corey pulled into the driveway. "He said we're under his protection."

"I caught him fish!" Cycling faster than his emotions had ever gone, Lon went proud. A wolf the size of Melvin might have needed a lot of dace, but Lon clarified, "A big fish! Wolf ate trout!"

"That was really nice of you to catch him some dinner." How had they communicated?

"He bit the bad wolf. Whit bit Lu. Melvin bit him." Lon demonstrated with snapping teeth. "Lu needed fish. And I ate one. Um, little fish."

"Dace?" Corey cared, but not as much as he cared that eating them kept Lon and his fellow fur person going.

"Yeah." Lon went small. "That was bad."

Corey'd had long hours to consider what he'd tell the otter, and getting Lon back in more or less one piece was worth a whole stream full of fish. A whole species. "You didn't eat them all."

"There's more!" Lon brightened, and maybe drooled a little. "Lots!"

"Lots" was more than "many," and "many" was more than eight, or maybe this wasn't otter counting. Didn't matter—either way there likely was a breeding population still swimming in that section of Whiskey Creek. "Excellent."

Lon bounced around the house, doing half a task or a quarter of a task, breaking off to tell Corey more details of his furry adventure. "I bit Whit's paw! Nasty!" He made a face to go with *Ptui!* and picked two more pairs of underwear off the floor. "Whit was sneaky. Mean and sneaky."

"He and his buddies put silver on Melvin, so yeah, sneaky." Also dishonest, underhanded, and a rotten son of a bitch, which Whit might or might not have seen as a compliment. Barbara hadn't been fazed by the insult. Lon's vocabulary was coming back, and might come back faster if

Corey stopped speaking like the parent of a three year old. "I'm not completely sure about their rules, but Whit and Jack sure seemed to be subverting them."

"Bad wolves."

Corey couldn't be sure if Lon understood what he'd said or not, but he'd try to keep to his usual vocabulary. "Will you please give Pumpkin her wet food?" Every task brought Lon that much closer to his old self.

"Won't make her like me." Lon's eyes went sad but he found the partial can in the fridge and scooped glop into her dish with the right spoon. "She won't ever like me."

"Keep feeding her, and maybe one day…." Even if it was only cupboard love, it would be an improvement over the distance Corey's marmalade kitty kept now, complete with sound effects. Corey drew Lon into his arms, and incidentally away from the dish, far enough that the cat would come to bury her face in her chow. "Anyway, I like you."

"I like you too." Lon snuggled into Corey's embrace, with his arms all the way around Corey's chest, not tucked between their bodies like paws. "You asked and I put my fur away."

Lon. Oh, Lon. A hitch in Corey's voice broke his words. "I was so scared you wouldn't. Or couldn't."

"It was… hard." A tremor ran through Lon.

"I'm glad you did." Corey spoke from the bottom of his heart. To never hold Lon again as a man… The tremor passed through his own body. Lon was Lon enough for a kiss, and maybe that would speed the return of other thoughts. Corey nuzzled into Lon's hair, pushing his way down the smooth skin of his cheek.

Lon lifted his face and their mouths met in a slow brush of lips. The nose bumping Corey's was dry and pale, human, and Lon's lips full, mobile. Torn between crying and rearranging his growing erection, Corey closed his eyes and lost himself in his lover's humanity.

Moving his erection had almost become urgent enough to break apart for a few inches when the doorbell rang.

Corey would have blown it off, but… Monday night. And he owed Steven. He nose-booped Lon and went to answer the door.

"Um, I'll just go around and feed the fish. Sorry to interrupt." Any conclusion Steven drew from Corey's appearance was probably right. "I thought Lon might like to practice that song before we, erm, I went to the session."

"Yeah! Feed my fish!" Lon appeared under Corey's arm. "Let's!" He slid out and led Steven around the side of the house. The guitar in the case on their neighbor's back disappeared with them, his legs flashing white from below his camouflage-patterned kilt. The session at Clancy's was tonight, and they'd planned to go.

Was this safe? Corey went through the house to meet them at the fish food bin on the back patio. Lon scraped food into the measure, chattering in two and three word sentences about his fish. Steven looked over him to Corey with his eyebrows bunched way up. He glanced at Lon and then back at Corey.

A full explanation wasn't on. Corey followed the anxious fish keeper to the shore, Steven at his side. Fooling a professional musician about his anxiety probably wouldn't work.

"Is Lon okay?" Steven murmured.

"He—hasn't been quite himself these last few days," Corey mumbled back. "He's doing better."

Lon flung handfuls of small pellets at the churning surface of the pond. Dozens of bright koi scuffled for the goodies, and Lon *hurr*'d his pleasure. Corey flipped some out toward the center where the less ambitious fish lurked, and watched them scarf up the fishmeal and wheat germ morsels with one eye on Lon.

"Oops!" Lon shoved the scoop at Steven and ran.

Corey fired, "Keep feeding, okay?" over his shoulder, and pelted after him. If Lon felt his two-foot self slipping, Corey'd shore him up, if he could catch him. Even with his longer legs, he had trouble catching the streak of lightning.

Knocking on the door got Lon to open up—he was leaning on it. "Lon, babe, let me in."

He shut the door between them and the pond, and enveloped his trembling lover. "Shh, it's okay, it will be okay. I'll keep feeding them for you. It will be okay…" Corey tried desperately to believe it. What did it mean that Lon's arms were folded up between them again? He rocked them to the sounds of his litany.

Lon had nearly stopped trembling when Steven let himself in through the back door. "All done. Hey, buddy, all those gaping mouths were a little freaky." He grinned, which had to be as big a performance as he'd ever done with a cello between his knees, because it disappeared when he slipped around them and only Corey could see him. Then he stretched his lips in an "Egads! What happened?" downturn. "Um, maybe this isn't a good night for learning a new tune?"

Lon loved the water, he had to run away from the water. The water called to him. Begged him. *Come play! Come splash! I have fishies!*

The fish. So pretty. So nommy. So easy to find in the dark water. They came to him. They begged for food. *Nom, nom, nom,* they ate up the bits.

Corey would see. Corey knew. Corey wanted… But the water called. Corey didn't want him to answer the water yet.

The water called.

Steven would see…

Lon ran. Away from the water, away from Corey, away from Steven. Away from the water that loved him as much as Corey did. The water wanted to keep him forever.

Corey never said keep you forever. He had rings, nasty silver rings. Maybe he meant… Maybe he meant keep you as people forever. But Corey…

Lon didn't doubt the water.

Rap, rap, by his ear. Rattles, make him stop leaning on the door. Make the door open, let in Corey, let in the water's call.

He couldn't hear the water while Corey held him. He folded into Corey's chest and listened only to the soothing *It will be okay.* What was okay? His fur itched beneath his skin. Okay would be to stop itching.

Corey didn't let go. Lon wouldn't leave. *It's okay, it will be okay* ran over him in Corey's words. His itch left him. It was more okay already.

Steven slid through the door. Little thump made music. Music! Music would be okay! Better than okay!

"Maybe this isn't a good night to learn a new tune?"

"Need loud," Lon muttered. "Louder than water."

"Uh…"

Corey rescued Lon from explaining more. "He should try. Let's go into the living room. Lon left his guitar out." He didn't take his hand off Lon's shoulder on the way. "I'd like to hear you play."

Steven could play louder than water. Steven could play his guitar. Or his cello. Or his uillean pipes, pipes were loud loud loud. But not his pennywhistle. That sounded like water.

Steven made the notes bend and settle, first on his guitar, then on Lon's. Lon took it back and had to think which way the long end went. That way. He walked his fingers up a string. Fingers had to go a certain way… *Plink, plink.* Plinks were louder than water. He tried again. *Plink, plink, blong.* Not that way. Blongs let the water talk. Two fingers made better notes. He strummed—*blong!* "Uh…" he looked from Corey to Steven and back. "I don't…"

"Do you mind if we stop dancing around this?" Steven stared at Lon.

Lon looked down. He used to play lots of notes. Good notes, not blongs. Steven wouldn't know where the notes went. Lon didn't know where the notes went. He wanted to call them back.

227

"Something happened to Lon, which you don't have to explain, but it has to do with water and fish and an otter who frolics around in your back yard. Am I right?"

Corey answered, "That's, ah, an interesting thought." He scooted closer to Lon, leg to leg, and ran tickly fingers up and down Lon's back.

Steven snorted. "It's more than interesting. I've seen an otter back here, and so have you, Corey. You play with him. With Lon."

"What?" Corey boggled. "Why would you even say…?"

Lon's jaw fell open. Steven knew? Steven saw? Did Hugh know too?

"When you nip into the bushes to peel down and come bouncing out, the kids can't see you, but, ah, the other neighbors can." Steven jabbed a thumb toward his house. "The human-shaped view is very nice, by the way. Hugh agrees."

That was for Corey to look at! But Steven knew, and he wasn't scared. He didn't smell scared. Or mad.

"Knew I should have planted more honeysuckles." Corey scrubbed at his face.

Steven whapped his guitar and made a horrible blong. "Oh, no, no, no! Those suckers are non-native and invasive! Fernbush or gambel oak or juniper. Natives. But"—Steven muffled his strings and the water got quiet again—"it's okay. I'm cool with you. Hugh's cool with you. And right now the pond's bothering you, so you're having some kind of otter problem. How can I help?"

"Music," Lon muttered. "Have to remember." He tried two fingers on the strings again. *Blong!*

Steven changed where Lon's fingers rested. *Plink!* "It does have power to sooth the savage—"

"He's not a beast!" Corey snapped.

But he almost was. Blongs made the colors go away. Easier for the water to whisper.

"Quote it right." Steven chuckled. "Of course he's not, and what Congreve said was, 'Music has power to soothe

the savage breast.' I assume you're having some turmoil?"
He ran his fingers up and down the strings. A tune poured
out, like water but—not. It called in a way that kept Lon's
fur from itching him, and made the colors come back. "Let's
soothe it."

Lon could play this tune once. He could play the
waterfalls of notes, and someone would dance. Not Hugh,
Hugh never danced, but others, who clicked their heels
against the wooden floor at… at… at Clancy's! Where
Hugh brought him a Coke and Steven a stout and Hannah
would play her fiddle and Emily would sing and play her
pennywhistle… Nope. Didn't even want to think about
pennywhistle music right now. Steven had his guitar and
was playing the water silent, and if Lon wanted that water
to stay silent, he'd better play too. He found a chord and
strummed it when Steven went past it in the runs. The
chord blended, and he found another. And two notes.

And two notes more. Steven began another repeat—
yeah, that's what he called it when the music looped around,
and Lon found the place to fit his chord and six notes, one
wrong. Corey relaxed beside him, and sniffled a little when
they played the second section and Lon got all six notes right.

Steven finished the tune, grinning up from his cross-
legged seat on the floor. "Sounds like you're remembering
it. Let's take a sec and look at some basics. A scale, walk
your fingers up the A string. Open, one, two."

Lon knew which one was the A string, didn't he? This
one? Or this one? Steven plucked a note—he matched it.
Yup, that one. He played three notes to match Steven's
example.

"Okay, the fourth note you switch strings." He played
an example. Lon could follow this! He played the four notes,
and then played them again, adding more fingers, and
switching strings again, counting, "Five, six, seven, eight."

Corey went tense, even though Lon played the notes
back down perfectly. He could relax. Lon knew more

229

numbers, lots of numbers. He played the scale all the way to the top and kept counting for Corey, "Nine, ten, eleven, twelve." He leaned against his poor worried lover, turning his face for a kiss. "Thirteen, fourteen. Fifteen."

"Wonderful," Corey choked out, and tightened his arm around Lon's waist.

"It's an otter/human thing," Lon told Steven, and winked. Boy was it. So many things were coming back! "Let's do a G scale."

He found his G string and plucked his way up two octaves and back down, Steven matching him note for note, and found the Kesh jig using the same notes, because… because… because it was in the same key! They whipped through the tune, although Lon had to pause in the B section the first time to see what Steven did with that tricky measure… It didn't give him any trouble the second time through, nor the third, and when Steven launched into Morrison's jig right after, Lon only missed a few notes.

It wasn't bad enough to make Corey cry! Lon turned to wipe his lover's face. "I'll practice more, I promise!"

"It's not that… It's beautiful. Keep playing, okay?" Corey smushed a kiss onto Lon's forehead and then bolted, wiping his arm across his face.

"More practice sounds about right," Steven commented and got up to join Lon on the futon.

That wasn't very nice of them to make a guy in a kilt sit on the floor. Steven dug in his beer pocket. He poked his phone and listened for a moment. "Hugh, hey, looks like I'm not going to be in for the session. Gonna hang out with Corey and Lon. I'll come get you at closing. Later." He put the phone away, and strummed out an E chord.

That sounded familiar… Lon added some As, and they were off. He remembered The Lilting Banshee with only a little help.

Three hours later, Lon's fingertips had deep valleys and he'd recalled a session's worth of tunes plus he'd learned the song Steven had come to teach him. Corey'd like this one. A noise in the doorway alerted them to their audience.

"Don't let me stop you." Corey's clothes were rumpled, but his face was damp and pale. He gestured for them to keep playing. Pumpkin ambled in to strop his ankles; he picked her up and burrowed his fingers into her coat.

Lon took it from the top. "Brown is the color of my true love's hair," he sang to the strum of his guitar, willing this wonderful man who'd stayed with him through all the crap to really hear the song. "His lips are like some roses fair." He'd kiss the pallor out of Corey's mouth as soon as Steven left. "He's the sweetest face," and the fiercest, and the most concerned, and the happiest, and right now, the most stunned. "And the gentlest hands," when wolves didn't need shooting or fences climbing. "I love the ground whereon he stands." Which was the honest truth. This man had walked through fire for him.

Steven dropped out between verses, putting his instrument back in the case. Lon sang on, loving the light growing in Corey's face. "...when he and I will be as one."

"You'll rock it at the session next week," Steven murmured on his way around Corey and out the door. "Byegottarun." The door shut behind him.

How he made it through the next few stanzas Lon didn't know, but he'd finish this for Corey, who'd died the ten thousand deaths he sang about. He ended with a trailing chord and set the guitar down still sounding. "It's been a hell of a few days, hasn't it?"

Corey let the cat leap to the floor. "Yeah. It has." He opened his arms and Lon was in them, to hold him close and kiss the last of the worry away.

They tangled in each other, squeezing, stroking, exploring each other's faces with lips and tongue. Lon kissed the roses back into Corey's mouth, his joy fierce for having the mobile lips and tongue to lick salt drops from his lover's cheeks. Corey's smiles and gasps went right through his sensitive whiskers, telling Lon more than words ever could about relief and love and fear.

"Are you back?" Corey whispered. "Are you really yourself again in there?" He thumbed Lon's whiskers down, and Lon sucked one of those doubting digits into his mouth.

Lon gave up Corey's thumb for his earlobe. "Yeah. Do you want me to recite multiplication tables or maybe do some algebra to prove it?"

"No, but I'm glad you can," Corey all but sobbed. "When you had such trouble taking your fur off, and then your words came back so slow…"

"Fur seemed like the way I'd always been, until you called me." He'd followed the sound and then followed the words, needing to make sense of them and needing to be two-footed to understand. Every bit as much as he needed to be two-footed to hold Corey now.

"I'm glad you came back." Corey twined his fingers through Lon's hair to pull his head back enough to nuzzle his throat. "I had visions of you putting your fur back on and going to live in Whiskey Creek because that was the best body for your mind."

"I thought about it a couple times too." Not in those exact words, but the longing for the water. Exact words were getting a little fuzzy under Corey's mouth, but that wasn't an otter problem, that was a "need to get Corey stripped and sucked" problem.

"I was so scared."

"Me too." But that was gone in the rising storm of lust. If they clutched each other any tighter Corey'd be inside what remained of Lon's clothing and it was much simpler to strip it off. "Take me to bed and remind me why I put my fur away."

Didn't have to ask him twice! Corey laughed all the way down the hall, checking over his shoulder to make sure Lon followed, as if he'd go anywhere else besides following the trail of the last few pieces of clothing. Even tripping over a shed shirt didn't slow him, and then they were flat in the bed, twining around each other and skin to skin.

Every inch of Lon that had been bare hide before was bare hide now, and no more of his fur remained than ever had—only the patches at his groin and chin, and his thick brown hair that never needed a trim. Corey tried to touch all of him at once, with hands and body and mouth.

They tumbled across the bed, plastered against each other in every way possible, knocking the pillows to the floor in their need to rub here and to lick there. He would have missed all this had he stayed in his fur. He'd never thrust his tongue into Corey's mouth if it was thin and flat—he needed his human tongue that made words like "I think I'm okay now," and "I'm glad you kept trying," and "Roll over, I need to see you."

Corey wanted to see him too—Lon ended up straddling Corey's thighs, their cocks batting together and then clutched in their joined fingers. Lon might have shut his eyes a bit for the firm touch of Corey's hand rolling the thin, velvety skins up and down their shafts, but every time he peeked, Corey's eyes were wide open.

"Stay with me," Corey whispered. "Most of the time."

"All of the time," Lon breathed back, thrusting his hips. "Just most of the time on eye level."

"Good enough."

Oh Lord, Lon needed his hands to touch Corey, his lightly washboarded stomach and the muscles in his arms. If he didn't have fingers he couldn't run one down the groove at Corey's hip or wiggle it into the tight spot where his buns came together. He needed his human form for touching and his mouth for talking, except he didn't want to talk now. Not when he could kiss Corey hard enough to curl four feet's worth of toes—that was twenty, and he could count that high and higher.

Would have been easier to keep his fur on, or let it come back on, but worthwhile didn't mean easy. He wouldn't give up his life with Corey without a fight.

The music did it—music was a human thing, and sex for loving's sake was a human thing, and every wonderful touch and nibble and caress in this bed with Corey was a human thing and it was all Lon's. The only fur he wanted now was the patch of hair at the base of Corey's cock. He ran his fingers—fingers!—through the coarse pubes so unlike his own, and slid downward.

Corey trusted his cock in Lon's mouth, with squared off teeth and a wicked tongue for laving up, down, and around. Corey trusted his balls in Lon's hand, with agile fingers and neatly trimmed nails. He trusted Lon with his most precious parts that he'd only share with another human. Even if human was relative and might change later. Later when Lon planned it.

Oh damn, he would have missed this if he'd kept his fur—the way Corey cupped the back of his head and thrust into his mouth. The way Corey cried out with the joy of his climax that Lon urged him to. And he would have missed being laid flat to the covers and Corey pressing down on him, body to like body, and covering his face with kisses.

And then covering all of him with kisses, neck and chest and hands and hips and cock, where he stayed. Ohh, yeah... He stayed. Not very still, not with the flicker of Corey's tongue or his lips and his warm brown eyes dancing up to hold Lon's gaze and to tease, tease, tease until he got real serious.

Lon forgot who he was or what he was in the incandescence of climax. Pulsing and exploding, he became nothing but joy, losing his control into the wet heat of Corey's mouth. He shattered and rejoined into himself, the Lon Corey called Babe and kept around in spite of, or maybe because of, his two-shaped self.

CHAPTER NINETEEN

Lon knotted the tie under his chin, not wanting to take extra days off when he and Corey would want vacation time in the summer. "I might as well, Corey," he argued for the fifth time. "I can't follow you around on campus all day long, and you have meetings. Staying home alone when I'm not sick will bore me to tears"—not to mention leaving him too close to the pond without the counterbalance of Corey's company. He wasn't sure his endurance could last eight hours, even with his guitar—"so you're going to take me to work."

"What if you misplace a decimal point?" Corey came up behind him to gaze into his eyes in the mirror, his hands on Lon's shoulders. "That could be an expensive error."

"If copy/paste, Excel, and the entire banking industry fail me that badly, the world will have bigger problems than me being furry." He turned to meet Corey's eyes directly, and tried kissing the doubts away. "The creek isn't that close to the bank."

"The creek runs between two banks," Corey jested, but his eyes betrayed his concern.

Lon kissed him again. "Please, let's let me get back to my regular life. Lasagna for dinner?"

What a nice normal day—Lon shipped off two big loans, took an application for another, and didn't see any werewolves. At his request, Petra double-checked his math, grumbling that he had it perfect and should trust himself more. Lon said nothing to that, and ate his peanut butter sandwich in the break room. Today was turning into the day without sunshine for him, but he'd let Corey talk him into not helping feed the fish this morning as the price of getting to work, and he'd promised to be careful.

Aside from a little too much attention while Lon set a pan of water to boil, Corey was doing great with his worry, and Lon felt nothing to worry about. He would have liked to look out the kitchen window at the pond, but Corey bit off an exclamation and turned away when he tried opening the blinds. Lon left the window covered and made do with artificial light. Some things were easier not to fight, if it was just for one day.

Lon picked up his guitar to work on his newest song. He swept his long human fingers over the strings and didn't follow Corey out the back door to feed the koi. The A, D and E minor chords swallowed the water's whispers. He hadn't finished the last verse when Corey came back in to sit with him, reading while he played.

That night in bed he could hear nothing but the pounding of his heart and Corey's soft cries, but he dreamed of scrabbling over boulders dark with snowmelt.

No arguments the next morning, only a tentative smile to go with their goodbye kiss in front of the bank. "You're going to be okay?" Corey asked, and kissed him again for the "Yes."

And Lon was okay, all day through piles of papers and meetings. At its end he could greet Corey with the kind of resounding embrace that meant the day really had been good, not the desperate clutches of one who heard the water.

Leftover lasagna was even better than fresh, and all he needed to make tonight was a green salad. Lon nearly caught his fingers with the knife when Corey roared.

236

"Damn it, Lon!" He appeared in the kitchen with his britches around his knees, holding what was left of the roll of toilet paper. Long shreds fluttered from the mangled cylinder and a flurry of gossamer fragments escaped his shaking fist. "This was the last roll!"

"Oops." Lon really had meant to replace his plaything with some useable buttwipe, but the days after his frolic under the sink had been seriously full of other things to think about. "Sorry about that. Um, I'll go get a new package."

"Never mind. I'll run by the grocery store. I need to pick up some razor blades and some half and half. We used the last this morning. I'll get a bottle of wine to go with your lasagna." He shuffled back whence he came.

Lon pressed his hand against his mouth to choke back the *hurr, hurr, hurr* his lover's righteous indignation and bare tush deserved. And neither of them commented when Corey departed on his errand and left Lon alone. Like nothing had ever been wrong.

All right! Corey was getting back to normal. Lon was ready and more than ready for his life to be calm. More of the same now: he'd had a great day, and the water was quiet. He sliced up another tomato and dropped some pine nuts on the greens. Dinner was ready.

Pumpkin was hungry enough that she scolded Lon from the doorway about the state of her dish. "Starvation!" she yowled, as if she didn't have half a bowl of kibble. He spooned out the glop and got out of the way. How long would it take her to decide otter contamination wasn't as important as her stomach?

The fish were just as hungry and much nicer about accepting their meal. Pumpkin kept one wary eye on him while scarfing nameless ground meat-stuff. He could wait for Corey to get back and feed the fish while the lasagna grew cold, or he could go make them happy and everyone could have a great dinner. He opened the back door.

The water whispered.

Shut up, water. Lon dragged the scoop through the fish pellets loud enough to quiet that insidious voice.

The water murmured.

Lon could turn off the aerator for an hour without creating havoc. Silence those enticing suggestions.

The fish were hungry and happy to see him, rising for the pellets he cast on the surface of his nemesis. He was staying up here, the fish would stay down there, he'd eat lasagna for dinner and the fish could have these nummy bits. The koi flashed orange and white under the surface, rising to snap at the flecks. He threw out another handful.

The water laughed. *I have your dinner.*

Nommy fish, right there. Begging to be caught. Play with the rest. Be the flashing shape among the bright colors, dealing death to the slow. Pull tender meat from flexing bones, lap the salty blood and spit the scales out. Twist in the water to wash his face. *Pfeh* on doughy blobs, and vegetables, ick. He could have fish!

Corey liked his... his... that stuff Lon made. Such a lot of work when dinner only needed to be caught. Why make that... that stuff, that...

Lasagna.

What was he doing? Lon hurled the rest of the fish food at the pond and fled back into the house. Back where only a cat door he could open would keep him dry.

He couldn't change, not now. His fur itched. His fur wanted out. The water wanted him. Lon slammed the door. Pumpkin screeched and fled.

The smell of warming lasagna hit his nose, every individual aroma of tomato, basil, garlic, and oregano. Each scent that meant Corey's dinner. Their dinner. The dinner Lon was supposed to eat with his human lover. He had to stay two-foot. He had to, he had to...

Lon stumbled to the bedroom, one leg too short. With brown hands he scrabbled in the oddments on Corey's dresser, searching. *They had to be here, they had to be.* His salvation lay in a velvet box.

Please let Corey have been too busy to take them back...

Here! Opening the box with fingers and claws, Lon flipped the contents out on the carpet. One he could find, and could slip it on, even on webbed digits. His hand stabilized and the colors jumped out, the carpet becoming a deep wine red, the quilt a cacophony of burgundy and green. A twinkle, the ring would twinkle in the light. He flicked the switch and dove to the floor.

There! On his knees, where he could let his fur come out, he fought. He crawled to the second ring, sliding into the circlet that had been his prison. Now it was his safety. Collapsing to his belly on the floor, Lon panted. The carpet told him no stories of who had walked where, even though his nose pressed against the twisted fibers. One silver ring on each hand, Lon could hear nothing but his tom-tom pulse.

The water was silent.

There was no water.

He couldn't hear the water. Water said nothing to him, just as it said nothing to Corey. Nothing called to him. Nothing beckoned to him. The fish were just fish, not at all tempting in the silent pond. They'd be pretty. If he looked at them.

On even but shaky legs, Lon hauled himself to his feet. His eyes complained of the bright colors Corey had strewn across their floors—the deep wine of the bedroom plush gave way to the striations of the oak laminate floors, trading brilliance for dizzying pattern. He stumbled down the hall to the living room, where he'd see Corey walk through the door.

How had he never noticed the kilim rug in its horrible screaming pattern? What had prompted Corey to defile his space with wild zigzags of red, yellow, and blue? Lon'd knelt on this rug a hundred times, immune to its craziness with his eyes shut in ecstasy for having Corey in his mouth, or a tune to play, or just because otters didn't see all this

239

vividness. He'd always thought the rug an interesting geometric exercise and now the damned thing was trying to pull his eyeballs out. Color was way, way overrated. How did Corey stand it?

Lon fell onto the futon, his hands pressed against his eyes. He'd have to get used to it. Sometime. Maybe next week. He didn't want to look at the rug again. Not when all this bright new color was the knife dividing him from his fur.

But his skin no longer itched. His hands were pale, with human fingers, no webs. His fur couldn't come out. Did he even have fur? He couldn't feel it waiting to be worn. Fur was an untrusty enemy, an ally of the water.

He was safe from all that. Half of himself, but safe. The water couldn't entice him into putting his fur on when he didn't want to. He didn't want to. But he did. He really did. But Corey didn't want him to, not yet, not when the water still wanted to keep Lon forever in its chill embrace.

But he was safe. He tried to hold to his invulnerability. The water couldn't steal him now.

If he had to stay like this forever… Would Corey even want him like this? He loved Lon as a two-foot, and he loved Lon as an otter. Didn't he? What if only half of him remained? Would Corey love him half as much? Or not at all? Or would he love Lon better for not getting into cabinets and shredding the toilet paper and never eating another ornamental fish?

A soft noise at his side wasn't enough to make him open his eyes. The pad, pad of thorned, velvet feet didn't make him look. The fuzzy presence at his side became a warm weight in his lap. He stroked her, not daring to believe she'd come within touching range, and had to look to be sure. Her fur was so soft. And such a terrible color.

Corey came home to a sight he'd hoped for but never expected to have. Lon sat with Pumpkin, who purred loudly enough to hear from the doorway. He stroked her, his eyes downcast.

Corey hadn't been gone very long, had he? Long enough for a miracle, apparently.

Or a disaster. A silver ring twinkled from Lon's hand. He looked up with none of the brightness he'd had when Corey left for the store.

"Oh, Babe." Corey dropped his purchases on the floor and came to put his arms around Lon. "Did the water get loud?"

"I tried to feed the fish." Lon leaned against Corey's shoulder. "I just wanted to be normal."

"You've been through a lot," Corey whispered. "If you aren't quite yourself yet, that's okay."

"No, it's not." Lon jerked up again, startling the cat out of his lap. He hissed at her passage—the little wretch must have sunk every claw for traction. She sat down on the wood floor to wash the rumple out of her dignity, oblivious to Lon now that he wasn't disrupting her rest. "I can barely function. I thought I was okay. I went to work. I came home, I made dinner. And then you left, and I probably should have picked up my guitar and kept playing every tune I know until it was time for bed. But the fish were hungry, so I went to feed them. And the water almost got me."

"But it didn't," Corey pointed out. "You're safe now, aren't you?"

"Now, yeah." Lon held up both hands, backs out. "With two pieces of silver to keep me on two feet."

Oh fuck. Both rings. "You won't have to wear them long, will you?"

Lon sprang to his feet, pacing across the kilim rug. "I don't know!" He dashed one hand across his eyes. "I don't even know! You can't babysit me forever, and we have this big honking hazard in the back yard, and I can't feel my face!" He scrubbed at his beard. "I can't feel anything with my vibrissae, and I'm seeing shit that... No wonder humans are weird, you have all this fucking color pounding at you

241

all the time." He looked down and jerked his head back up much faster. "Do you have any idea how mean this rug is? It's like it wants to destroy my brain."

"We can roll it up until your otter sight is back," Corey offered. That wouldn't be enough, but he had nothing else to offer. If it wasn't the rug, it would be the quilt, or the geometric pattern of the dishes, and he couldn't make the sky stop being blue. And it wasn't the problem, only a symptom.

"But will it ever be back?" Lon demanded. "Just normal? I don't know. You can't know. And here I am half of myself because I don't want to be only the other half of myself." He snatched Pumpkin up from the floor. She *mrp*'ed her startlement but stayed in Lon's arms. He buried his face in her coat, and maybe wiped tears on her. "What if this is the closest I dare come to fur again?"

Corey stood up to catch Lon in a hug. "You were doing really well until you went to the pond without me. Or without your iPod. You said I help, and the music helps, and you can have one or the other or both, and then you can feel your face again. It will be okay."

"Really? It's two steps forward and two steps back." He let the cat flow to the floor and nestled closer into Corey. "And this isn't fair to you—you made the pond for me and I can't ask you to leave your home, and you shouldn't have to watch me like a toddler, and you deserve someone who doesn't destroy the last roll of toilet paper or get your nads half chewed off by werewolves."

"I still have my nads, and I still want you."

They ate dinner, eventually, with Irish trad tunes blasting from the speakers, bands with pipes, guitars, fiddles, and more box accordion than Corey ever wanted to hear. He'd let the damned squeeze box shake all his fillings out if it would just give Lon enough confidence to take off the rings. But he flicked away every tune with a pennywhistle and went to bed with a T-shirt, underwear, and silver on both hands.

"You've been lots more yourself these last couple of days," Corey whispered into Lon's hair. "This is just a setback. It's not permanent."

"If I thought it was permanent, I'd head back to Whiskey Creek and put my fur on." Lon sniffled. "But I don't want to die yet."

"Wait, what did I miss?" Corey broke his own rule on asking about otter things—he had to know this. Death?

"When one of us gets old, or ill, we go to the water. Everyone goes, and we put our fur on, and we play. We have fun." Lon ran his hand down Corey's side. "Everybody together. And after a couple of hours, most everybody takes their fur off and goes home. Except one. Who stays and plays."

"Stays…" A stone grew in his throat and crushed his words. "How long?"

"Nobody knows. We go back to the water and the earth, and it's happy. To just never take your fur off again. There's some kind of thoughts you can't have in your fur. You can be afraid of something like a wolf, you can worry about getting hurt, but you can't think about dying the way you can as a two-foot. So it's not scary. Except I'm not wearing my fur now, I can't even feel my fur, and I know what can happen."

He hugged Lon more tightly. "You aren't going to put your fur on forever, and you aren't going to die, or even live a long time in the creek. We'll talk about this again in thirty or forty years, okay?"

"I love you, Corey, but not even for you can I live like this for thirty years." He held up his hand, the silver catching the blue light from the digital clock on the nightstand.

"You won't have to." Corey put a CD of Gaelic harp on endless repeat. "You have tunes, and you have me. It's not that bad." He tried persuasion with caresses, but both rings stayed on Lon's hands. Corey bought the rings hoping they'd wear them forever, but not out of fear. He left off his coaxing and loved Lon to sleep.

Chapter Twenty

They got through the rest of the week somehow. Lon handed over one silver ring, and wore the other. He also kept his sunglasses on indoors, and had no trace of his usual bounce.

Corey counted being given one ring as a victory, and shot down every one of Lon's gloomy predictions. "You'll be okay, Lon. Really. You'll find your balance," he murmured every morning in front of the bank, and every morning Lon mumbled something that wasn't exactly agreement.

"You didn't sign up for this kind of shit," Lon told him while flipping pellets at greedy fish that didn't make him drool, sprout fur, or even smile.

"I sort of did," Corey reminded him. "Nobody said it was all going to be good times." Even reinforcing his words with kisses didn't budge Lon's gloom.

"What if it's never going to be good times again?" Lon twisted the ring on his finger. "If I can't take this off? Mom and Dad didn't know, and hearing about Aunt Trudy's disappearance wasn't reassuring."

"You don't know if you can because you haven't tried it yet," Corey argued, suddenly terrified at the thought of an Aunt Trudy. He'd found Lon stroking his beard too often to think he wouldn't remove the ring eventually.

"Then I get to be the crazy wild animal who eats all your ornamental fish instead of Donny Downer the two-foot. Either way I'm a craptastic boyfriend. You'll get tired of me not being fun like I used to be. I'm already tired of me not being any fun." Lon pulled away and headed back to the house, leaving Corey standing at the side of the pond with empty arms.

He found Lon in the bedroom piling shirts and socks into a cardboard box.

"What the fuck?" Corey snatched handfuls of jersey and shoved them back into the drawer. "You can't give up like this."

"I don't know how I can go on, Corey, and I won't make you watch me disintegrate. I'd rather go to the water and stay forever than lose everything I am." Lon sat heavily on the bed and stared at his knees. "I don't feel like an otter, because if I do then I'm all otter." He rubbed his thumb along the silver band. "I'm so fucked up. I've turned into… a man who works at a bank."

"Nope." Corey flung the last sock into the drawer and slammed it shut. "You still have a lot of otter in there, because you're seeing this in black and white." He tapped the side of Lon's sunglasses. Lon jerked his head away. "It's all or nothing, and the way it is now is the way it will always be. Maybe that ring trapped some of your human side where you can't get at it, because you aren't seeing that the future could be different than now." He slid to kneel between Lon's thighs, crushing him in a hug that had to squeeze some sense into him. "Hope, it's a human thing."

"Then I'm a crappy excuse for a human too, Corey, because I don't see a lot to be hopeful about." He rested his arms on Corey's shoulders and didn't squeeze back.

"You don't? We found our dace, we thwarted the werewolves—I'm still having issues with the concept of werewolves but the evidence is pretty convincing. We saved Melvin, I'm not going to be a werewolf, and you got your words back. It's all good." Corey launched himself up and over, knocking Lon flat to the mattress and lying

245

down on top of him. The sunglasses had to go—nothing on Corey's head or the ceiling was bright enough to be a distraction—he hoped—and the damned things kept him from trailing kisses across the bridge of Lon's nose and over his cheekbones. "You'll find your balance, and tomorrow is Sat-fur-day."

"You say that like it's a good thing." Lon crushed his mouth against Corey's like he'd never have another chance.

Even after Corey was up and moving, Lon stayed huddled under the covers. Pumpkin pussyfooted up his legs and across his back, to recline against his shoulder with one paw on his ear. Maybe that's all he was really good for now, to be a cat bed. He wouldn't mind at all if she hissed and swatted at him instead—that would mean he was back to normal.

The silver ring weighted his hand like lead. He'd have to take it off. He never wanted to wear it. Who would he be without it? The Lon he'd been eight days ago seemed so far away. The cat didn't mind if he stroked her now. A pitiful trade.

Corey came back into the bedroom with a cup of coffee in hand, lightened with cream. "Hey, sleepyhead." He sat down and made an arm for Lon to snuggle into. Pumpkin grumbled at being moved and sprawled across their ankles instead.

Lon hadn't been asleep for a couple of hours and was pretty sure Corey knew that too. Nice of him not to say, "Hey, coward." He buried his nose and his reply in the mug.

"What do you want for breakfast?"

Lon spilled coffee down his front at the thought of eating. "This is fine. For now."

"You sure?" Corey wiped the mess away with a handful of tissues. "I'll put cream cheese on your bagel. Breakfast in bed?"

Lon's stomach flipped over at the idea. "Very, very sure."

"Okay." Corey kissed the side of Lon's head.

Lon snuggled into Corey's embrace, feeling the minutes flowing past like water. "Guess I should get up." He groped around on the bedside table for the polarized shades that kept the colors from battering his brain.

"Uh, Lon." Corey stopped him before he'd unfolded both earpieces. "Maybe instead of putting the glasses on, you take the ring off?"

Eyes shut, Lon let his head flop back. "Are you in such a hurry to find out if I can't control my fur? I'm not."

"No, of course not." The hurt in Corey's voice chastised him. He reached across Lon to punch the iPod's docking station. A fiddle and a guitar noodled a slow air through the speakers. "More like, do Step One inside with me touching you. Get used to that much, see how you do."

"I… I guess you're right, but I'm scared." What if he'd cut part of himself away with a silver knife and the ring no longer mattered?

"Me too, but I'll hold the ring and give it back if you say you need it." Spreading his fingers to make the light play off the plain band, Corey pointed out, "You can have both of them back if it looks dire."

"If it's really dire, rings won't fit me." Lon shivered. And if things got to that point, he wouldn't have the kind of mind that cared. "If… if it gets that dire, Whiskey Creek would be an okay place to…."

"To visit," Corey cut him off. "On Saturdays with no full moon. That's all you're going to need." His hug turned fierce, squishing Lon's shoulders sideways. "Think positive."

"I'll try." If doubly negative made a positive, he'd be fine. Twisting the ring around and around on his finger, he could delay the inevitable a little longer.

"I'm with you."

Corey meant that to be soothing but… "Why didn't you come for me sooner?" Lon twisted to look over his shoulder into his lover's eyes.

"I tried, Lon, I tried." Corey tipped his head forward, his eyes closed. "I found the cavalry, and I tried to get them over the hill earlier, but... And when that failed, I tried to steal Ray's truck. So I could come after you."

"You did?" Corey? Steal a truck? No way.

"And I did a shitty job of it and spent the night hand-cuffed to a piece of furniture too big to move."

Way.

Corey didn't lift his face until he came to the last words. "I fucked up. I'm sorry."

Okay, maybe it meant more than he'd thought to have Corey here now. Lon took a deep breath and removed the ring.

His face was back! He dropped the ring in his excitement, needing those fingers to stroke his vibrissae. Every pass and flick sent messages through his face. Oh, he could feel all those missing signals! Corey was right there, perfect for a face strop that said *I can feel again!* Best face rub ever!

Corey caught his breath and let it out with a little sob. He nibbled a kiss at Lon's goatee, and Lon could feel it! He bounced a little with his joy.

That disturbed Pumpkin. She slapped at his toes through the blanket. But she didn't get up! Was something missing? Had his otter smell not come back yet? Would it?

Her fur was the color he'd learned to call marmalade last winter, a nice, warm, stripy beigey-brown, not the horrible, eyeball-pulling orange he'd hated looking at the last few days. He wiggled his toes again, and they both laughed when Pumpkin abandoned her snooze to pounce on them. "My eyesight's back," he whispered, making ridges under the comforter to give her a target. "The kitty's the right color."

Also armed and dangerous. She hunted his feet through the bedding and stabbed them with daggers. "Ack!" he yelped, and she raced away, startled but not fearful. Would that last?

"See, better already!" Corey laughed and then rolled over to pin Lon to the pillows. "Isn't it?"

"Yeah," Lon breathed, trying not to say the good news loud enough to give the universe ideas. "I can smell you again."

"Is it bad?" Corey made a face at his armpit. "'Cause we could get really sweaty before…"

They had to. Now, while his senses worked right, before he let go of this man who'd become his anchor. Before he risked anything else changing. "It's your usual morning smell. Soap, deodorant, coffee, a little sweat, and you." Lon dragged in a lungful of air just to savor it. "You smell right. Good."

"You smell right again too." Corey nibbled his way down Lon's neck, swiping his tongue across the big strap muscle. Tilting to make it stand out, Lon let Corey nibble there too, accompanying each familiar caress with fingertips across flesh. "A little muskier? It's…" Corey lifted his head to ponder out loud. "I don't know, fuller? I don't know how to describe smells."

"You never had to." Lon didn't describe smells with words either. And who cared when Corey-feeling tingled up his whiskers with every brush of his face against the top of Corey's head?

Okay, Lon might miss the subtle gold and brown hues of Corey's eyes when they got up close, but he'd live with that if he could just smell Corey, his bottled scents and his natural scents, the way his hair was different from his armpits were different from his neck were different from his belly was different from his groin only inches away. Lon could smell them all, mixed into the wonderful mélange that was this smiling being made of hope and effort, who pinned him down and rubbed him with his whole body.

And then words went pointless, swimming around in his brain like the koi at feeding time, because they'd explore each other with hands and tongues and cheeks. If Corey couldn't feel the ripple of Lon's muscles the way Lon could

249

feel Corey's, he didn't sound at all upset, not the way the "mmm's" and the "ah's" and the "oh's" rumbled out of him. Every sense Lon had was on high alert for Corey's pleasure, and for what Corey was doing back.

Bare skin to bare skin, and fingers to work into Corey's muscles, to wrap around his stiff cock, to grab his muscular cheeks and spread them. And Corey was trying just as hard to find every inch of Lon—if he didn't want to touch Corey so badly he'd lie back and luxuriate, but he had hands, he had Corey, and he had—everything. Everything he was before, everything he was used to being—like putting on fur, only backwards. Putting on hide. He was wearing his hide, and Corey was licking it and moaning.

Nothing in the world sounded like Corey in bed. The water couldn't talk through him or over him—all Lon heard was "Yes" and "more, yeah" and "you feel so good" if there were words at all.

Lon kissed his way down Corey's abs, getting jabbed in the cheek with the best blunt rod ever—he turned to take Corey's cock in his mouth. He had to follow his leg—Corey all but slung it over his head to be straddled in the best position. Surprise—Corey's mouth was as warm and his tongue as mobile as Lon remembered, and if he couldn't concentrate on what he was doing and what Corey was doing—it didn't matter. With large hands splayed across Lon's hips, Corey could just... for as long as they could... which might not be long... but there was tonight. Everything that was best about being human happened all at once, and Corey's fingers drove deep into Lon's glutes with his climax.

How could he not follow his lover into bliss? When the small cries of orgasms rumbled around his own cock, and his mouth captured every salt drop?

And when he turned to lie against Corey's chest, to hold him and catch breath, all Lon could hear was the human thudding of his lover's heart.

When they did finally get up, the music had changed to something fast with fiddles. Lon scrubbed his teeth and the only water he could hear came out of the tap. A shower seemed superfluous, but Corey ran through the spray and found some sweat pants and a T-shirt. Lon didn't bother. Maybe he could get all the way to the kitchen. If Corey didn't get too far away. They could turn up the speakers—the music would carry.

The kitchen blazed with the morning sun, warm with the scent of coffee and the echo of a toasted bagel. Corey'd offered cream cheese. Lon started to take him up on the offer, but the sight of the pond through the window brought him to a halt. He leaned against the sink, staring out at the bright ripples where his fish kissed the surface. A corner of the netting flapped. They'd have to secure it. Maybe he could even help.

Corey slid his hands under Lon's arms, reaching up to grip his shoulders. Lon leaned back into the wall of strength who'd had his back. Everything felt so normal; surely something would shatter in a minute or two.

"Is the water calling?" Corey murmured into his ear.

"Just—like 'I'm here, you could join me.' Not roaring." Lon smiled—the water hadn't sounded this friendly since he'd brought the babies out of the den. He turned to wrap his arms around Corey's neck.

"Good."

And even better, Corey held him and kissed him for long moments that still ended too soon. He jerked out of the kiss with a double take over Lon's shoulder and a "Hey!"

Lon whirled to see disaster through the kitchen window. "Hey! Those are ours!" He dropped to the floor and pushed his fur out. Was the cat door locked? Corey was right behind, flinging open the whole door.

Dumb heron! Lon bounded across the grass, charging for the pond. No stupid bird got to eat all the fish. Maybe one or two, but herons were greedy greedy greedy. Growling didn't help—the heron darted its long neck out to stab the water. It raised its head with a flapping orange and white fish. It tossed the fish to aim down its gullet.

Lon pounced. Dumb slow bird! The fish fell back and disappeared. The heron flapped wildly, jabbing at Lon. Didn't matter. Lon grabbed a feather and slid down into the water. Pullpullpull, make that heron sorry it stole his fish. Ow! Sharp beak! Two could play—he let go the feather and bit one skinny leg. Ow! He bit again.

Flapflap, the bird struggled to get airborne. Fly away, dumb bird. Lon growled at the retreating wings, paddling to keep his head and neck above water.

"I think it got a fish, but it lost the second one. I see what you mean about herons and stocked ponds—it was fast." Corey knelt and grabbed the loose corner. Lon swam over to see what he was doing. "You really scared it."

Lon whuffled. He'd scare that bird. Didn't want it coming back all the time. He could still get out of the pond, the way Corey fixed the net. He was all wet, so time to shake shake shake all the water away. Start at the head, go to the tail shake. Felt nice!

"Hey!" Corey hid behind his arms. "You wretch!"

Lon shook some more. He couldn't remember what "wretch" was but it sounded playful mad. Corey wasn't really mad, was he? Rub against his legs and chase the mad away.

When Corey got all folded like that it was easy to reach his face. Lon rested his paws on Corey's knees and sniffed his wet face. Nope, not mad, just drippy.

"Since you're wearing your fur already, you might as well keep it on." Corey gave such good neck rubs! "I'll keep time and start talking to you at the hour mark. You have fun swimming, okay?"

Have fun—that's what Lon did best! He stuck his tongue out at Corey and bounced back to the water.

Lovely water! Pretty fish—lots and lots. Oh my goodness lots. Twist and turn, nose the bright shapes, do flips in the deep part. Such fun to be in fur. Why had he worried about fur? Fur was great! He chased a white and black torpedo and made the rest scatter.

Corey came out to sit on the bench with his flat noisy picture thing. Company! Lon scrabbled out of the pond to come say hi. Oops—he was wet. Shake!

"Agh!" Corey hid his noisy picture thing behind his back. "Not again!"

Well sure. Every time he got out of the water. His nice oily coat was nearly dry once he shook it. But okay, for Corey. He found a rock from the garden, just the right size to juggle. Lying on his back in the grass, flipping his rock from paw to paw, he was much cuter than anything on the noisy picture thing. And fun! Lon juggled his new toy. Corey would probably scold him not to leave it in the grass. Hmmph. Lon juggled some more and Corey smiled.

Enough of that. Lon tossed his rock back into the garden. Maybe he'd try it with a pine cone.

"Thanks."

Corey watched him investigate the bushes and flower beds. He kept watching, and Lon wanted him to relax. Okay, he'd stretch out on the grass and pretend to take a nap. Then Corey would look at his picture thing and not at Lon. He came to plop by Corey's feet. With half an eye open he stayed quiet, and Corey turned the sound on low.

This trick needed time. Lon yawned, rolling over closer to Corey's feet. Corey watched his picture thingie. A soft whiffle and a half roll, and Lon could keep an eye on his target and still look asleep.

His target wasn't paying attention. Oh darn for him, oh good for Lon. Bare skin showed where his shoes and jeans didn't meet. Lon dozed, or pretended to. Corey looked at his thingie.

Fast as the heron, Lon stuck his nose against Corey's ankle.

"Ack!" Corey jerked his leg away. "You set me up!"

Sure did! Lon bounded back to the pond, chuckling *hurr, hurr, hurr.* What a good joke on Corey!

The water was his friend again, glad to see him and full of fish. Lon's tummy growled—no breakfast. Well, not 'til he caught some. Lon started a slow exploration of the bottom of the pond. Around and around, finding schools of fish, passing by. He really shouldn't, but...why? He was an otter, otters ate fish.

Sounds came through the water, sounds that meant something. "Lon! Lon! It's been an hour!"

He could probably take his fur off now, but he didn't like to do that when he was hungry and breakfast swam past his nose. A burst of speed and he'd caught his snack. Crunch! His fish stopped wiggling. Yum! He hopped out of the water to eat it.

"There you are, Lon. Oh ick!" Corey loomed over him. "Why'd you do that?"

Well *phoo*, Corey didn't want his fish, Corey never ate the fish Lon caught for him. Lon took a bite, slicing off flesh with his sharp teeth. His fish wasn't ick, it was yummy.

"Did you have to do that now? I was calling, it's been an hour. I could have made you..." He waved his hands.

Lon wouldn't stick around to be scolded. Okay, Corey wanted him to go in. He'd go in. And see if the cat still liked him. The cat might want a bite, and then she'd like him! Lon grabbed the tail end of his prize and bounced to the back door.

Why was Corey yelling? He had so many rules.

Lon left most of the water outside and slipped in with his prize, a couple steps ahead of Grumpy Human, who kept calling his name. "Lon, Lon, Lon...." *Pfeh.*

Oh right—he was supposed to do something.... Oh yeah. Put his fur away. He went past the stinky shoes this time, dropped his fish—maybe he should gobble it down first— and pushed. He tingled everywhere as his fur disappeared, his tail went...wherever his tail went when he wasn't using it.

Oops. Lon stared at the back half of a koi. Definitely his koi, with gnaw-marks. Unmistakable at close range. Shit.

Corey blasted through the door. "Lon! Are you—"

"I'm sorry! I'm so sorry!" Why couldn't he have waited another ten minutes? Lon rose to his knees, what was left of his victim cradled in his palm.

"Are you okay?" Corey hauled him to his feet.

Lon stared at his victim. "I didn't know it was so close to time. I was holding off but I was so hungry—"

"I'll make you an omelet." Corey cut him off and started pulling him this way and that. "Are you okay?"

"Fine, perfect, but I—oh dear, I ate it and I wasn't going to!" Maybe Pumpkin would help him hide the evidence: she wound around his ankles, mewing hopefully. "I only wanted to chase the heron away and then—"

"You were going to put your fur on today anyway." Corey grabbed Lon's face in both hands and tilted him up, staring deeply. "You put your fur on, you took it off, and how loud is the water?"

"It's just there." Lon pulled away. Corey wouldn't kiss him now. He'd want toothpaste first.

"Great!" Corey pulled him back. "Put that down."

And never pick it up. Don't be an otter, don't hear the water, don't trash the house, don't don't don't. Lon stared at the half a fish in his hand.

"It's still dead. You can't stare it back to life. Come on, put it down." Corey lost patience and took his fish away to drop on the counter.

At least he didn't drop it straight down the disposal or into the trash. Like Lon was a wild thing and his food was dirty. He reached for it, not sure what he'd do with it now, but unwilling to let it go yet.

"I can't hug you if you're holding the fish." Corey tugged at him.

"You won't kiss me since I've eaten some." He remembered that part only too well.

"Well…"

Corey's arms were Lon's haven, but he knew better than to put his face up now. "I'm sorry. I might be back to my usual, but that's still ottery."

"I know! Isn't it great?"

"Yeah, but…" Why was Corey holding him so tight? Didn't he know that Lon couldn't be a good boyfriend, what with killing paper goods and fish and needing so much hand-holding?

"What's for 'but'?" His words rumbled through Lon's ear, what with his lips close enough to nuzzle the ridgy human shell. "Come on, kiss me!"

"Can't." Lon mumbled his refusal into Corey's collarbone. "I have koi breath."

"Uh…" The nuzzling stopped.

Might as well get it all out now. "And I may be back to my usual, but that's destructive and impetuous and higher maintenance than I ever thought I'd be, and you don't like koi breath. I should move out."

"You aren't going anywhere. I thought we established that." Corey started running his fingertips up and down Lon's spine. Gee, that felt good, and was hard on the resolve. "You're adventurous and brave and I don't mind the maintenance. Which isn't that high."

"I still have sushi breath." That would be a problem every week for the rest of his life.

"Hey!" Corey whirled around to seize a knife from the block on the counter. "So what?" The butcher block cutting board rang loud against the counter—he slammed the fish down and whittled at it, shredding the skin off. "I don't care. You're you, I love you, and I want you to stay for now and for always."

"I love you too, but…" Lon could only stare at the pile of shredded flesh growing under Corey's knife.

"But what? We like a lot of the same things, we teach each other new stuff, and I hope you'll be okay with me

256

asking more questions now— " Corey's knife flashed over the fish. "I won't push, but I could have been more effective if I understood otters better. Or knew how to contact your parents. Or both. Also, I promise my folks will like you." Corey picked up the shreds—could they be called sashimi now?—and held them up before Lon's face. "We're more alike than we are different."

But, but… After everything, all the danger and every impulse Lon couldn't keep to himself? Corey still wanted them together? Lon stared at the fragments of pale flesh and Corey's face. No "ick"?

Corey popped the fish into his mouth. He chewed slowly and swallowed. "I eat sushi too."

EPILOGUE

The sign at the turnoff to the Full Moon Conservancy hung askew, though the scent markers were likely intact. Corey turned down the freshly churned track. He hadn't expected to be back here any time soon. If Lon hadn't taken Ray DeLuty's call and then pitched the project hard, Corey would have declined. But no, Lon wanted to make a party of it, and had been so enchanted that he'd called his parents to join them.

"They'll love you," Lon said for the thirtieth time. "Because I do. They're good people."

"Can I ask them otter questions?" Having his lover's parents' phone numbers in his list reassured Corey a little about further adventures with their son, though they both had lingering questions about Aunt Trudy.

"Nope." Lon grinned, spreading his whiskers. "You ask me first. If I can't answer, you ask them."

Corey parked next to a familiar Fish and Game pickup truck. A blue F-250 with ladder racks and a tool chest had the spot between a fir and the pickup. "I'm not going to be a terrible pest? With ten million questions you don't want to answer?" Lon had fretted about a thousand questions, but the weekend with the werewolves led Corey to apply a serious inflation factor.

"If you are, you're my pest." Lon pulled Corey across the console for a smooch. "Let's go see Ray and the otters."

How many members of his family was Lon including in that term?

They were the last to arrive, mostly because Corey'd spent three times his usual in the shower, trying to remove traces of an enthusiastic morning greeting. He'd rather meet his lover's parents smelling of woodsy soap than semen. Even if it didn't fool them one bit.

Lon bounded down the path, his arms wide. "Mom! Dad!"

Corey hung back from the group hug, until Lon pulled back and grabbed his arm. "This is Corey Levigne, and Corey, my mom and dad, Jackie and Seth Ewing. Don't worry, nobody bites."

Corey wasn't too sure of that, but their wide grins and big hugs went a long way to convincing him no one would bite right now. Seth looked like his son, brown-haired and bearded. Jackie had combed a part into her short brown pelt, and her smooth face silently answered one of Corey's questions: now he needed to know how female otters knew they were mature enough to shift. A question he'd keep firmly to himself.

"The party can start now that the MacGregor's here!" boomed from the far side of the pickup. Ray DeLuty came around to slap Corey on the shoulder and grin at Lon. "Slugabeds."

"They had the farthest to come." Melvin Vadas, dressed in his own jeans for the first time in Corey's memory, marched up the path that led to the creek.

Corey should have expected to see the land's owner, but was still taken aback. Had Vadas given Seth and Jackie grief for being otters on wolf lands? Which now looked like the rest of the woods.

"You took the fence down." The memory of fencing stuck up in a long row through the pines, but the evil chain link was gone.

"My exiled idiots spent more on the fence than they

would have spent on the population studies," Vadas commented. "I have hundreds of feet of useless wire."

The sun warmed another few degrees when Seth eyed a fencepost. "I'll send a pal to make you a bid. He'll be fair."

"Excellent." The gleam in Vadas's eye translated to another bedroom in the wolves' lodge. "Lon, you never mentioned your father was in construction."

Lon's grip on Corey's arm tightened. "I had every reason to keep you two far apart." Lon relaxed, and the blood flowed back into Corey's hand. "Then."

"Maybe you talk business after we do what we came for?" Ray dropped the tailgate on his pickup. "Getting this girl and a couple of slippery brats into the cage wasn't nearly so easy this time."

The squeaks and hisses emanating from the carrier said Lu and her babies wanted out, and they wanted out now. Corey wouldn't risk his valuable fingers on the project, no matter how he sympathized. Two weeks of rehab for werewolf bites, even with catered meals, had to be wearing on her. Maybe not as bad as that first week had been for him and Lon, but she had to be more than ready to get back home. "Are the smells of forest making her crazy?"

"Probably." Lon ran to help Ray lift the carrier out of the back of the pickup.

"Are we going to release them here?" Three appetites would nibble "oh my goodness" endangered fish down to numbers an otter could count.

"Not if you value your silverscale dace population." Ray flashed a grin and flicked a thumb downstream. "We'll take her back to her home range. Too bad the wolves dug her original den out."

At a low growl from Melvin, Ray blurted "Present company excepted, of course."

"Of course." Melvin didn't reach for a handle. Instead, he led their motley parade along the stream. Ray and Lon carried the otters between them, and Corey brought up the rear with Lon's parents. Could get awkward...

"Lon says you've been very, very good to him. You got him through that difficult time." Jackie slipped her hand through Corey's arm, though whether to improve her balance or keep him from running was an open question.

"It was pretty scary," Corey admitted. "I wish I could have called you." By the time Lon could call, they'd been in uncharted territory, but having support around in the preverbal hours would have been nice.

"Now you have our numbers, so you call any time, and we expect to see the two of you for dinner now and then." She squeezed his arm. "Since he says he's keeping you."

Corey let his breath out very slowly. One hurdle down— she wasn't angry for his nearly losing their son into the water. Two hurdles—he could quit worrying about Lon running to the bedroom to fling socks and underwear into makeshift moving boxes. "Good. Because I'm keeping him too."

Especially after the bright white grin Lon threw over his shoulder at Corey's words.

The stream chuckled at snowmelt jokes beside them, and the trees creaked with the breeze playing in their tops. Pine duff and rocks crisped beneath their boots, mixing with grumbles and squeaks from the carrier. How far was Lu's old den, and wouldn't they need to find her another stretch of bank for her den?

Churned earth and overturned stones with dried mud clinging to their sides announced where Whit, Jack, and/ or Barbara had done their evil work. Huge paw prints and human-shaped tracks mixed in the dirt. Melvin's lips thinned out, and everything from *tsk* to "Damn it" to growls said all that needed to be said about his former minions' destruction.

"Jack and Barbara will have to work harder to make a new home in Wyoming. Rough justice." Melvin glanced back at the group. "But where should we release the otters?"

"Keep going downstream." Seth pointed at an outcropping. "We'll find something suitable."

"This looks good!" Lon announced fifty yards later. "Rocks and pools and a hill!" He and Ray set the crate down.

"You and your mudslides!" Jackie rumpled Lon's hair.

"You like them too! Both of you!"

"Yes, we do." Seth eyed the hill and the water.

Corey got a glimpse of his lover in thirty years' time. Could he hope to keep up then?

"Glad to let you go, Lu, old girl." Ray reached for the latch on the crate. "Those babies outgrew the paddling pool."

"Oh! That's right!" Jackie turned and stopped. "You two get started on renovations. Lu and I have swimming lessons to teach!"

She dashed away. Corey wouldn't turn around for love nor money right now. Much as he loved watching Lon's shifts, he did not want even a glimpse of his lover's mother doing the same bit of magic. Lon and Seth had no such modesty, though Ray turned red enough he might be wishing they did. Lon barely paused between naked and furry.

"Wow!" Guess Ray would survive a few seconds of nudity. Melvin didn't twitch, but then, he sported a plumy tail at intervals.

Three otters romped around the two-foots' ankles for a moment, and then Lon—Corey could pick his lover apart from other otters now—poked his nose through the wire mesh and whiffled. Lu squeaked back. Ray released the catch, and the door swung open.

Lu stepped out daintily, to rub noses with Lon and then the other two. They sniffed and groomed, and Lu didn't hustle the babies away from the adults, but let them tumble and boing out of the carrier. That had to be Jackie, grooming a rumpled ear on a little squeaker.

"Two weeks bigger, two weeks cuter." Ray grinned.

"Two weeks hungrier," Melvin observed. "You're going to lose some dace."

"There's enough for everyone, I think." Corey had plenty of time to consider what he'd tell the otter. "If nobody takes too much."

Two of the adults left for the rocky outcropping, sliding around boulders and disappearing. Lon knew digging in both his forms, and apparently came from a line of experts in making a den. Corey'd have to ask Lon a few pointed questions when they got home. Maybe their den wasn't to Lon's liking. What had he said about the rug?

One of the babies escaped, running down to the creek's edge. It stuck its nose into the water and backed up with a yip.

"Yup, colder than the pool at Wildlife Rehab." Ray chuckled. "You'll learn to rough it, little guy."

Jackie slipped into the pool, rolling over and waving paws. Good times here! Lu nosed her child into the water under Jackie's vigilant gaze. The baby paddled furiously, keeping its face out of the water. That wouldn't last long, not when brother tumbled in on top of him. The adults kept the babies in the shallows, guiding and demonstrating.

Corey watched his family, for weren't they all connected in some way? His family, with four feet, and sometimes two. He couldn't hope to join in so many of their games, big, clumsy two-foot that he was, but he could enjoy them enjoying themselves. Lon shared so much with him… Even this wonder.

Corey, Ray, and Melvin watched the swimming lesson. "Are they going to be safe in wolf territory?" Ray asked. "Maybe we should have gone up Little Jug Creek."

"Safer here than anywhere," Melvin commented. "They're under my protection too." He glanced at Corey. "Get that paper written and sent out. Tenure hearings are coming up."

"I'll get right on that." Security! For him and Lon! He could even buy golden rings of a purity that wouldn't disturb his lover. Husband. If Lon said yes. Lon would. He had to. He'd said he'd wear a cigar band, if Corey gave it to him. Well. They could do better than cigar bands, and Corey would wear both rings while Lon wore his fur.

The otter in question reappeared about an hour later, streaked with mud. With a quick dip into the stream and a playful pat at one of the babies, he washed his efforts off in flowing water. Corey backed away from the stream—ten paces should be enough.

Melvin and Ray didn't.

Everyone climbed out on the bank. And everyone shook.

Corey didn't even try not to laugh as Ray and Melvin yelled. Warding off the shower, hands before their faces, didn't keep them dry.

"You could have warned us!" Ray grumbled.

"More fun not to." Lon was definitely rubbing off on Corey's sense of humor.

Lon picked up one of the babies and waited for Lu to grab the other. The group scampered off toward the new den. Presently three adults returned, swimming strongly upstream. This time everyone backed away from the water's edge.

Seth and Lon put away their fur, while Jackie ran back to her shelter and clothes to change back. With everyone dressed and talking, the air filled with chatter about the new den, soft grasses, one of the babies was a boy, one was a girl, they were so cute, and everyone would have to come play with Lu and the kids.

Family talk. His family. Corey wrapped his arm around Lon's shoulder and heard all about enough room to grow into and a population of cutthroat trout downstream.

"It's like being a grandmother," Jackie sighed happily. "Spoil them and give them back to Mama." She found an idea Corey'd barely turned over. "Speaking of which…" She pinned them with a steely gaze. Corey clutched his lover a little tighter.

Lon clutched back. "Motherrrrr…"

264

"It's early days for you two, which give us time to figure out how, but I do expect to be given some granddaughters. Eventually."

Eep! This was going way too fast! He'd only just met Lon's parents! Couldn't they wait for a wedding first? He seized on a possible objection. "Erm, what if they turn out to be grandsons?"

"Girls, boys, we don't care." Prospective Grandma smiled an accord at prospective Grandpa. "We just want some grandotters."

About the Author

P.D. Singer lives in Colorado with her slightly bemused husband, two former rowdy teenage boys turned young men, and thirty pounds of cats. She's a big believer in research, first-hand if possible, so the reader can be quite certain Pam has skied down a mountain face-first, been stepped on by rodeo horses, acquired a potato burn or two, and will never, ever, write a novel that includes sky-diving.

When not writing, playing her fiddle, or skiing, she can be found with a book in hand.

Also by P.D. Singer

Pro cyclist Luca Biondi lives for the race. For the star of Team Antano-Clark, victory lies within his grasp—if he can outdistance 200 other hopefuls, avoid suspicion from race officials, and keep his lieutenant more friend than foe. Luca also has secrets, and eyes for amateur cyclist and journalist Christopher Nye.

Christopher understands Luca's need to keep their relationship under wraps, but chafes at hiding in the shadows of his lover's career. He's ready to cheer Luca's victories, but he knows too well how triumph can turn to tears. While Christopher's heart sees Luca the man, his inner journalist—and his editor—sees the cycling world's biggest scoop.

From the jagged curves of the Colorado Rockies to the viciously steep Belgian hills, Luca can ride out any bumps—except rumors about his loyalty.

A few words in the wrong ear could crash everything. With miles between them, hints of scandal, and Luca's fierce need to guard his reputation, a journalist might have to let go of the biggest story of his career or risk forcing

266

his lover to abandon the race. Christopher and Luca face a path more treacherous than any road to the summit in the Italian Alps.

Senior year of college is for studying, partying, and having fun before getting serious about life. Instead, Chad's days are filled with headaches and exhaustion, and his fencing skills are getting worse with practice, not better. Then there's his nonexistent love life, full of girls he's shunted to the friend zone. Is he asexual? Gay?

Grad student Warren Douglas could be out clubbing, but his roommate is better company, even without kisses. He's torn up watching Chad suffer, gobbling ibuprofen and coming home early on Friday nights. If Chad weren't straight, Warren would keep him up past midnight. They're great as friends. Benefits might answer Chad's questions.

A brief encounter with lab rats reveals Chad's illness—he needs surgery, STAT, and can't rely on his dysfunctional parents for medical decisions. Warren's both trustworthy and likely to get overruled—unless they're married. "You can throw me back later," Warren says, and he may throw himself back after his husband turns out moody and hard to get along with, no matter how much fun his new sex drive is. Surgery turns Chad into a new man, all right…

…but Warren fell in love with the old one.

Hedge fund trader Ricky Santeramo has it all: money, looks, and fellow trader Jonathan Hogenboom. The two couldn't be more different: Jon is from old money, while Ricky clawed his way out of blue-collar New Jersey. Jon hedges his positions; Ricky goes for broke. Jon likes opera and the Yankees;

Ricky prefers clubbing. Jon drinks wine with dinner; Ricky throws back a beer. Jon wants monogamy… but Ricky likes variety.

Bankrupt airlines are facing strikes, the housing market is starting to crumble, and Jon can't wait any longer for Ricky to commit. One last night alone and one last risky trade make Jon say, "Enough." Then Jon's old friend Davis comes to New York City, ready for baseball and forever. The whole world is chaos, but there are fortunes to be made—or lost—and hearts to be broken—or won.

Faced with losing it all, Ricky must make the savviest trades of his life and pray for a rare event. His portfolio and Jon's love are on the line.

 Take a break from academics, enjoy the Colorado Rockies, fight a fire now and then. That's all Jake Landon expected when he signed up to be a ranger. He'll partner with some crusty old mountain man; they'll patrol the wilderness in a tanker, speak three words a day, and Old Crusty won't be alluring at all. A national forest is big enough to be Jake's closet—he'll spend his free time fishing.

Except Old Crusty turns out to be Kurt Carlson: confident, competent, and experienced. He's also young, hot, friendly, and considers clothing optional when it's just two guys in the wilderness. Sharing a small cabin with this walking temptation is stressing Jake's sanity--is he sending signals, or just being Kurt? And how would Kurt react if he found out his new partner wants to start a fire of a different kind? Jake's terrified--they have to live together for five months no matter what.

Enough sparks fly between the rangers to set the trees alight, but it takes a raging inferno to make Jake and Kurt admit to the heat between them.

Read the other books in the Mountain series:

Other works from Rocky Ridge Books

There are good guys, bad guys, and then there's Lucky.

Former drug trafficker Richmond "Lucky" Lucklighter flaunts his past like a badge of honor. He speaks his mind, doesn't play nice, and flirts with disaster while working off his sentence with the Southeastern Narcotics Bureau. If he can keep out of trouble a while longer he'll be a free man—after he trains his replacement.

Textbook-quoting, by the book Bo Schollenberger is everything Lucky isn't. Lucky slurps coffee, Bo lives caffeine free. Lucky worships bacon, Bo eats tofu. Lucky trusts no one, Bo calls suspects by first name. Yet when the chips are down on their shared case of breaking up a drug diversion ring, they may have more in common than they believe.

Two men. Close quarters. Friction results in heat. But Lucky scoffs at partnerships, no matter how thrilling the roller-coaster. Bo has two months to break down Lucky's defenses… and seconds are ticking by.

Read the other books in the Diversion Series:

The lights go down and stage lights up. The Dark Angels have arrived. With his come-hither voice and body made for sin, lead singer Angel Luv draws lovers like a magnet. And when he caresses and taunts shy guitarist Darius Stone on stage, well…it's an act, right? But every touch lights a fire, and every flirtatious glance chips away at Dare's certainty that he's straight. No one else has so captured his imagination.

Temptation beckons. It's hard not to notice the want in Dare's eyes, the way he stares when he thinks Angel's not watching. One wrong move might scare him away, but a work trip to exotic Bali might be the perfect place to let Dare explore his sexuality, with none to be the wiser. But their "friends with benefits" pact has an expiration date, that just might sour their friendship.

Read the other books in The Dark Angels series:
Tied Together
Finally Fallen
Happy Holidays

www.ingramcontent.com/pod-product-compliance
Lightning Source LLC
Chambersburg PA
CBHW052036240626
47153CB00006B/2102